KING OF TIDES

IMMORTAL IRON BROTHERS SERIES
BOOK THREE

BLUE SAFFIRE

PERCEPTIVE
ILLUSIONS

PERCEPTIVE ILLUSIONS
PUBLISHING

King of Tides

Immortal Iron Brothers
BLUE SAFFIRE
Perceptive Illusions Publishing
Bayshore, New York

Blue Saffire/Perceptive Illusions Publishing, Inc.

PO BOX 5253

Bayshore, NY 11706

www.BlueSaffire.com

Publisher's Note: This is a work of fiction. Names, characters, places, and incidents are a product of the author's imagination. Locales and public names are sometimes used for atmospheric purposes. Any resemblance to actual people, living or dead, or to businesses, companies, events, institutions, or locales is completely coincidental.

Ordering Information:

Quantity sales. Special discounts are available on quantity purchases by corporations, associations, and others. For details, contact the "Special Sales Department" at the address above.

King of Tides/ Blue Saffire. -- 1st ed.

WORDS FROM BLUE

Be the tide that sets the motion.

—BLUE SAFFIRE

Tanri

Changing Tides

Balance is yet another word humans use without the full comprehension of the term. It is understandable as they have not grasped that as it is below, so is it above. Everything is a reflection.

I've created the sky to reflect the ocean and vice versa. Moisture is the balance of the earth, air, and sea. They flow as one to create the balance of the whole—to keep humans complete. You cannot have one without the other.

The clouds are but a reflection of the rolling ocean and turbulent sea. A way for the gods to look at their true selves and see the truth that brings them back to themselves. Balance—a measure of the emotions we allow to go unkept.

The tides roll in and crash upon the sands as a reminder of our existence. It can be a force that drags everything out into the deep, or it can force the creation of more grains of sand and life. The driving force behind the ecosystem that makes up the sea creatures Su-Vaha created and so loves.

Tides provide an energy of their own that, when mastered, harnesses a current of its own that's unstoppable. From the moment I looked into my third son's eyes, I knew he would master true power, strength, and the ability to harness this balance.

However, control of the mirrors of the gods is something to be shared and not burdened on the shoulders of one. I chose the one who would be that balance. I was ready to help him shoulder that burden.

My sons have been on an odyssey of their mother's and my creation. This journey has brought them pain, and at times, they have returned the favor. Habun and I have many wrongs to right.

Just because one is absent does not mean their love isn't there. Love is like the tides of the ocean; it's continuously flowing. The love of a parent is the greatest current.

It will transcend time, space, and all understanding. Agape love is what I wanted for all my children. The intentions of a good heart. The empathy of a pure soul.

I thought I was building that as I shared my essence with those I deemed my siblings. Yet, the individual mind is what moves the tides, not the collective intention.

I learned this too late, and my heart has suffered. Now, I will right all wrongs and shift the tides as the grains of time mark a new time, a new era.

"She did this out of love. We must honor her memory by doing our part." I hear Habun say as I enter ethereal pools.

I find her and Su-Vaha on the floor between the pools as Habun holds a sobbing Su in her embrace. I should have known Su-Vaha would take this hard.

She and Güç have always been extremely close. Su-Vaha has been to Güç as the sky has been to the ocean. Their friendship has no measure. However, this needed to be done, and it had to be done just as it has occurred.

"Why didn't she tell me? Why wouldn't she warn me before doing something like this?"

"Would you have stepped aside and allowed her to carry this through?" I say, alerting them both of my presence.

Su-Vaha looks up at me and wipes away her tears. I hold out my hand to her. She places her four-fingered hand in mine.

Su prefers this form she is in. She often tends to be in sea creature forms. However, at the moment, her hands and eyes are more like those of an amphibian. Like the creatures humans call frogs—her eyes and hands take on the animal's features while others appear more humanlike.

When not in this form, she's often in the form of a mermaid. I'm assuming she's currently in this form after feeling the loss of our sibling and needing to surface from the pools.

She sniffles and looks up into my eyes with her amphibian ones. There's pleading and sadness in her gaze. I can feel the hurt filling her being.

"No, I don't think I would. If I had known, I would have taken her place," she says tearfully.

"And this is why she could not tell you. This was her sacrifice to make."

Su shakes her head before I finish my words. "I wish to understand. Why?"

"You will understand as things unfold. For now, as Habun has said, we must do our part. Is she ready?

"Will her gift manifest? Will she be able to harness İntikam this time?"

"We made sure she kept her virginity. It was a task, but it's been done. As a result, her gift is already manifesting, and because of him, she will be able to control İntikam this time. He will begin to sense her now …"

Her words choke off. I already know what she was going

to say. Güç's sacrifice has lifted the veil. My sons' mates will no longer be hidden from them. Nor will their mates' gifts be shielded from everyone.

They will come into who I meant for them to be from the beginning. This was Güç's gift to me. The ultimate sacrifice for the greater good.

"Are you sure Kenji can handle this task?"

"Yes, he has done right by us and will continue to do so," Su-Vaha replies.

"So it has begun, my love," Habun says as she moves to my side.

I look to her and smile. She has waited as long as I have to right this wrong. A mother's love is a powerful thing.

Habun's sheer will has done so much for our sons and their well-being. All I've done has been for her happiness and to restore my sons to their rightful place.

"Yes, it has," I say as I place my free hand against her soft cheek.

"What of Hizmetkar? He cannot go unpunished. Allow me to—"

"No. He was manipulated into this."

"But his actions are his own."

"Yes, that they are. Because of that, he will know the pain and frustration the others have grown to experience. Don't worry, my love. I have a plan for him."

Pain and conflict fill her eyes. This has all become more complicated than it should have. However, the guilt and pain in her eyes is something I wish to erase. None of it deserves the opportunity to mar her beauty.

My love is still as beautiful as the day I created her. I fell in love with her as well as the idea of her. My perfect creation. This is what I wanted for my sons. This was my goal in the beginning.

Billy

Job & Neighbor

It's been a long day. This call should be my last, but I'm not counting on it. I can't wait to get back to my place and have a cold beer. A book, a beer, and a bath are all calling me.

Since I was a little girl, I've loved to escape into a good book. This day is escape worthy. I'm looking forward to getting lost in my e-reader.

I was already halfway home when I got the call. Our squad has been shorthanded, and they've been working me like a dog. The amount of paperwork alone has me questioning my life.

If I couldn't see for myself that our team has been light, I would think my captain has been punishing me to keep me from digging into the case I can't get him to approve me to make a move on. I know Candido and Pauly Ricci are hiding something. All I need is a task force to nail them for a RICO case to put them both away.

Especially Candido, he's the type of asshole I became a cop to put away. He may have everyone else fooled, but I see right through him. One of these days, he's going to fuck up, and I'm going to be on his ass. That's a promise.

"What do we have, Jenkins?" I ask as he lifts the yellow tape to let me through.

"Homeless guy found a body behind the dumpster. Female, early twenties," he replies.

"Fuck. Any ID?"

"Nope, Jane Doe looks like she's fresh. I'm thinking she was dumped here just after the rainstorm. Looks like cause of death was asphyxiation. She has a contusion to the left side of the head and her clothing was torn, indicating there may have been a sexual assault before the time of death," Jenkins rattles off.

I go to step toward Jane Doe and step into a puddle of water. I look down at the puddle and it's like I'm sucked into its reflection. That's the best way I can explain it.

I lift my head, and a couple appears before me. He's a lot taller than her that's the first thing I note about them. As he has her pinned to the wall, I home in on everything about them.

She shoves him back and her face comes into view. She doesn't look very lucid. As he stumbles back, she actually falls to the side as if drunk or high—maybe even drugged.

"Come on, you little slut. You were in there shaking your ass for me all night. Don't try to be hard to get now," the guy snarls.

He closes in on her and she pushes at him once again. This time, he punches her on the left side of her head. She stumbles back against the concrete wall behind her and hits her head again. That's when the guy grabs her by the throat, and she grabs his wrist.

I note they both have a stamp on the backs of their hands, probably from a nightclub in the area. I want to draw my gun and pull the trigger when he tears her dress and proceeds to violate her.

6

However, the vision is popped and I'm brought back to the present. "Detective Salvado," Jenkins calls. "You all right?"

I take a step forward and shake my head to clear it. "Uh, yeah, I'm fine." Lifting a hand to my head, I try to figure out what the heck is going on with me.

I move to where the body lies covered by a sheet. Jenkins squats to pull the sheet back and reveals the young woman beneath. My mouth falls open as it's the same woman from the vision I just had.

I take a calming breath as my thoughts spiral. What the fuck is going on? How did I see her face? Was that what happened to her?

I squat to check for the stamp on the back of her hand. The moment I see the same stamp from the vision, I purse my lips. This is the same girl.

"I want to know which club in the area uses this stamp for their patrons. Get me their CCTV footage and get me the footage from those cams as well," I say, nodding my head up at the surveillance cams I've noted since stepping into this alley.

"Tanner, Robinson, and Jones, y'all come with me. My gut is telling me this guy hasn't called it a night. Let's go party," I start to bark out orders, knowing I plan to head into the local clubs for myself.

I already know who I'm looking for. He probably thinks he got away with this, so he'll be partying without a care. I'm counting on it.

My little squad follows me out of the alley. I turn right and find a club down at the end of the block on the other side of the street. Holding my hand up to the oncoming traffic, we then jog across the street and move toward the club, bypassing the line awaiting entry.

I flash my badge at the bouncer. "We'd like to speak with the manager."

He nods curtly and lifts his wrist to speak into the comm. "We have PD out here asking to speak with you." He looks back to me and says. "He'll be right out."

"Good, he can talk to my officers here. My partner and I will be heading in," I say, waving Jenkins to follow me in.

Jenkins isn't really my partner, but he is in plain clothes, so he won't stand out as much as the uniformed guys we have with us. I'm the only one who knows who we're looking for, but it won't hurt to have someone inside to watch my back.

We walk into the club. Once we step through the door, the music thumps so hard I can feel it in my chest. I keep my gaze sharp as I look around for the big guy from my vision. I know this is crazy, but my gut is telling me to go with it.

"What are we looking for?" Jenkins leans to whisper in my ear.

"White male, around six-two, dark, medium-length hair, light-blue T-shirt and blue jeans," I murmur back.

"And you got all that from a hand stamp?"

I turn to look him in the eyes. "Just trust me."

He shrugs. Then his eyes go wide as he looks over my shoulder. I turn to see what he's looking at. A grin comes to my lips as the perp comes into view.

It's him, the guy from the vision. His shirt is now damp. One would think he's been sweating. I know better. It had been drizzling just a bit while he was in the alley with our vic.

I nearly growl as I watch the asshole slip something into the drink of a young woman at the bar. He's actually going to try this shit again tonight. Jenkins calls for backup.

Without a word, I saunter over to the bar to stand beside him and get a good look at his face and hand. I signal for the bartender once there and order a beer. The perp turns his attention to me, forgetting his intended target.

His gaze drops to my badge as he gives me a once-over and his eyes light up as if I'm a new challenge. The sick bastard. Up close, I know I have my guy. He has scratches on his wrist and his face is the same as the one in the vision.

"How about I buy your next one," he says cockily.

"How about you turn around and let me put these cuffs on you?"

"If that's what you're into. Although, I'd rather be the one doing the restraining."

"Too bad, the only one you'll be restraining will be your cellmate. You're under arrest for murder. You have the right to remain silent—" I begin to read him his rights as backup surrounds us.

However, he turns to bolt before I'm done. He shoves by my officers and takes off. I'm hot on his heels as I find my second wind for the night.

I follow him through the club to an emergency exit he ducks out of. His long legs are carrying him forward fast, but I'm faster. I jump up in the air and kick him in his back, sending him flying forward onto his face.

Before he can roll over and fight back, I'm on him with my cuffs. I grin as he calls me every name in the book. I've been more bitches from better mouths, so I'm not fazed in the least.

ARDAN

"YOU HEADING OUT, BROTHER?" Dagger asks as I stand from the table and rap my knuckles against it.

I've been drinking with a few of the captains and some brothers tonight to pass the time. I can feel the eyes of the club bunnies on me, hoping I'll entertain them for the night.

Most wouldn't dare try to sleep with me, but many have offered to blow me in hopes to get closer to me. I've allowed it with a few, but not often. I have held out hope that my mate will someday appear. That's the reason I ignore the stares and the flirting.

"Yeah, I need to go for a ride to clear my head and then I'm going to my place," I murmur back to Dagger.

"I heard you haven't been using your room here at the clubhouse. Too good for your brothers, eh?" Brass says with a taunting smile.

I snort. "If that's how you want to take it."

I don't bother to tell him that I've been spending more time at my apartment these days because something is drawing me there. It feels more like home than anywhere else, so I'm there most nights. I purchased the building about a year ago.

Then I moved into one of the units. None of the tenants know I own the place. I like it that way.

"I'm not offended. These motherfuckers around here can get unruly. Don't blame you one bit for wanting to get away from them," Dracon says through a laugh.

I snort at that one. "You brothers have a good night."

I turn to leave as they continue to throw jeers at me. I stroll easy, in no real rush. While my apartment does feel like home, it's still lonely. A grin comes to my lips.

Maybe I'll run into my little neighbor. She's a hot little cop. If humans were an option, I would have been all over that months ago.

I may not be able to do anything about the attraction I feel toward her, but I love when I get to see her. She's pretty

and gives off this independent vibe that I love about her. I've tried to help her with carrying her bags into the building or offering to hold a door for her, but she manages to sidestep me or decline my offers for help each time.

Not that I don't see the lust that often fills her eyes. Now her … I'd allow her to wrap those sexy lips around my dick any day of the week. I'd give anything to have those eyes looking up at me as she takes me in deep. I have to adjust myself as the thought crosses my mind.

I shake my head clear and throw my leg over my hog. I might need to get laid sooner rather than later. That mermaid Oasis has been giving me the eye. She might be worth a try. I'll have to ask about her the next time I meet up with Amadeus.

As I ride, I begin to think about club business. The books have been looking good. Everyone has been paying their dues and turning in earnings.

We're thriving and that's always a good thing. I'll be able to approve quite a few requests for financial assists from those needing help. Not all supers are great at money management, much like humans.

The club also foots the bills for things like new schools, repairs to our neighbors, and business start-ups for those who relocate. I mentally make a list of the requests that have come in that deserve priority.

By the time I pull into the parking garage of my apartment building, I have a firm plan in my mind and I'm ready to head upstairs to find a book to read.

However, I'm not the only one to pull in. The black sedan that belongs to my pretty little neighbor pulls into her spot. I take a glance at my watch.

It's almost three in the morning. I honestly hate that she keeps such late hours. If she were mine, I would make sure to

be waiting outside her precinct every night to see her home. Heck, I don't think I'd be able to take her career if she belonged to me.

For the millionth time, I wonder if she has a boyfriend who waits up for her calls at night. I've only seen one guy come by her apartment in the last year. He seemed to be into her, but she was indifferent from what I could tell.

It wouldn't have been hard to take her from him if he were her man. I swing my leg over my bike to dismount with a smile on my lips from the thought. She climbs out of her cage and releases her hair from the ponytail she had it in.

She looks tired but sexy as her wavy locks fall into her cocoa-brown face and she reaches up to push them out of her eyes then scratches her scalp.

I would love to take her up to my apartment and draw her a bath to let her soak. Then I could be the one to scratch and massage her scalp as she relaxes.

"Good evening," I say as we reach the elevator at the same time.

She shivers, then looks up at me as if just noticing my presence. "Hey," she says with a smile.

"Long day?"

She scoffs. "You have no idea."

We step into the elevator silently. I can't take my eyes off her. She leans against the wall and closes her eyes. I take in her full lips and the way her T-shirt hugs her breasts.

As if feeling my eyes on her, she opens hers and stares back at me. A sweet smile comes to her lips as she takes me in from head to toe. I return the smile and the gesture as I stand with my legs set wide and my arms across my chest.

"You make sure to get something to eat before you go to bed. You're looking a bit hungry over there," she says.

I release a laugh and smile wider. "As long as you drink plenty of water, gorgeous."

She shakes her head as the elevator dings on our floor. "Yeah, right." She smiles. "You have a good night, neighbor."

"You too."

Billy

Water Visions

I sit on the side of the boxing ring, taping my hands as Mack and Carson are locked together in conversation. I don't mind; I want to be left alone with my thoughts.

I have a lot on my mind. I have three sisters, and we all share the same scumbag father. I haven't been able to tell the family I grew up with about them because I'm embarrassed about who my father is.

Candido isn't someone to be proud of. My sisters are lucky not to have known him. Well, all except Ray. However, none of them seem to know the kind of man we come from.

I'm staring off into space as Mack comes over and sits beside me. He's the closest thing I have to a father. He's the only father figure I've ever known. I still remember the day I turned up on his gym's doorstep.

"You look like you have the weight of the world on your shoulders, sport. What's up?" he says.

"Nothing, Papi. It's all good."

"I know you better than that. I'm here to listen. Go on, tell me what's on your mind. I might be able to help."

I lean my head on his shoulder and release a heavy breath. He reaches to palm my head and holds me in place as he kisses the top of my head.

That's the closest I'll allow to a hug. It took years for us to get there. Mack has been patient with me since day one. He has demonstrated the patience of a saint with us all.

Now this man I can be proud of. Has he always done the right things? Not at all. Not with three mouths to feed and a business to run to do so.

However, this gym was once my home. I've watched Mack do what he needed to do to make sure Hydra keeps its doors open, not because of greed or power.

This man took in three runaways and made us a family. He gave us love when the world refused to treat us like human beings who deserved to be safe and protected. There is no way I could ever repay him for that.

"I'm fine, Papi. I promise. Let me get into this ring with Carson and I'll prove it," I say to reassure him.

"*Hija*, you know once you're in my ring, you need to be fully focused. Don't get in there with a monkey on your back."

"Ugh, Papi, I said I'm fine."

"Still my little girl," he chuckles and gets up.

I punch my fist into my palm and roll my shoulders as I stand. Carson comes to hold the ropes open for me to step in and then he follows. I bounce around in the ring to loosen up and get my thoughts together.

"You all right?" Carson asks.

"Not you too. What the hell?"

"We know you, mommy. You wear your feelings on your

face when you're around family," he says as he searches my face with his gaze.

"Less talk, more of me kicking your ass. Let's get this started," I say and nod at Mack to call the fight.

We bump knuckles and the fight starts. I dodge Carson's first attack easily. Mack has been training us from the time he took us in.

Carson is another of Mack's strays. He's been like a brother to me. The other cop in the family. He works uptown with them bougie folks.

If I wanted a shot at Ricci, I needed to land midtown. That's just what I did. I mean, how is it no one else sees Candido or his brother for who they are?

"Come on, Billy, keep your hands up. Don't let him outfight you," Mack calls into the ring.

I had been dirty and hungry but determined to make it on my own when Mack came into my life. I couldn't stand the foster home they had placed me in and had the right mind to get the hell out of there before something happened to me.

The social workers were getting tired of me. I had been through at least three by that time. Mrs. Perkins was nice; she had been the last one assigned to me, but I didn't think she was going to be so kind once she found out I ran away.

Mack found me trying to dumpster dive in his cans. He took me into his gym and gave me a sandwich and a soda. I probably shouldn't have taken either, but I was so hungry, and he gave off good vibes.

I've always been able to read the vibes of others. That's why I ran away. That family was evil, and they were going to hurt me if I stayed.

"Billy," Mack growls. "Focus. Whatever's going on in your head, you need to save that for later. Your opponent isn't going to hesitate to use your distractions against you out there. Keep your guard up and stay focused."

Carson throws a punch and lands it right on my jaw. I dance back, shocked he was able to land a hit and pissed that I allowed it. Carson grins and begins to move with more swagger as he circles me, looking for another opening.

"You're going to pay for that," I hiss.

He shrugs. "If you say so."

I move in with a combo and land it swiftly. The impact of the blows sounds around the gym, but I don't get cocky. Carson is a good fighter.

I'm just better. I keep attacking his weak points until I've tired him out. However, my mind goes back to my rambling thoughts as I think of last night.

That whole crime scene and arrest were crazy. I'm still trying to figure out how to best submit my report. I don't want to come off looking crazy.

Then there was my run in with my neighbor. My fine-as-fuck neighbor. That man just looks like he knows how to take care of his woman. I'm even digging the nose ring.

Too bad his club's name has made its way onto my radar. I think they're in cahoots with Ricci and his operation. I don't have any proof yet, but it's only a matter of time.

My captain can't block me for forever. I'm going to get to the bottom of this and put Candido Ricci behind bars once and for all.

"Damn it, Billy," Mack growls as Carson takes advantage of my lack of focus.

"Got you," Carson breathes in my ear as he holds me in a headlock, his chest heaving against my back.

I curse myself for losing focus and allowing him to best me. This one was mine for the taking. I don't know what's wrong with me lately.

Carson releases me. I frown and run my forearm across my sweaty forehead. These sessions are to keep me sharp out there in those streets. Failing is unacceptable.

"I'll treat you to lunch. You can tell me what's on your mind while we eat," he offers.

"Nah, I have a ton of shit to do. Maybe next time."

I don't miss the disappointment that comes to his face. Carson is handsome, with a great physique. I don't think Carson has ever seen me as family—at least not like a sister as Mack always wanted.

I know he's not my blood, but we've always been close. We've just never been more than friends. Not for his lack of trying.

I've been down once or twice to allow him to take my V card, but something has always stopped it from happening. Freak floods in the bathroom.

Fire alarms going off and setting the sprinkler system off. After the first two times, I figured it was a sign it wasn't meant to be. I mean, I care about Carson.

He knows that. He also knows I'm not emotionally available. Together, we would never work out.

Sometimes, I wonder if I'm just asexual. I mean, I have no real desire for sex from either gender. I never feel like I'm missing out on anything.

The times I've tried to go there have always been botched. There were the times with Carson, then Mike, Lou, Andre, and Vernon. I think I was more concerned with the fact that I've never done it instead of actually wanting to do it.

However, once things fell through for whatever reason, I didn't much care. Sex is more of a curiosity for me. I'm not really pressed to have it.

"Billy?"

"Huh?" I say, looking up at Carson.

"Next weekend. Do you want to come on a date with me?"

I knit my brows. I haven't heard a word he said. I look

around and Mack is on the other side of the gym, barking out orders.

"I ... I ... uh."

"Never mind. You know, you can't do life alone, Billy. I get that you're strong and you can do it by yourself, but you shouldn't have to. You don't have to. I'm always here," he says as he reaches to brush his thumb against my cheek.

"Car, you're like a brother to me. I know you want more, but I don't think it's a good idea. I'm okay with my life. I like having my own space and not having to answer to anyone.

"Be honest, you're a cop. I'm a cop. In what world will that work? The job will always come between us. We'd be like ships passing in the night. You're bound to get tired and want to move on," I say.

"I would never want to move on from you. You're the reason why I stay."

"I shouldn't be. Listen, I need to go. See you next week?"

He takes a step back and nods. I feel like shit for not being able to give him more, but I'm not about to force a relationship I'm not feeling. That will never be me.

"Yeah, next week," he says. "Or we could have a few beers sometime this week after work."

I shrug my shoulders. "Maybe."

He gives me a blinding smile. "I'm going to hold you to that. I'll text you."

"Cool, later."

I turn to leave the ring and sigh. You can't say I haven't tried to tell him it's never going to happen. This wouldn't be the first time. It's like he's convinced himself I'm going to change my mind.

I'm not. I never want to settle. When people settle, they wake up one day miserable as they look around at their lives. Then the home is broken.

I would never want to do that to a child. There is nothing worse in the world than being small and feeling alone. I know that feeling too well.

I grind my teeth. Candido Ricci isn't just scum. He's the worse kind of scum. A criminal and a deadbeat father.

I'm ashamed to know I come from him. As I step into the locker room to shower and go home, I glance in the mirror, trying to see if I can find a trace of that scumbag in my face. I must have gotten my warm cocoa-brown complexion from my mother.

Although Ricci is a tanned Italian man, he's not anywhere near as dark as I am. I'm clearly a Black woman even with my reddish-brown wavy hair and reddish-brown eyes. I have never passed the brown paper bag test and couldn't pass for white even if I tried.

I've seen two of my sisters and they are both lighter than me. A frown comes to my lips, and I roll my eyes. My father wouldn't be able to deny any of us. When I look into his eyes to lock him up, I will be looking into eyes I've seen almost every day of my life.

"Of all the assholes in the world, you would be my father," I mutter to myself.

A gasp leaves my lips as I stumble back a step. I could swear that the mirror I was looking into just rippled before my eyes as if made of liquid. Lifting my hand to palm my forehead, I shake my head clear.

Maybe I'm pushing too hard. I'm spreading myself thin. Between my work hours and the hours I put in investigating my sperm donor and his family—I might be driving myself crazy.

I still can't explain what happened the other night. I groan and turn to strip down and wrap my hair up before grabbing my towel and heading for the shower stalls.

The place is empty today. Mack has been complaining about the lack of female clientele. I've been wanting to sit with him to brainstorm to fix that. This place is his life.

I would hate to see him struggle to keep the doors open. Maybe I can leave some flyers around for him or lead a self-defense class for the ladies or something.

I turn on the shower spray as ideas begin to run through my head. The warm water begins to cascade down on me, loosening my muscles. Releasing a moan of relief, I lift my face to the spray.

Suddenly as the water hits my face, it's like I'm sucked out of my body and I'm plunged into water. Bubbles pour from my nose as I begin to move my arms and legs. Looking around, I try to figure out what's going on.

Schools of fish in all sorts of beautiful colors float by and gorgeous reefs of coral are all around me. A dolphin swims up to me and it's like he's assessing me.

I laugh as it begins to bob its head as if reading my thoughts. I reach out to touch it, smoothing my hand over its head. The dolphin looks me in the eyes and it's like I come out of my body once again.

This time I'm looking at the scene from above. I'm watching myself look around in confusion. I can see the dolphin still floating before me as I stroke its head.

Then something catches my eye from behind me. It's creeping forward slowly. I open my mouth, trying to warn myself as the creature rises up behind me.

However, I can't make a sound. I blink a few times, trying to make sure I'm seeing what I think I am. I'm frozen as I watch what looks like a huge dragon floating behind me before my eyes.

The thing looks like something out of some Japanese artwork. It seems to be glowing, giving off a blue hue. It's large and menacing looking, but it doesn't seem like it's going to attack.

The dragon is observing me floating before it, much like I'm doing them. I tilt my head as I process what's happening. The me before me turns and reaches up to place a hand on the side of the dragon's face.

The two look familiar with each other. In my confusion, I take the creature in some more. It's much bigger than I originally thought. I can now see its body fully. It has large wings resting against its sides and a long body with a tail floating behind it.

Suddenly, the dragon's underbelly begins to glow brighter than the rest of it. Out of nowhere, it opens its wings and engulfs me within them. I cover my face with my arm as a blinding light emits from where they are.

I gasp as I pop back into my body and I'm back in the gym shower. I look around frantically. I'm still alone as the water cascades down on me.

I think I'm losing my mind.

My heart is racing and I'm more confused than ever. I make quick work of my shower, wanting to go home and get some sleep. This is getting out of hand.

What the hell is wrong with me?

ARDAN

I NEEDED THIS RIDE. I'm in a shit mood. I spent the morning handling club business just to have Ricci summon me to handle some shipment coming into the docks for him.

I grow tired of this shit. I've wanted to be done with the Ricci family for decades now. In all honesty, I resent ever being locked into servitude in the first place.

If only I had done as Kendrick asked and been on time that night so long ago. The '20s were a fun time for me. I had to be in the mix of things. Running with stars and legends like Babe Ruth, Charlie Chaplin, Duke Ellington, Josephine Baker, Coco Chanel, and Al Capone —who had no idea what I was—had been fun. Times were changing and I was right in the center of that change.

I was more interested in a good time than being where my brother asked me to be. I fucked up royally that night. When you bind one brother, you bind us as a bloodline. You don't get one; you get us all.

I've accepted that as my punishment for leaving Kendrick vulnerable that night, but Bradan and Reilly didn't deserve this. I will forever feel responsible for what has happened to my brothers. However, the only thing that can fix this now is for all four of us to find our mates.

"That seems like it's never going to happen," I mutter to myself as I pull into the docks and head for the loading area the Iron Brothers own.

Amadeus, the captain of the merfolk, usually handles all dealings we have down at the docks. However, Ricci wants me to make sure everything goes smoothly with this particular delivery. I loathe that guy.

After coming to know real gangsters in my past, I can't find it in me to hold an ounce of respect for that asshole. He's not as smart as he thinks he is. If it weren't for me and my brothers, he would have lost everything his father and those before him built a long time ago.

I pull up to the main office, where I know I will find Amadeus and cut the engine. Swinging my leg over my bike, I roll my shoulders back and take a look around. I can tell the human workers from the mermen.

It's never hard to tell the difference, at least not for me.

Merfolk have a glow about them. It comes from the energy they pull from the atmosphere.

"Hello, brother," one of the workers says in Mermish, the merfolk language—not to be confused with Aquan, the language of the royal merfamily and ancient water folks.

His name is Conway. He's one of the brothers and spends enough time at the clubhouse for me to know him by name and face. From what I've seen, he has a thing for one of the water fairies. I give him a nod as I continue to head into the warehouse.

Despite the rumors and myths, merfolk aren't weakened when on land. They're magical beings. Their magic is always at work. When outside of water, their magic pulls from the moisture of the atmosphere. There's always moisture in the air.

Sometimes more than others. You're just not likely to find them in Vegas, Arizona, or any type of desert. As long as they can pull from that moisture, they can survive just fine on land.

However, we thought it wiser to protect their species by starting the myth centuries ago that they need to be in water, or they become weak and can die.

Amadeus is one of the oldest of his kind. I've known his father before him and a long line of fathers before him. They all come from noble blood, direct descendants of Kenji, one of my most trusted friends—not a merman, but born of their blood.

His mother was the daughter of the original merking, back when merfolk were known as sirens or water nymphs. His father was a shapeshifting trickster with the gift of alchemy.

That's what makes Amadeus the perfect captain for his people. He's the first in several generations to display the talents of Kenji and his parentage. In addition, he and his

fathers before him have been loyal for as long as we've had ties with them.

I step into the main office of the warehouse as Amadeus steps from his office while speaking with one of the young mermaids. Kai is his assistant and one of the fiercest warriors among his people.

"Ah, Ardan. It's good to see you," Kai says.

"Always a pleasure, baby girl. You staying out of trouble."

She gives me a mischievous smile. "I'm trying."

I give a laugh and shake my head. Kai can be a handful. Amadeus and I have had to get her out of trouble on more occasions than I care to count.

"What brings you here, brother?" Amadeus asks, interrupting our exchange.

I turn my gaze to him. He takes after his ancestor Kenji with his white hair and monolid eyes. Over the millennia, Kenji and his family settled in what is now known as Japan. They have since taken on the features of the humans in that region.

His broad upper build fills his Iron Brothers cut well. His lower body tapers in as his natural form would, with his fin visible. His aura is greater because of his heritage and the manifestation of his inherited gifts.

I've only known six of Kenji's descendants who have shown signs of inheriting his gift. Five of whom he has chosen to lock those gifts within. I completely understand why—that type of power can be dangerous—and that's only one reason for his decision.

"He comes to see me. You know this," Kai teases.

"Mind your mouth, Kai. This is the king you are speaking of," he bites out. "Why don't you go wait in my office?"

I can't help the scoff that leaves my lips. He is very protective over Kai, not that I'm interested in the young girl. I have enough years on her to be the start of her lineage.

Gorgeous girl and exquisite when in her mermaid form, but not my type.

"I'm here on business. Need to collect a shipment for Ricci and run it through the tunnels for his guys to collect," I say, turning my full attention to him.

"That container just came in. I'll have a few guys load it up and take it down to the tunnel for you. Do you need a driver?"

"No, I'll handle this one myself."

I can use my magic to drive the truck while I ride my bike. We hate involving others in Ricci's business when we don't need to. This is a simple drop. There's no need to involve anyone else.

Besides, I want to make this quick so I can head to my apartment. I've been feeling restless, like that's where I need to be. My mind goes to my neighbor.

I would love to talk to her again. There's always been something familiar about her. The other night was the most we've ever spoken to each other. Her voice was like warm honey, and she smelled as good as she looked.

If only …

"Ardan?" Amadeus calls my name, pulling me from my thoughts.

"Sorry, brother, what was that?"

"I have been summoned by Kenji. I leave within the next few weeks. I wanted to let you know Kai and Ocean will take over things here for me," he repeats.

I nod. "I will keep an eye on things here as well. You never take time away. Try to enjoy this, brother. Time with Kenji is always an experience."

"I will try." He gives a bow and turns to handle the business I've come for. Amadeus has never been one for many words. This is why we work well together.

I glance at my wristwatch. If I'm quick, I can catch my

little neighbor before she leaves for her shift. A frown comes to my face.

I shouldn't know her schedule as well as I do. Perhaps it's time I start going to the apartment less and not more. Who the fuck am I kidding? I look forward to my sightings of the pretty human.

Amadeus

Apprentice

Two weeks later ...

I am curious about this trip to Japan. Kenji is my great-grandfather many times over. Although if we stood side by side, you would think we were brothers.

My grandfather doesn't call for me often. His dojo is his life. He has taken his skills and gifts to the next level and built wealth and a reputation to match.

They call him the puppet master. Kenji is more than a merman and greater than a siren. He outranks all of my kind.

"Ah, you are here," Kenji says as I'm led to the room he's waiting in.

I remove my shoes and step into the room before I bow and take the seat I'm offered. I cross my legs and place my hands palms up on my knees.

"Thank you for having me, Master Kenji," I reply once seated.

"Call me *Sofu* or grandfather. Do you know why I've called you here, Amadeus?"

"No, I'm afraid I have no idea, grandfather."

Out of my four cousins and my brother, I'm the only one here. I'm not surprised not to see my cousins. With their human mother, they have not been raised much around magic or the supernatural. To this day, I don't believe they know I'm their cousin or that I'm other than human.

"I have felt your gifts growing. It is time you master them. It is time you become my apprentice. You have become powerful enough to protect yourself from those who would want to take that power from you or use you for it.

"I have watched you closely over the years. I have guarded you and your life well. Now I believe it's time you know how to harness what's inside of you."

"Why now?" I ask with my brows drawn.

"Because now is when Ardan and the others will need you."

"Ardan? What does he have to do with anything?"

"We are all woven together. Our family has been chosen to serve and honor Ardan since before these lands existed. Have you learned of the siren brothers? Have you been told the stories?"

"Forgive me. I don't believe I have."

"Sirens were not all female, as we have led humans to believe. The original sirens were two males. Brothers.

"The goddess Su-Vaha was their creator. From the beginning of time Su-Vaha has made a mirror image when she creates. Some say it is because she needs balance.

"Others believe she made one for Tanrı and one for the goddess Güç as a gift. I have also heard that Su-Vaha and Güç were once one and split into the two gods. So Su-Vaha shared everything with her sister.

"The brothers took after Su-Vaha's playful spirit and

mischief. As well as her ability to shift forms. Both Tanrı and Güç favored their gifts from Su-Vaha.

"The brothers became their friends. Güç fell in love with Tanrı's companion Yakışıklı. As Güç and Su-Vaha did everything together, Su-Vaha fell for Sevimli, Yakışıklı's brother.

"This is where our lineage started. We are born of sirens. The original tricksters. Su-Vaha would take the form of a mermaid to roam the ocean with Sevimli.

"This is the form they mated in. However, when Yakışıklı was murdered, setting off the war. Sevimli transformed into an angry and bitter sea beast. So angry they changed his name and now don't speak it aloud."

"Okay, but what does that have to do with me or Ardan?"

"İntikam will return. This is why your power is awakening. I have sealed away all my decedents who have displayed my powers to protect them, but not you. I was told to leave you unbound. You will be needed for İntikam's return. He awakens as I speak."

"Within me?"

My grandfather shakes his head. "No. İntikam cannot take on another male being. This time, the gods will place him within a female. They will match this time. He will not overpower her."

"How do you know this?"

"Because this time, I will right the wrongs." He claps his hands together. "Let's begin."

Billy

Triggered

I've been trying for weeks to trigger one of those visions again—that's the only thing I can think to call them. I haven't had one since the one in the shower at the gym. The problem is, I'm not entirely sure what triggered them in the first place.

If only I could figure it out and use it to prove to my commander once and for all that we should have a task force on Candido Ricci and his organization. I have no idea how everyone is so blind to this guy and his family. I didn't know he was my father the very first time I ran into him, but I did know he was more than a businessman. That was clear as day to me even then.

I had been seventeen at the time. Back then, Mack used to hold illegal fights at the gym. All types of seedy characters would make their way through the doors of Hydra and a lot more went on than fights and betting.

It was how Mack made sure to keep the lights on. At the

time, he had three of us runaways to look after. In those days, Hydra was where the nightlife was. He didn't much like us kids around all of that. Especially not me. Eddy and Carson loved to sneak downstairs from the apartment we lived in over the gym.

That particular night, Eddy had dared me to join them as they snuck to watch one of our favorite fighters in a match. I took the dare and ended up in the middle of Candido extorting that same fighter—trying to get him to throw the fight. Candido and his men had threatened to place a duffel full of coke in his locker to frame him. One of his men caught me watching in shock and brought attention to me.

To this day, I can't remember the face of the guy who stepped in to save me. I can remember the cut he wore, nothing else. It was an Immortal Iron Brothers cut—something I only remembered after running into my neighbor for the first time.

Since running into him, a few things about that night have come back to me. I remember the guy being upset because Candido wanted to off me. They argued about making me forget if they weren't going to kill me. The biker had been upset about both options.

While I can't remember what the biker looked like. I never forgot that Candido Ricci was an asshole and an evil man. Whatever the biker did, he didn't erase what I had learned about Ricci.

That's what made me become a cop. I remembered his evil ways and wanted him to pay for what he did to that fighter and what he tried to do to me. I have seen Candido for the man he is since that night.

The problem is no one else does. People sing his praises all the time. I know better and have been trying to get my commander to see what I know deep down inside. If we were to dig into the Riccis, we would find so much more.

"Hey, you going for a swim or are you just going to investigate the water? What crimes did it commit?" Eddy taunts, pulling me from my thoughts.

I place my hands on my hips and frown as I turn to look up at him. He has a smile on his handsome face. Eddy was Mack's last stray but he's the oldest out of the three of us.

"Shouldn't you be flying a plane somewhere? I thought you were going to Fiji or something."

He releases a short laugh and shakes his head. "That was two months ago. At least you care enough to know I'm a pilot."

"I care, you know I care," I say and scowl.

He opens his arms and waves me over to him. I go to move into his embrace. He engulfs me in his big, strong arms.

I still remember the day I allowed him to hug me for the first time. I had been upset about a fight I had with some girls at school. It wasn't actually a fight. They tried to jump me and failed.

I had broken down and cried after I whipped their asses and made it home, where I could lick my wounds. I hadn't done anything to any of them. One of them had been a friend, or so I thought.

Eddy had just been the first to find me. I was vulnerable in the moment, and he took me by surprise when he hugged me. It was foreign at the time, but something I needed. We've had a bond ever since.

"I know you care in your own way," he says into the top of my hair as he towers over me. "Mack's worried about you. He feels like you've been pushing everyone away more than usual. What did I tell you about that shit?

"We're your family. I know you can handle yourself, but we're always here to protect and support you. You don't have to be alone, Billy."

"I'm fine. You guys can stop worrying about me."

"We will always worry about you. You're our little sister and Mack's little girl. Besides, I get it. I know where we come from and how important it is to do things on our own." He pulls away and looks me in the eyes. "We just need you to remember that you have people who care. Don't let the job consume you, sis.

"It's okay to keep up with us and know where the fuck we are. Fiji?" he snorts and shakes his head.

"I know you were in London. I just don't want you thinking too much of yourself," I say with a smile.

"You're the only woman who hasn't had a crush on me and demands to cling to me. It's why I love to see this face."

"Ew, you're my brother and that's totally gross."

"Not your brother by blood and Carson has known you longer than I have."

I shrug. "What's that supposed to mean?"

"You know he's crazy about you. Yet you keep shutting him down."

I roll my eyes. "You guys are upset that I'm shutting y'all out as family? Could you imagine what it's like dating me? I'm doing him a favor, trust me."

Eddy places a hand over his belly and laughs. I punch him in the shoulder. With a smile, he wraps the crook of his arm around my head and tugs me in.

"Come on. I want some tacos. Let's hit our spot."

"So you're in town for a few days then?"

"Shut up. That happened one time."

"One time you're never going to forget. I'm sure no one who was on that flight ever will."

"Be quiet before I make you treat me."

"You wouldn't," I mock gasp. "Trying to take my little cop salary with all that money you make. I'm telling Papi if you do."

. . .

***

Dinner with Eddy was fun as always. However, I still need to clear my head and figure some things out. So here I am, back at the gym. Mack put this pool in when I was around nine.

I'm a good swimmer and love to swim to work out my thoughts. Tonight, that's exactly what I plan to do. Swim until my thoughts are clear.

I dive into the water and push forward then begin to stroke. I slice through the water as if that will allow me to slice through my frustration and thoughts.

As I swim, my mind goes to my neighbor. Why can't I connect his gang to Candido? I know it was an Iron Brother who saved me. I remember the cut. However, I can't get a solid lead that connects me to something I can use.

The Immortal Iron Brothers come up cleaner than Ricci does. It's like they don't exist. I swear, I've been running in circles.

Suddenly, I get this feeling in my stomach. I stop stroking and halt. When I look before me, it's like a sheet of ice has formed in front of me.

I reach out a hand to see if I can touch the surface. I'm not crazy. There is a panel of ice in the water that came out of nowhere. It's like an underwater mirror.

I blink a few times as I swim in place and stare at the barrier. That's when images begin to form as if the ice were a TV. I ball my fist as Candido comes into view.

It's that night all over again. However, the biker in this

frame has his back to me. I still can't see his face. He's a blond, that much I can tell.

He's no small guy either. The way he fills out that cut feels so familiar to me. If only he would turn so I could see his face.

Who are you?

I think the words and he does turn as if he heard them. I'm met with blue eyes I know well. It's him, my neighbor.

There's no way he's the one who saved me that night. That was thirteen years ago. From the image before me, he hasn't aged a day. My neighbor doesn't look older than thirty or so. Exactly the same age as the guy in the image before me looks.

How could this be? How do these visions work? As my mind reels with questions, the vision changes.

It takes a few seconds for me to realize I'm looking at the docks. I'm looking at one of the warehouses. The image before me moves as if a drone is flying, catching the footage.

Candido comes into view. A woman is on her knees before him with her hands tied behind her back. I grind my teeth, wanting to strangle this motherfucker.

I still can't believe this asshole is my father. Fucking piece of shit. I narrow my eyes and look at the woman. She looks young. As I look closer, I notice she's working her hands out of the zip ties on her wrists.

A grin comes to my lips. Hopefully, she'll be able to take this asshole and his men. She pauses as Ricci says something to her.

I become frustrated because I can't hear. Then suddenly, as if someone has unmuted the vision. I can hear everything.

"What did you say to me?" The young woman hisses.

"I said where's your fucking boss, bitch?"

"Trust me, you don't want to know where he is. How dare

you come in here like you run this place. Do you know what they will do to you?"

"Who, the Iron Brothers? Sweetheart, I own those biker fucks. They ain't gonna do shit. Now answer the fucking question."

"I'm not answering shit. What do you want with Amadeus anyway?" She bites out.

"You think I don't know you all are some type of freaks? Everyone connected to that club is. That's where you all come in handy to my business.

"I have a friend who needs distribution and transport. I'm going to get a nice kickback from the deal, but first, I need to have an understanding with your boss."

"Let me guess? Whatever you're up to is something the brothers want nothing to do with."

"Smart girl. The problem is they're only obligated to be loyal to me. I can't force them to do anything for a family outside of mine."

"You have no honor or loyalty. Amadeus will never work for you."

"You let me be the judge of that. Stop wasting my time. My little girl's engagement party is tomorrow night. I need this deal done by then. So where the fuck is he?"

"Shove it up your ass, human. I can smell your fear. You know he's going to kill you, and if he doesn't, one of the brothers will."

"In that case. Since I've told you way too much, I can leave you as a warning," Candido says and pulls a gun.

He aims it at her head and pulls the trigger. I lift my hand to cover my mouth as my eyes go wide.

A bright light appears and the ice shatters before my eyes. I push up to break through the surface of the water and gasp in a breath.

I shake my head and punch the water, biting out a curse.

So the Iron Brothers are connected to Ricci. I have a million thoughts running through my head.

I try to remember everything I saw so I can find that warehouse and gather evidence of the crime. Then I pause and knit my brows. That wasn't the present or the past.

Candido said his daughter's engagement party is tomorrow. Ray told us about her engagement party last week. It's not for another month.

"Oh my God, I have time to save her," I say and begin to swim to climb out of the pool.

Billy

Shut It Down

I chew on my gum as I watch the warehouse down at the docks, which I was able to connect to the Immortal Iron Brothers club. It took some doing, but I was finally able to uncover the connection. Still no real connection to Ricci, but I'm a hundred percent that it's owned by the bikers.

A few guys in cuts step out of the warehouse and I take a few photos. I'll run them through facial recognition later. The odd thing is, I've been surveilling this place for two weeks and taking photos of these guys as they come and go. They're a biker gang, but not a single one of the guys I've photographed has come up in the system.

How can they be affiliated with Ricci and be this clean? I place my camera down and take a few notes. I look at the time. I wish I could sit on this place all day, but I need to get to work for my shift.

I go to start my car when two bikers pull up. Quickly, I

reach for my camera. My breath catches as I see it's my neighbor and a redhead. The two look a lot alike except for the hair. The redhead also has a fuller beard as opposed to my neighbor's mustache and goatee. They even move alike—that easy stroll and swag that oozes something dark and sexy.

My anticipation begins to build. I'll finally learn more about him if his face comes up in the database. I can at least figure out his age.

I know, I know, I should just ask the guy all these questions I have brewing like a normal person. I just haven't been able to since I crashed into him the day he moved into the building. That day, for the first time ever, I felt a real attraction to a man.

I probably would have explored it too, if not for the memories that rushed me of that night when one of his brothers saved my life. I shake my head as I remind myself it had to be one of his biker brothers because it couldn't have been him.

While his face is sharp and hard, it still has a youthful look. I'd peg him for his midtwenties, early thirties, max. I may not remember everything, but the one who saved me was a man. This guy would have been around my age back then—still a boy.

I have no idea why I saw him in that vision. To be honest, I don't know what to think of anything I saw that night. I've been going on a hunch even coming here.

I jump and yelp as my phone rings. My camera drops into my lap as I chide myself. Glancing at my phone in the cup holder, I curse and place a hand over my chest to calm myself.

"Damn, this is the last thing I need," I mutter as my captain's name flashes across my screen.

I wipe my suddenly sweaty palms against my thighs. A

quick look back toward the warehouse tells me the bikers are gone. However, I don't know if they went inside.

I bite out another curse and pick up the call. "Hello."

"Salvado, why aren't you in my office? I thought I told you to get in here early today. I need to talk to you now," Captain Gates growls through the line.

"Sir, I'm sorry. It slipped my mind. I'm on my way," I say quickly.

"For your sake, you better hope you're not getting into any more shit I have to clean up. I have enough on my plate. I don't need to babysit your ass."

I jerk my head back and look at the phone with a frown on my face. We've always clashed when it comes to the Ricci organization, so I haven't mentioned anything about my investigation. I plan to have them dead to rights before I reveal my hand.

"Not sure what you're talking about, but I'll be in soon," I mumble.

Just as I go to hang up, my neighbor and the other biker step from the building with a woman who looks a lot like the one from my vision. I bite my lip, trying to decide if I should remain and try to learn more or if I should get to the precinct for the dress down that's waiting for me.

I roll my eyes and mutter to myself as I take off. I'll just have to come back. At least I have a location, and I know for a fact this woman is real.

I still have time to save her from Candido. Now, if only I could figure out the connection to the biker club.

ARDAN

.   .   .

"New receptionist?" Bradan asks as we go to leave the warehouse after our meeting with Kai.

I glance back over my shoulder. An older woman is at the main desk. I narrow my gaze as I take the woman in.

"I guess so," I say to Bradan as I turn back to look forward.

"Is she registered? She's not human and I didn't receive paperwork for Amadeus to take on a new super as an employee," Bradan says.

"That's on me, brother. Kai and Ocean have been handling the place in Amadeus's absence. I'll let them know they have to file the proper paperwork and clear her as an employee through the brotherhood."

"What did Kai say her name was?"

"Shit. Was it Güç or Pouch or something like that?"

"Güç, that was it," he says and chuckles. "Pouch. Get the fuck out of here with that."

"What? I wasn't really paying attention, and she only called her name, like, once."

"Normally you would have caught it that once."

"Well, I didn't this time. Besides, when was the last time you heard of someone named after one of the gods," I mutter.

I wasn't paying attention before but now that he's brought attention to her name, I do find it odd that she has it. Granted, the supers haven't completely forgotten the gods, but not many honor them as they used to. Not like the wolves honor the moon goddess.

Some are too afraid to utter their creator's names. My brothers and I don't use our father's name by choice. He abandoned us. I, for one, have no use for his name.

"Truth, but that's still not like you. Everything okay?

You've been staying at your apartment more lately. Anything you want to talk about?"

"I'm all good," I reply. "On second thought … let me ask you something."

I've been wanting to bring this up for a while now, but I didn't want my brothers to question me. It's already odd that I've purchased the apartment building and chose to live elsewhere.

We do it from time to time, but it's not often and normally happens after we've been through something traumatic. Reilly was the last one to break off to take some alone time from the family. However, we never stay apart for long.

"Go on," Bradan says as he straddles his machine.

"Have you ever felt a pull somewhere, like that's where you always need to be?"

"Sure as shit have and still don't know why. Shit is driving me crazy."

I think his words over. It dawns on me that I have noticed he's been taking off at random times over the last few months. We are close, but I haven't questioned him on his comings and goings, as Bradan tends to need to blow off steam every now and then.

We all get that and try to back off to give him his space. Kendrick believes Bradan has a hidden place. I know he does. As his twin, I can feel when he goes there to fully release. However, I know that's not where he's been taking off to, because I don't feel him releasing his powers while he's gone.

"Is it me, or does it feel like change is coming?"

Even as I ask the question, there's something in the air telling me the answer. As if for the first time since I was a young boy, the gods have tuned in to listen to my words and feelings. My brothers and I haven't just felt the absence of our mother and father. They have all gone silent on us.

"I'm no Kendrick or Reilly, but I feel it. Something's brewing."

I shrug. "Maybe we're just getting anxious for the bond to run out. I think we're all at the end of our rope with Ricci."

"I know I'm ready to be done with them, you feel me?"

"Oh, I feel you, brother. He has a lot of fucking nerve asking us to do shit for another family as if he doesn't know the rules."

"He knows the fucking rules. If it's not in direct connection or a direct benefit. It's our call and we can deny it.

"He knows how much we hate the drug and sex trafficking business, so he knew we would say no. How much you want to bet his pussy ass tries to go around us?"

"You know I don't like to lose, brother. I wouldn't take that bet for free," I say then climb on and start my bike.

"Let's go," I say through our mind link.

BILLY

THIS IS NOT my damn day. Traffic was a beast and added at least another hour to my travel time. I didn't even have time to eat.

My stomach growls as I walk to Cap's office. I can tell by the vibe in the precinct that Captain Gates is on one today. That man can sour everyone's mood by breathing.

To be honest, it could be worse. Our cap can be a dick, but I've heard stories of real tyrants who are a trip to work under. Gates will get in your ass, but he's a decent guy when he wants to be.

I knock on his door and wait for him to call out. "Yeah," he rumbles.

I pop my head in. "You wanted to see me?"

"Come on in."

That doesn't sound too good. I take a deep breath and step in to take a seat. I already have a feeling I know what this is about.

"Salvado, can you explain to me why I'm getting calls about you sticking your nose places I've told you to stay away from? Tell me you're not using city time to investigate innocent people when you have plenty of cold cases and cases fresh off the streets that need your attention. Cases like that young couple who went missing two days ago or that homicide from the other night," Captain Gates bites out.

He's right. I do have those two cases on my desk. While I'm still digging into the homicide, the missing couple is bull-shit. I'm not wasting my time with those two. I could see from the moment I stepped on the scene at the apartment of those two it was a game they were playing with the friend who made the call.

"Cap, with all due respect. That couple was wrapped up in a love triangle. The friend who made the report is just the last to find out the other two decided to go it solo. Or should I say as a duo.

"The *blood*." I make air quotes with my fingers. "Was pig's blood and I tracked the two to a little house upstate. Both breathing and looking like they're living their best lives."

He purses his lips at me. "Fine, and the homicide?"

"I'm circling back to the restaurant owner. He failed to mention he was dating our vic. Our pregnant vic, who I'm sure was carrying his baby. Which will be easily proven with a DNA test. If he didn't do it, it was the wife. I'll be able to nail the truth down as soon as I log in for the evening, Cap," I say with a bright smile.

I do my fucking job. I have never allowed my investigation into Ricci to deter me from getting my job done. I don't know who's trying to blow the whistle on me, but they can suck it.

Gates sits back in his seat. "Good job, just stay the fuck away from Ricci. Whatever you're up to, can it."

"What makes you so sure he's clean?" I say, getting pissed.

"It's above my pay grade, which means it's way above yours. Candido and Pauly Ricci are off-limits. Stay away from them. That means their properties and any connected to them—that includes the docks and warehouses surrounding theirs.

"Drop it, Salvado, or I'll be forced to suspend you. Since I'm already short-staffed and you're one of the best I have on the squad, I'd appreciate it if you could just listen for once."

Gotcha. So the Iron Brothers are connected somehow. I know it.

"Understood," I mutter.

"Now get the fuck out of my office and do your job. I want your reports on my desk first thing tomorrow morning."

I go to leave until I realize what he just said. He has lost his damn mind. There's no damn way.

"But I won't be able to get all that done before the end of my shift and get out in the field to make that collar," I protest.

"Looks like you'll be earning some overtime. Don't tell me you went out and got yourself a boyfriend."

I have to bite down on my tongue to keep from cursing him out. If I were a male officer, he wouldn't dare say some shit like that to me.

"Fuck off," I say under my breath.

"What was that?"

"Nothing. You have a safe shift, sir."
Asshole.

Billy

In the Deep

I smile as I get up from my desk chair and close my laptop. I enjoy my online chats with my sisters. We have this bond I wasn't expecting.

At first, I think we were all nervous and awkward. Now, I feel like they've been a part of my life all along. In a way I feel closer to them than I do Mack and the guys.

"Meeting you guys should be fun," I mutter to myself as I think of our plans to finally meet up.

In just a few days, I'm going to meet my sisters face to face. I'm nervous and excited. This will help me to keep my mind off what's coming and the fact that I can't do anything about it.

I sigh and shake my head. Blowing out a breath, I look around my apartment. I never thought I would have this—a place all my own.

I head to the fridge for a beer. Once I finish it, I plan to take a nice long bath and read a good book. My muscles

ache from the punishment I put my body through to ward off the stress of having to back off the warehouse before I got what I needed or being able to save the woman from the vision.

I've been trying to figure out how to save her when I've been forbidden from going back to the docks or any of Candido's properties. I'm trying to wrap my head around how he has so much pull.

I swallow down a sip of beer as an idea comes to me. "Bingo. Now that's how you use your head, Billy," I say to myself with a sly grin.

With my beer in hand, I head into the bathroom as my thoughts begin to come together. Cap said I had to stay away. I know someone who can make sure that woman isn't harmed and if Candido shows his true face, he'll end up right where he belongs.

I begin to hum to myself as it all comes together. I'll make the call after my bath. Ricci is going down one way or the other.

As the water runs, I pour in some milk bath. I'm going to treat myself. I bop my head from side to side happily. It's going to be so sweet to nail Candido.

"Should have killed me when you had a chance," I sing as I pull my hair up and cover it.

After, I grab my shower bag and head for the shower as I've decided to hop in and shave before my soak. As I'm shaving my legs, the water begins to feel like a warm caress on my skin. A gasp slips from my lips as my skin becomes hypersensitive.

I bite my lip and run my hand over my stomach. For the first time in a long time, I think about shaving my bits. I bite my lip as my neighbor comes to mind.

I've never seen him with a woman at his place. The way he looked at me that night in the elevator was enough to

make me wonder what his type was. I cut the thought off as I remind myself he could be affiliated with Ricci.

"What a shame," I huff and proceed to shave so I can sink into the tub.

I'm pleasantly surprised to find the water is at the perfect temperature as I step into the bath. I groan as I submerge myself into the water. The milk bath has a hint of honey in the scent that's welcoming. I lie back and close my eyes as I allow the feeling of the warm water to carry me away.

What I'm not expecting is how far it carries me. One moment, I'm in my bathroom alone. The next, I have someone between my legs.

"Oh my God," I cry out as I look down and find a blond head bobbing beneath the water as broad shoulders rest beneath my legs.

This feels so good I don't want it to stop. I reach to tangle my hand into his hair and hold on tight. When his blue gaze lifts to mine, I take in a sharp breath of air.

I don't even know this guy. How is this happening? I throw my head back and nearly buck from the tub as he reaches to pinch my clit. Reaching behind me, I claw at the tub for something to anchor me.

He hums as if he's tasting the best thing he's ever had in his life. I try my best to pull away, but he follows my hips down beneath the water.

I furrow my brows as I wonder how he's breathing under there. However, that thought is lost as the buildup inside me comes to a crescendo and I cry out so loud I'm sure everyone in the building can hear me.

I lie back, panting as he comes up out of the water and pushes his blond hair out of his face. I'm in awe of him as water ripples down his chiseled chest. I take my gaze lower to see what he's working with, but I don't get the view I'm expecting to find.

Instead, I find myself alone once again, panting and

needing more. What in the entire fuck just happened? Was that real? Can it be real sometime soon?

"Fuck, he would be the only dick I've ever wanted. This shit is for the birds," I grumble to myself.

I decide to end my bath and make my call. Anything to get my mind off what just happened. My pussy is still pulsing.

ARDAN

As soon as I step off the elevator, the scent of something delicious hits my nostrils. A hint of honey with something else that's mouthwatering. Instead of heading for my apartment, I pull in my energy and follow the scent.

My groin tightens from the sight I find as I get to the trash shoot on my floor. My little officer is before me with her phone between her shoulder and her ear as she tosses out her trash.

However, that's not what has my body hardening. She's in a thin tank top with a pair of Crocs on her feet. The tank top she has on has risen in the back to reveal a pair of boy shorts that her cheeks are just barely contained in.

"Fuck me," I mutter under my breath.

I've never been interested in a human the way I'm interested in her. I want to push her up against a wall and fuck her senseless for coming out here looking so fucking sexy.

"Thanks, Carson. I know I'm right about this. It's going to go down on Friday. My captain won't listen to me, and I've been warned to stay away. When you nail that douchebag for

attempted murder, I'll have all I need," she says into her phone.

She pauses to listen to what's being said on the other end. I grin and allow my eyes to roam over her toned legs and plump ass. Damn, I wish she could take me.

"No, I appreciate this. Just keep me posted. I want to know that asshole gets what's coming to him. Good night, Car. Thanks again."

She ends her call and picks up the last bag of trash to toss it down the shoot. Not able to resist, I move to stand behind her before she turns from throwing the bag out. That's when I release my energy once again.

She jumps as she feels my presence and looks over her shoulder at me. I catch her phone she has dropped in surprise. I smile down at her and hold her phone out to her.

"You smell amazing," I dip my head to say into her ear.

"How the hell did you sneak up on me like that?" she breathes.

I give her just enough space to turn and face me. Looking into her eyes, I forget her question. This … this is what I want my mate to look like. Her reddish-brown eyes pop from her face and her lips. I want to taste them so bad. Why the fuck does she smell so fucking good?

"Are you going to answer me?"

"I'm a light walker," I say close to her lips.

She clears her throat and shakes her head. It's not lost on me that her eyes fill with a ton of lust and desire. I inhale deeply and the scent of her arousal fills my head.

I place a hand on her waist and draw her close to me. I know I can't take things far with her, but I want a taste so bad my jaw is ticcing as my mouth waters.

She searches my face with her gaze. I bite back the smile that wants to come to my lips. She clenches her phone to her chest as if that's enough to keep her from touching me.

"Why do you look so familiar to me?" she asks as the silence stretches between us.

"I don't know. I would have remembered coming across a face like yours."

"Are you sure about that? I feel like I've run into you in my past," she says, still searching my face.

I'll admit. Now that I'm this close, something is tickling my brain, but I've lived so long there's no telling where we could have crossed paths. In a playful mood and because I know we could never do more than give each other head, I decide to push the envelope.

"Trust me, had you crossed my path before, your pussy would be wet every time I got near you. Your body would remember my tongue and how good I made you feel," I lean to say into her ear.

I love the gasp that comes from her lips. I close my eyes and imagine that sound coming from her as I slide inside her for the first time.

"Not going to happen," she pants as if reading my thoughts.

I open my eyes and look into her face. "Why not? You have a boyfriend?"

"No." She shrugs. "I'm not interested. That's why."

"Lies," I say and release her. I look down at her thin tank top and note her hardened nipples pushing at the fabric. She has goose bumps across her collarbone and down her arms. If I couldn't smell her arousal, her body sure is giving her away. "You shouldn't be out here like this."

"I hadn't planned to run into anyone or to be out here long."

"Let me walk you to your door."

"Why?"

"Because I want to make sure you get inside safely. You

know, I'm only ever trying to be nice. We're neighbors. I'm looking out."

"So you want me to start coming by for sugar and shit?" she says, sounding amused.

"Sugar, a hand with opening a jar, fixing other shit that comes up. I'm here for it all," I reply.

"And what are you looking for in return?"

"Nothing at all. Seeing your pretty face is enough for me."

"Um … whatever. Come on. I'll let you walk me to my door this once."

I'm taken by surprise by her acceptance. She has shut my help down any other time I've offered. Images of walking into her place and trailing kisses down the back of her neck fill my head.

I put my palm on the back of her neck and start for her place. She glances at me as she bites down on her lip. I would love to be the one to have that flesh in my mouth.

Once at her door, she reaches for my wrist and pries my hand from her skin, turning her palm to place her hand in mine. I look down at our joined hands. This feels so right, but I know it isn't.

"How long have you been with your biker club?" she asks, looking up at me.

I reach for the top of the doorjamb of her apartment door and hold on to it as I look down into her eyes. I watch as her breath hitches and her gaze rolls over me. That desire seems to increase tenfold as she takes me in.

She cranes her neck to look up at me. She's about five-eight, give or take. My brothers and I tend to shrink down to fit in our human forms, so I tower over her at six-seven at the moment.

"Almost all my life. Why? Not into bikers?"

"Does that really matter?"

I snort. "No, gorgeous, it doesn't."

"Can I ask one more question?"

I reach for her waist and pull her toward my heat. I love that she comes willingly. Something I'm sure isn't the norm for her.

"You have my attention. Ask away."

"Do you have an older brother?"

I lean in to nuzzle her ear. "Want to come meet my family, do you? I love a woman who knows what she wants."

A shiver runs through her as that delicious scent begins to rise more. She places a hand on my chest. "Just answer the question."

"Yes, I have two. My oldest brother and my twin."

She seems to relax, causing me to look down into her eyes curiously. I'm so tempted to kiss her. Yet I know if I do, I'll be inside her apartment in the next breath with her riding my face.

"Do you all look alike?"

"What was that?" I say as she pulls me from my thoughts of devouring her sweet-smelling pussy.

"Do you guys look alike?" she repeats.

"I guess you could say we do. I'm the only one with blond hair and blue eyes."

"Oh," she says as a confused look comes to her face.

"What's going on in your head? Am I not good enough for you? Looking for something else? They're all bikers as well, so you're not trading out for much."

She forces a laugh. "It's nothing. I was just curious."

I laugh too. "You have a good night. Looking forward to talking to you again. You keep that sexy ass covered when you come out of that door. I don't need you trying to arrest me for what I might do to someone for staring or trying to touch," I say with a grin.

"Good night, neighbor."

"Ardan … and you are?"

"Billy Ann, but you can call me Billy."

"Good night, Billy. You go on inside and lock the door."

"You just said you know I'm a cop. You know I can handle myself, right?"

"I do. I'm still going to make sure you make it inside. Unless you're thinking about asking me to come in. I'm great with my mouth. I can do all the talking if you like."

Her chest begins to heave, and her cheeks take on a darker hue. It's pretty on her. I wouldn't have thought I could make her blush.

"Good night, Ardan. It's nice to finally know how to pronounce your name."

"Good night, baby girl. See you around."

Billy

The Veil is Lifted

Two weeks later ...

I lift an arm and give my pit a sniff. I know I'm being ridiculous, but I would rather have taken a shower for tonight. Too bad for me, something is going on with the water pressure. I'll have to call maintenance in the morning.

I stand in the mirror, looking myself over. I have on makeup and I'm wearing a dress. I bite my lip, wondering if I'm doing too much with the red lipstick.

I don't normally dress up like this, but I want to look nice when I meet my sisters for the first time. Since this is sort of like a bachelorette party, I went with this little black number; it's flirty and cute.

It stops midthigh and pours over my curves with the right amount of everything. The sleeves are sheer and puff just a

bit. The patent leather pumps on my feet are the right touch to pull it all together.

"Look at you, Billy. Maybe you'll run into Ardan on the way back in," I say and wink at my reflection.

I haven't been able to get that man off my mind. After that vision in the bathtub, I was sure I was hallucinating when he came up behind me in the hall. I have never been so turned on by anyone.

That body and his face. Good Lord, he said I smelled good, but that man smells divine—like the ocean mixed with a clean breeze. I could sit and allow him to talk in my ear for hours and probably would come from that alone.

The way his voice rumbles like the roar of the ocean rushing does something to me. I clench my thighs and chide myself for getting lost in my thoughts of him again.

Yelp, these panties are ruined. I'll be changing them before I leave. I roll my eyes and turn to pull a new pair from the drawer. My phone rings as I get the new pair in my hand.

I glance at my phone on top of the dresser and see it's Carson. My heart begins to race. This is it.

"Hello," I say into the phone as I answer.

"Hey, I'm sorry, Billy. We did catch him in the act. I mean … we had him. Everything was going as you said it would. Then … *fuck*," he roars into the line.

"Car, what happened? Are you all right?"

"I'm fine, but none of this makes sense. One minute, we had him with the vic. The next, all our surveillance and comms failed. I'm talking about total blackout," he says in frustration.

"Is she safe? Is she still alive?"

"Yeah, she is, but Candido got away and she's not talking. Billy, I swear there was another woman there. Then puff she was gone."

"What? Did she escape with Candido?" I breathe as I knit my brows in confusion.

"No. I called in some pretty big favors for this. I look crazy as fuck right now."

"So they're shutting it down?"

He sighs. "No, lucky for me, the rest of the team saw what I saw and had the same questions. The FBI wants to continue looking into Ricci."

"That's good, right? That's what I wanted."

"Yeah, Billy, but how do I explain the things you told me?"

Oh shit. I groan. Carson had trusted my word when I asked for the favor. I had been so sure Candido would be caught red-handed, so I didn't think that far ahead.

"Shit, Carson. Let me cancel my plans. I'm on my way. I've got you."

"You better. I'm looking at losing my job if I don't come up with some answers tonight."

"I promise I'm coming. Hold tight."

I hang up and dial Lee. She was the one to suggest we all meet. I'm disappointed I'm not going to make it, but I can't let Carson go down for helping me. I'll figure something out to help him.

I have to.

The Bishop

Our Time

I hate weakness. Since I was a boy, I've learned to find it and cut it out. My master can't count on me if I allow weakness to distract me from the course I'm on.

The fact that I'm still chasing this task because somehow, I've been made blind to where those bastards are digs in deep, but I will never give up. It is my life's mission to find them and free my lord once and for all.

Once he's free, we can right all wrongs that have manifested over the course of time. Everything has gone to shit. My kind aren't the only ones who have suffered. There's no longer a species that's pure among us.

I bare my teeth as I get lost in my thoughts and not the release I'm supposed to be enjoying. I grab Azar by her red hair and tug her head back.

"I summoned you for business. You offered this release to relieve the stress. Can't you do better?" I snarl as I glare into her eyes.

"You have to allow me to do better. You're making me work without my hands. Relax, focus on me. Not what needs to be done. We will get to business once I give you a much-needed release," she purrs.

"You used to be able to get it done without your hands. Figure it out," I hiss.

Azar is one of those weaknesses I need to get under control. If not for that curse, I wouldn't even have a mate. I wanted to ignore her from the first time I ran across her. I didn't have time for her then and I barely allow myself to indulge now.

I already know I can't trust her fully. Never again will I allow myself to let my guard down around her. If I didn't know I would be ending my own life, I would have taken hers then.

I nearly did until I realized my life force was draining with hers. That's when I healed her and allowed her to flee back to the fairy realm. That incident is where I got the idea of finding the mates of those bastards.

I don't know if their kind has the same weakness—probably not, as Tanrı has granted them exceptions the rest of my people never had. And here lies the problem. They have never been held to proper standards.

Even if I can't use their mates to kill them. Once I find them, they will lead me to them. Most importantly, I will also have the child. The child is the key to freeing my master.

"Argh," I groan as Azar places more vigor into her task, effectively pulling me from my thoughts.

Placing a hand behind her head, I push her head down further. She begins to choke, bringing a smile to my face. I groan when she relaxes her throat and takes me deeper.

My resentment rises as I feel myself about to come. How I allow this fairy to reduce me to this, I will never know. As

my rage boils over, I tug her from my cock and force her to stand.

I bend her over the desk and thrust into her treacherous cunt. She moans like a whore as I seat myself. This bond may force me to desire her, but I don't have to like it.

I take her body with the force of my anger. My hips slap so hard against her ass, her front is knocking against the desk. I'm sure she will have bruises later.

That's nothing new. It's par for the course for our trysts. Always rough, never after I've ingested anything around her, and I finish on her and not in her. She will never trick another being from my loins.

"Shut up," I bite out as she begins to moan and keen loudly.

"Please, more, please," she begs.

I hadn't planned on stopping anytime soon. However, I do need to slow my pace to throw up a sound barrier. I don't need one of my hunters to hear her.

They need to continue to believe I have no weaknesses. I have served the church for centuries to hide my true purpose. It has suited me well. And then I met her. Her tempting lips and supple skin drew me in like a weak-minded dog.

The fever of the mate bond made me sick for a week before I gave in. That fever is treacherous. I'm counting on that firsthand knowledge for my plan.

I know if I have control of their mates, I will own them. Even the sons of Tanrı will be no match for the mate bond. I've had more than one witch tell me they will find their chosen ones, including this one squealing beneath me.

She stiffens against the desk, at the same time, I feel a shift in the ethers. I know right away she's felt it too. I pause and pull out.

"You felt that?" I say. "What has happened?"

Azar has made herself useful to me. When I needed a witch to assist me in my mission, I went to the coven she was raised in. That was when I first saw her.

A week later, I destroyed the village but took her with me. She was skilled enough to do all I needed and as she was my mate, her powers were heightened, causing me to have no need to mingle with those poor excuses for witches.

I've never told her that my powers were diminished as punishment for my part in the wars. I honestly didn't think I had anything left to share with her.

However, there was just enough left for her to gain. While I had to use alchemy and other dark methods to restore myself, she's been able to wield my powers for her own effortlessly. I'm sure our spawn would be just as gifted wherever she may be—if I had not locked her powers away at birth.

"A veil has been lifted. You must find their mates now. The ones who have kept us blind are weakened. One of them is gone," Azar says.

A smile comes to my lips. I wasn't the only one blocked. It's as if everyone had been made blind to them, if not within their circle.

"Are we not going to finish?"

"No. We are done. It's time you do your part. I need my army ready. We are coming upon the hour. Don't come back until you have managed your tasks."

"But—"

"I said go," I snarl.

I don't even wait for her to leave before I fix my clothes and head to my prayer quarters. No one would ever suspect what I have hidden in this room.

Before the war, Master Harb gave me a source stone. It's the only reason I didn't completely lose my powers when he

was sentenced and locked away. I have used the stone to communicate with my lord.

I grin when I enter the space, and the stone begins to glow. Even my master can feel the time growing near. He shall be free soon.

I kneel before the stone and bow my head. It doesn't take long before I'm pulled through the ethers to the realm between here and where my master is imprisoned. Always just out of reach.

"My Lord, I can feel your power increasing. The time is coming."

"Yes, I can do more to influence emotions and thoughts now. I feel it. It is time you use Eden and Asher. Their gift will serve you in this hour. You have to be quick.

"Send them to inhabit the ones who hold trust. You will see who I mean as you return. Play every angle you have to succeed.

"I am sure Tanrı is watching your every move. Do not become complacent in this hour. You are right. I have grown stronger.

"He has to know this as well. However, he will be too late to stop me once you unlock this cage. I will push my energy to help as much as I can," he says.

"I will not fail you, my lord. I will have Eden and Asher do our bidding right away."

With that, I open my eyes and stand to my feet. I will not waste valuable time. In my mind's eye, I see exactly who to send the twin hunters to.

Their gift of invading bodies and minds will come in handy. They are invaluable as they are able to take over a being completely and harness their memories and mannerisms.

My top hunters all have special purposes. Their gifts were

chosen to play a part in this mission. They are the first line in this war.

"Yes, this is war. We will finish what was started," I say as I move to find Sister Eden and Brother Asher.

PAULY

I JUMP out of my sleep and look around. My heart is racing. Something doesn't feel right.

Reaching for my chest, I rub at it and take a deep breath. I furrow my brows and try to gather my bearings. What the fuck is going on?

Turning my head, I look down at my Gianna. She looks like she's still asleep. Good, I don't want to wake her.

I can't believe this woman is still with me. Marrying into the Ricci family hasn't been so great to her. Money doesn't fix all things. I've caused her hurt I never intended to—things I can never fix.

Pursing my lips, I shake my head. I've put her through enough. This is why I have to ensure Candido doesn't fuck this up.

I can't take this life away from her. What will all her pain be for if it all disappears? We lose the Iron Brothers; we lose this cushy life and all that comes with it. One way or another, we have to turn this around.

I might hate summoning those biker fuckers, but they have done their part to make sure my family has been prosperous. I can't deny that. However, the one thing Gianna wanted, I couldn't get from them.

This woman has allowed me to bring a child into our home to raise when I couldn't give her one of her own. A child who hates us both. Charlie Ann has looked at us with scorn from the time she was a baby.

"Never should have agreed to any of this shit," I mutter under my breath.

I turn to roll out of bed to head to my office. I know I'm not going back to sleep. As I roll from the bed, it groans and creeks loudly under my weight.

Annoyed, I grind my teeth. They don't make furniture like they used to. This thing has been making more and more noise lately.

"What's wrong, Pauly?" Gianna murmurs sleepily as she stirs from her sleep.

"Forget about it. It's nothing, go back to sleep."

"You want me to make you a sandwich? I can heat up some pasta or something. I made some of Ma's gravy last night."

"No, thanks. I'm fine."

My phone rings before she can say anything else. I grab it from the nightstand and move from the room to answer. Still rubbing at my chest, I know something is wrong.

"Hello."

"Pauly, it ain't good," Marko says on the other side of the line.

"What happened? He didn't lose them, did he?"

I'm going to hurt Candido if he causes this bond to be broken because of his stupidity. He always calls me the slow one. I don't have to be quick to see what's coming from his actions.

"No … no, but I can't tell you what just happened. I ain't never seen no shit like it and I've seen some crazy shit working for you guys."

"Just spit it out. What has Candido done now?"

"We were down at the docks to make that deal with Lombardo work. He was trying to meet with the brothers' guy down there. Some other shit went down and the met went sideways.

"Feds were there, and we almost got busted. We escaped but I couldn't tell you how or what the fuck happened," Marko says, sounding completely confused.

I've had Marko watching my brother for the last three years. I don't trust Candido not to fuck this all up. He's getting us into some shit I don't know if either of us knows how to get out of.

Fucking with those genies was just one of his dumbass ideas I know will come back to bite us. His desperation is a problem. He's making bad decision after bad decision. I need eyes on him.

"I knew him wanting to make that deal was going to be a problem. He's grasping at straws to keep those bikers under our thumb. He is going to cost us everything with this reckless bullshit."

"I thought you would want to know," Marko says.

"Good job. You made the right call. Keep me posted," I say and hang up.

I pinch the bridge of my nose. I knew something wasn't right. Candido is going to get us both killed.

"*Fuck*," I roar.

Ardan

Different

I still haven't been able to wrap my mind around the fact that Kendrick has found his mate. She's not what I expected, but I like her. She suits him.

I rub at my chest, wondering if I will be next. I had to stop by to see the sea fairies—not to be confused with water fairies. They'd have your ass for that.

Sea fairies provide us superbeings with seaweed. It's nothing like the human stuff. Sea fairies grow some pure shit. Not the type of stuff that needs to fall into the hands of any human—not without being diluted with magic dust.

I was in desperate need of some hydro to calm my nerves. Knowing my mate is out there and could be on her way has all kinds of energy rolling through me. I can't even get off my bike to head upstairs.

Instead, I roll up right here in the lot. I've just placed the joint in my mouth and pulled out a lighter when Billy pulls in. I squint as I light up and watch her step from her car.

"Shit, my mate better show up soon before I say fuck it and pin her ass to a wall and eat her until she's dry," I say as I stare at my little neighbor.

She's in heels and a dress that shows off her sexy legs. She looks tired as she heads my way, but never more gorgeous. I knit my brows and pull a hand down my face as a breeze blows through the garage and her scent is carried on it.

It's different. Almost as if not human at all. I tilt my head to the side. Ray sort of has the same scent. As a matter of fact, Billy came to mind earlier when Kendrick introduced me and the others to Ray.

I knew Ray reminded me of someone, but I couldn't nail it right away. Then Billy's face popped into my head. I don't want to be a dick and say all Black women look alike, so I shook the thought off.

"Well, look at you. Getting high in the basement of our building as if you don't have an apartment right upstairs," she says with a sleepy grin.

"You plan on booking me?"

"Not if you're willing to share. I haven't been home since last night. I want a shower I can't have and something greasy and comforting to fill my belly that I know I don't have in my fridge."

"Why can't you have that shower? Where have you been since last night? Hot date? You've been cheating on me, baby girl?"

I should feel guilty for flirting now that I know my mate could be on her way, but there's something about this woman. Her scent is driving me fucking crazy.

"I wish. I would much rather have been on a date than where I was. We'd have to be dating for me to cheat," she says and rolls her eyes.

"You going to tell me what's going on with your shower? You need to come use mine?"

"Not going to happen," she scoffs. "Something is going on with the water pressure in my place. I was going to call maintenance first thing this morning, but I've been in an interrogation room since last night."

"I'll come up and look at it," I say and swing my leg off my bike, then put my joint out.

"You don't have to do that."

I step closer to her and place my nose in her wavy locks. I inhale deeply and my pants grow tight. Shit, she smells good. My throat tickles a bit, causing me to back off.

I look down at her, narrowing my gaze. If she were my mate, I would be in full fever right now. I chalk it up to wishful thinking.

"Come on, it's no problem. I'll even give you a few hits of my joint after I get you that greasy food you're craving."

"Oh, so you're really trying to act like my man now," she laughs.

I place my hand on the back of her neck like I did that one night. I swear to the gods she feels right in my palm. If I didn't know any better, I would claim her as mine regardless.

Too bad we're not able to choose our mate for ourselves. She'd be mine in a heartbeat. When she leans into me as I guide us to the elevator, I have to hold back the groan that rises in my throat.

"I have a question. Why are you all dressed up?"

"I was going to meet with some friends before I got a call. I didn't have time to change. I had to get to my brother to help him."

"Is he all right? Is there anything I can do?"

"He'll be fine. I sort of got him into a jam. I hope I said all the right things to cover his ass. I'll never forgive myself if he loses his badge."

"I know people in high places. If you need some help, come to me. I'll do all I can," I say.

"Aren't you sweet."

"Gods, Billy, did you change your perfume?" I groan as we ride in the tight space.

She looks up at me in surprise. "No. I mean, I'm probably a little ripe right now since I haven't had a real shower in over forty-eight hours."

"There is nothing ripe about you. You smell like ocean candy," I say before I can think better of it.

"Ocean candy?" she blinks at me in confusion.

"It's … never mind. I used to eat it as a kid."

I thank the gods when the elevator dings open. We step out and I lead her to her apartment. Once inside, she steps from her shoes and heads for the kitchen.

"Want a beer?"

I go to say no because human beer tastes like shit and does nothing for us, but she's welcoming me into her space and this pull to her is enough to make me question everything. Instead, I smile and nod. She grabs two longnecks and comes over to hand me one.

"I'm sure you're wasting your time. The least I can do is offer you a drink."

"No time with you is wasted. Besides, you said you were hungry. Once I fix the water, you can take your shower while I order something to eat. What are you in the mood for?" I reply.

The heated look she gives me brings a smile to my lips. We'd be so much trouble together. All the things I'd do to her without penetration would blow her mind.

"I'm good with a Philly cheesesteak and fries. That place on Broadway is okay when you can't get the real thing," she says.

"A Philly cheesesteak and fries you shall have. Let me get that shower fixed."

I take the beer and saunter my way into the bathroom up

the hall. I know the layout of her place because I've been in the units above and below this one when I looked at the place to purchase.

I look over my shoulder to find her watching my ass. I grin and shake my head—glad she's not following me. She looks tired, so I'm not going to do this the human way.

Once in the bathroom, I close the door and take a sip of the beer. I grimace at the bottle and pour the rest down the sink. The shit is horrible.

Pulling the joint from my pocket, I go ahead and reroll it with magic dust in case Billy does decide to take a few pulls. As I do that, I work on the water pressure with my magic as well.

It only takes a few seconds, but I knock around in here for a few minutes to keep down her suspicion. After about ten minutes, I reach into the shower to turn it on. When I open the door, Billy is standing there with a towel clutched to her chest and a smile on her face.

"You fixed it," she says as she peeks into the bathroom, where the shower is still running.

"I told you I would," I say as I lean into the doorway.

"Thanks. You have no idea how much I appreciate this."

I bite back the slick comment that floats to my lips. I couldn't bear for my mate to have another woman she had to compete with. As much as I want Billy, it's not fair to her either.

So I keep my mouth shut and reach to grasp the back of her neck and kiss her forehead. I'm no saint. I'm using all the restraint I have as it is. Not to mention, I just want to inhale her for a moment.

Whatever she's done to her scent has an intoxicating allure to it. I want to suck down as much of the aroma as I can. I keep my lips pressed to her skin for a few beats just so I can.

"No need to thank me. Take your shower. I'll have your food waiting for you when you're done."

"Okay."

I step out of the way and allow her to go into the bathroom. I think to cleanse her place of my essence. I've used enough magic to leave an imprint, but there's something about her being wrapped in my magic that makes my chest swell with pride.

I shake the thought off and go to sit in the living room. I'm lost in thought as I pull my phone and scroll through messages. I have one from Kai. Which I find odd. She has the ability to mind-link me.

Only human brothers and hangarounds need to communicate with me through text. I throw up a barrier around myself so my call can't be overheard. Then I dial Kai back.

"Hello."

"Kai? What's up, baby girl?"

"Ricci tried to kill me. He was looking for Amadeus."

"Did you take his fucking head off?" I growl.

My brothers and I aren't allowed to kill Candido or his brother, but Kai could have done it easily. I hope she did. Kendrick has his mate, but the rest of us would need to find ours to be free once and for all.

"No, he had his men bind my hands. They also injected me with something to keep me from mind-linking. Ardan, Güç gave her life to save mine. She came out of nowhere. One minute, Candido had a gun pointed at my head; the next, she appeared and covered me with this light.

"I didn't know she was a super. I didn't know there were others with that type of power. She shielded me, but it cost her her life."

"Hold on, you didn't know she was an other? Bradan mentioned it and I was supposed to talk to you about it, but you mean to tell me you didn't even know?"

"No, I couldn't sense it at all. The cops are involved, Ardan. I called you earlier from jail right before they released me.

"I didn't think they would. They kept me for hours asking questions. I wouldn't say anything. I called you as soon as I could to get some help," she explains.

"Where are you now?"

"I'm home. I wasn't sure if I should show up at the club-house. I didn't want to bring trouble to the brotherhood's doorstep."

"Good girl. I want you to head there now. You can tele-port. I will open a portal for you so you arrive at the club safely without being followed. I'll be there first thing in the morning. We'll talk more then."

"Thank you, My King."

I hang up and growl. I think to tell my brothers what's going on, but these are water folk. It's my prob-lem. Kendrick went to that party with his mate and Bradan and Reilly already have enough on their plates. I'll handle this in the morning, and if I need to share then, I will.

I'm lost in thought when I feel Billy enter the room. Lifting my head, I find her standing watching me. She's in a T-shirt with her legs bear again. She's killing me with this shit.

I clear my throat and stand. "You're right on time. They just delivered your food," I say.

I move to the door as I use my magic to leave the bag of food outside her apartment. When I open the door, the bag is sitting there with her piping-hot food. I turn back into the apartment and find her sitting on the couch with her legs tucked beneath her.

"God, that smells good."

I carry the bag over to her and place it on the coffee table.

She leans forward to grab the bag and peeks inside. I stand watching her as she looks up at me.

"You didn't order something for yourself?"

"Not hungry. You enjoy, baby girl."

"You seem like you're having as rough a day as I am."

"This is more than a day."

"You want to talk about it?"

I scoff. "You would need to give me your entire life to tell you all I'm dealing with."

"Let me grab a beer and you can give me the CliffsNotes. It's the least I can do. My father says I need to make more friends and let others in."

I give her a tight smile. For decades, that's all I've ever wanted. Someone other than my brothers who I could open up to. We've been hidden for so long it's become a habit not to share or open up.

"You and I have more in common than you might think."

She tilts her head to the side as she munches on her food. "You're emotionally unavailable too?"

"Something like that. I have as many secrets as I see swimming in your eyes."

"Do you now? My secrets are innocent. Something tells me yours might have a little bite."

That should be my cue to leave. I can never tell her about my world. Her place is in the human world, far away from me and all that comes with me. Not to mention, the secrets I hold could send her running for the hills.

That's what I should want. I have a mate out there somewhere. This little thing is only a means to pass time.

Yet even thinking that feels wrong and sounds worse in my head. I definitely need to clear my mind. I stand to do just that and start for her kitchen.

"That they do, baby girl. That they do. Let me get you that beer."

My secrets have more than a little bite. They'd take a chunk out of her. Not willing to allow that; I'll have to change the subject.

BILLY

I'M SITTING HERE LAUGHING like a little schoolgirl as I get high with my sexy biker neighbor. That food was torch. It hit the spot for sure. The best I've ever had from that place.

"You're nothing like what I expected," I say as I take the joint from his hand and take a puff.

This stuff is good as well. It smokes so clean. I have a nice high. Just what I needed to get my mind off the shit that went down. I lied my ass off for my brother.

If this shit blows back, it's going to roll back on me as it should. I can't allow Carson to take the fall for me. Candido is a piece of shit and should pay for everything he's done.

"What were you expecting?" Ardan says, pushing into my thoughts.

I shrug my shoulders. "I don't know. You come off as rough and gruff. Instead, you're down to earth and kind of funny. The alpha male shit, that doesn't surprise me as much.

"My attraction to it is more of a surprise to me. Actually, my attraction to you, period, has caught me off guard," I say before I can shut myself up.

It has to be the weed. My foot is in my mouth and my brain isn't connecting to shut me the fuck up. My cheeks heat as I start to feel stupid for talking so much.

I cut my words off by taking another pull and handing

the joint back. He takes the joint with one hand and lifts his other arm as if welcoming me into his side. There's this pull to him that's been calling to me all night.

I couldn't ignore him if I wanted to. I move over close to him and settle into his side. He's warm but cool at the same time. I don't know how to explain it. It's almost like sitting next to a warm spring while a breeze is blowing.

He wraps his arm around me as he puffs at the joint. I allow myself to relax and wonder what it would be like if I had someone to let my guard down with. I don't know how to let someone take care of me.

However, I wouldn't mind trying with this guy. I'm totally thrown by my train of thought. The last thing I need is to fall into some relationship.

I'm going to need my focus to help take down Candido Ricci. Nothing can get in the way of that mission. He's going to pay.

"I should probably go," Ardan says, jolting me out of my thoughts.

I look up at him in confusion. That is not what I was expecting him to say after my confession and him drawing me in close.

"Um … you don't have to."

"I should though. I have some business to handle in the morning and you should get some rest. When this stuff hits, you're going to pass out anyway. I want you to lock up behind me before you fall out."

I get angry that he doesn't want to stay. Just when I am ready to let my guard down, he's rejecting me. This is why I take care of myself.

"Yeah, fine. Thanks for everything," I bite out.

"Billy, I—"

"You don't owe me anything. See you around."

He clamps his mouth shut and stands. I pull back into

myself and shut down. I don't need him and one night isn't going to miraculously make us the perfect match. He can go.

"I'll see you around," he says as he nods to himself and turns for the door.

I stand to follow him to lock up. Anger fills me as tears sting the backs of my eyes. He turns to look down at me as we reach the door.

"Billy—"

"Good night, Ardan."

He sighs heavily. "Good night, Billy."

Ardan

Unexpected Guests

"*D*o you need anything? How are you feeling this morning?" I ask as Kai enters my office.

"I'm fine. Still a bit shaken up. Güç only worked for us for a few weeks. Why would she give up her life for me? What was she doing there? Better yet, what was she that I didn't know she was a super, and where did her body go? Could she have been some type of fairy?"

"All great questions. It's not uncommon for some to hide their identity when it comes to lower-level others. No offense."

Kai wouldn't have felt what Bradan and I were able too. I can't blame her for not knowing she had an other around who was hiding their identity. It really wasn't her place to.

"None taken. Amadeus said I could hire help while he was gone. I thought she was a human."

"This is my fault. I was supposed to tell you she wasn't about two weeks ago. Reilly and I are going to head down to

the warehouse to see what we can learn. I will inform Amadeus of what's going on."

"What about Candido? He wants to get in touch with Amadeus in order to strike a deal up because you guys will never agree to what he's asking for," Kai says with concern in her voice.

I scoff. "He won't have to worry about what we won't agree to. He's cut off. No one under our charge is to do anything for him. No one," I say firmly.

"I'm fine with that. Fucking prick was going to shoot me in the head. He's lucky I don't break into his place and put Octo poison in his food."

"Not a bad idea. Let's keep that on the table for now," I chuckle.

I would love to watch Candido take his last breath. I don't care for his brother either. He fears us too much to summon us as much as his brother does, but he has asked for things in the past.

He usually has a laundry list, so he only has to summon us once until the next time his coward ass gets up the courage to call for us again.

Kai's stomach grumbles, pulling me from my thoughts. Her cheeks glow as she bites her lip and holds a hand to her stomach. I give her a warm smile.

"Hungry?"

"Yeah, it's been a while since I've had anything. I was too wired to find something once I arrived last night."

I stand from my desk. "Come with me. I'll get you something to eat and we can talk some more."

"Okay. Thanks."

We exit my office and head to the main hall. Once there, we get Kai something to eat, and she finds a corner to sit in. I'm about to go sit with her when I see Bradan with a tiny woman clinging to him.

So he's found himself a new fairy. I grin as I watch the two. However, I make note that she's not a fairy at all. My curiosity gets the better of me.

"Kai, you eat as much as you want and stay for as long as you like. I'd prefer to have you here at the clubhouse for now. At least until I speak with Amadeus. I'll check in on you later," I say as I start in the direction of my brother and the mystery woman.

"I'm cool. You don't have to worry about me," Kai calls after me.

I lift a hand to acknowledge her words. There's something about the look on Bradan's face that's holding my attention. This little woman is more than a warm body that has filled his bed.

This will be interesting, I tell myself. Could this be his mate? If it is, I was right to walk away from Billy last night. Her confession of her attraction was the final straw. I had been ready to strip her bare and devour her.

If I hadn't put an end to things when I did, I would have taken things too far and hurt her in the end. She may not be my mate, but I have more respect for her than to do something like that to her.

When I get closer to my brother the first thing to hit me is the woman's scent. It's so familiar. I can smell her human blood, but there is something else, like Kendrick's mate Ray and ... Billy. That's what was different last night.

That hint of something other. I had ignored it because of the high from the joint and my hope to finally find my mate. There's something sweeter about the way they smell, with a hint of something familiar.

Could I have been with my ... no.

BILLY

"HELLO," I groan into the phone as I snatch it up from the nightstand.

"Billy, we need to talk. Can we meet up?"

"Carson?"

"Yeah, I can come to you if you want."

I palm my forehead as my head clears, and I begin to become alert. Last night comes back to me. I remember crying myself to sleep after letting Ardan out.

That's so not like me. It had to be the weed. I don't smoke often.

I've had a few smoke sessions with Carson and Eddy when we were younger, but I haven't smoked much since. I thought it would help me get my mind off things last night.

Boy did it, but what the hell was the rest of that. I haven't cried over someone leaving me behind in years. I shake it off and focus on what Carson has asked.

He wants to come by. Bile rises in my throat at the thought of him running into Ardan or Ardan seeing him entering or leaving my place. I don't want to come off as petty—because he rejected me or worse as some slut—who jumps from guy to guy.

Not that it should matter. I just can't get the feeling out of my head—Carson and Ardan should never meet. I grow protective of Carson and shake my head as if he can see me.

"No, no. I'll come to you. I'm just waking up, so give me an hour or so to head your way."

"I'm already up and on the move. I can be to you in twenty."

"No. I'll meet you at your place. I have errands to run anyway."

"I can bring you coffee and breakfast. It's no big deal. If I stop for breakfast, that will give you more time to get ready," he pushes.

"Carson," I huff. "I'll be ready in thirty and we can go to breakfast together. How does that sound?"

"Perfect. I know this place you'll love. The food is great. We can talk in the car on the way," he says with way too much hope in his voice.

I frown. There's something off about the way he sounds. It's not just the eagerness. Something is different in his voice.

As my Spidey senses go off, I decide to use our secret code. Mack made us come up with it years ago so we'd be able to let the other know something was wrong. As runaways it was a necessary precaution.

"Car?"

"Yeah?"

"Not my blood …"

"But always my family," he responds.

I blow out a relieved breath. Thank God. I have enough weird shit going on.

"Text me when you arrive, I'll come down to meet you. See you in a bit," I sigh into the phone.

Hanging up, I then flop back against my pillow and close my eyes to think. I don't allow myself to think of last night or Ardan. I need to get my head together to figure out this mess I've gotten Carson and me into.

I growl and punch the bed as I kick my feet. This is why I never ask for help. The one time I do, I get Carson into some shit and we could both end up losing our badges.

"Fuck me," I groan as I open my eyes and stare up at the ceiling.

I was so focused on nailing Candido I didn't think about how this could blow up in my face. Yes, we saved that woman's life, but how do we get out of this without me ending up in a straitjacket.

"Why me?" I mumble and force myself to get up and head for the shower.

I smile as I remember Ardan coming to fix the water pressure for me. Immediately, I frown and chide myself for my thoughts. I mean, I confessed that I was attracted to him.

I was expecting him to flirt back or something, not rush to leave. I'm not begging for anyone's attention.

I don't know what his problem is, but I guess it's for the best. I don't need to get involved with him anyway. He could be a potential suspect.

I make quick work of taking my shower. Then I jump out to lotion my skin before I throw on a pair of jeans and a loose-fitting T-shirt. Looking in the mirror, I decide to leave my curly waves out.

I run a hand through my locks and pull them to the right side, then go to plug in my flat iron to set my part. Once I have a clean part and my hair is resting to the right on its own, I blow out a breath and head to the kitchen to find something to drink.

I glance toward the lockbox where I keep my guns, but my stomach growls and acid rises in my throat. Damn, I didn't realize how hungry I am. I can't wait for breakfast with Carson. I need something to eat now.

I move into the kitchen and go to make some toast. Once the bread is in the toaster, I decide to grab the kettle to fill it with water for some tea. As the water runs, I stare at it, filling the clear glass. My vision begins to ripple.

I gasp as the head of that dragon from the other vision

rises from the water in the kettle. My hand shakes as I place the kettle down in the sink. Covering my mouth, I try to hold my scream in.

Its whisker-looking things curl at the tips as they float through the air and glow with a light of their own. Its blue skin looks almost iridescent. Yet, it sits there as if it belongs.

What the fuck was in that shit we smoked last night? I'm never smoking again. When it seems like it tilts its head to study me, I nearly laugh. This is some crazy shit.

"What the fuck?" I breathe when I finally calm myself.

The dragon remains silent at first as it looks me in the eyes with its deep-blue ones. I take a few steps back, bumping into the island behind me.

The dragon becomes larger and places its forearms against the edge of the sink as if it were an old friend leaning in to have a chat. Its elbows look hard and sharp, like horns or something. I shake my head as if that will be enough to clear it and make the vision go away.

"Don't be alarmed. I have not come to harm you but to join you. It is time, young master."

"Time for what?"

"Time for you to connect with your inner self, the part of you that has the power to accept me. Time for you to find your strength within so my place can be prepared. You and I will connect at the core.

"They are coming, and you will need to be ready, young master. Soon, you will learn to count on others once again. When you return home, you will fully understand," the dragon says.

I can't believe I'm standing in the middle of my kitchen talking to a fucking dragon. Scratch that, a dragon who has half its body sticking out of my damn tea kettle.

"Return home? This is my home."

"Yes, but not the home I speak of. You were touched with

power; it is time for it to awaken. Water and ash are within you. Your power is pushing at the surface. Just reach for it," it replies.

My toast pops up in the toaster, breaking the vision. The dragon disappears, leaving me baffled and confused. I really need to have my head examined.

Muttering to myself, I change my mind about the tea. I'm no longer interested. I'm grabbing the butter for my toast when there's a knock at the door.

I roll my eyes. Carson never listens. Good thing he didn't arrive a few moments ago.

That shit would have freaked him out. I wonder if he would have seen it in the first place. This could be my own brand of crazy.

Lost in thought, I head for the door to answer it before someone sees Carson in the hall. Nervously, I bite my lip as I think of him and Ardan running into each other.

"I told you to text me," I say as I open the door to rush him inside.

I'm taken by surprise as I'm pushed back into my apartment by three large guys. I stumble back in shock. However, it only takes a second for me to snap into action.

I turn for the lockbox to grab a gun, but I'm grabbed by the back of my hair. This guy is huge and so much taller than me. The tight grip he has on my hair causes me to panic for a second.

My heart races as I think of how this can all go wrong. I bet these guys belong to Ricci. He's finally going to finish me off. I wonder if he knows I'm his daughter or if he even cares.

I throw my head back as I'm lifted off my feet, hoping to connect with this bastard's face. When I don't make the connection, I begin to panic more. He starts to head for the door with me still in tow.

My instincts begin to kick in. If they get me outside of

this apartment, I'm fucked. The vision from the kitchen comes back to me. Maybe this has nothing to do with Ricci.

These guys seem a bit off and uncharacteristically tall. I really start to panic as I think this could be some unnatural shit happening to me.

I kick at the guy nearest me, and he stumbles back. I then kick out at the one holding me and connect this time. He drops me and I spin to kick him again.

As I drop him to his knees, the third one comes at me. That's when I get this feeling to just hold out my hands. As soon as I do, an axe and shield appear in my palms. I don't know how, but I know exactly what to do with them.

I twirl the axe in one hand as I hold the shield in front of me with the other. The first guy I kicked recovers and throws a bolt of light at me. I knock it away with the shield and throw the axe at him.

It catches him in the forehead, and he falls back. I grin with satisfaction as his body drops to the floor. The one who grabbed me is now back on his feet and looks like he's about to toss an orb of light at me.

I block the attack just in time as I cross my arm in front of me. The orb bounces off my shield and returns to the sender. The asshole bursts like a water balloon and falls to nothing more than a puddle on the floor.

With a quick glance, I note that my axe is now sitting in a pool of liquid as well. The guy whose head it was lodged in is now gone. The last one comes at me, but my fighting skills kick in and I kick his ass using my shield like a weapon instead of a guard.

I tire him out quickly, then wish the shield had a sharper edge so I could slice his throat and be done with it. As I hit him in the side with the shield, it comes away with blood on the edge. I narrow my eyes and see the edge gleaming like the edge of a sword.

I take a chance and swing for his throat. Suddenly, his neck is slashed and then he too bursts like a water balloon and falls to the floor in a puddle.

I bend at the waist, panting. My mind is reeling and now my heart is racing ten times as fast as it was when I was fighting for my life. I knit my brows in confusion and reach to clench at my T-shirt.

My veins feel like they're on fire. My skin feels like it's going to peel right off my bones. I may have bested those assholes, but did they slip me something to kill me?

This is madness. I've gone twelve rounds in the ring and have never been this winded. My mind races for answers.

What the fuck is wrong with me? I start to become light-headed. That's when a slow clap begins from behind me. I turn quickly to find Ardan standing in my living room, looking back at me. I hold my hand out and the axe comes to me.

"Did Candido Ricci send you and those fucks to finish me off?"

He tilts his head to the side and studies me. "I'm not here to do Ricci's bidding, baby girl. I'm here for you."

I snort, then freeze. "Hold on a minute. Did you just stand there and watch me get jumped?"

"I stood here and watched you take them down without batting an eye. Impressive. I wasn't going to allow them to hurt you, but I got the feeling you would have fought me if I jumped in," he says as he looks me over with a heated gaze and amused smile.

As my adrenaline starts to come down, I can think more clearly. I jerk my head back as I stare across my apartment at him, leaning against the wall with his arms across his chest. None of this is making sense.

What the fuck just happened? How did I get these weapons in my hands? I don't know how I know they will,

but I drop my hands to my sides and allow the axe and shield to vanish.

Placing my hands on my hips, I speak my thoughts as I try to get my heart rate under control. "How did you get in here? You didn't come in with them and you couldn't have come through the front door."

"You pulled me to you. I didn't need to come through the door."

"Ardan, what the hell are you talking about? Am I tripping off that shit you gave me last night?" I say with a grimace as I reach to rub at my chest.

One minute, he's across the room, leaning against the wall. The next, he's in front of me and has me pinned to the wall behind me. My heart begins to race more and not because I'm afraid of him.

"You feel the fever too," he says against my lips.

"What?" I ask in confusion.

"For me, it's like a punch to the gut. My powers are humming to break free. It's a high that comes with pain and excitement.

"So much excitement because I know it's you. Baby, my veins feel alive, my heart is beating double time. If I thought I wanted you before, I'm sure I'll go insane if I don't have you now," he breathes into my mouth as he has a hold of my throat.

I shake my head. "I don't know what's going on, but you lost your chance. You left last night after I told you how I felt. I'm over it."

He snorts a laugh into my ear. "You. Will. Never. Be. Over. Us," he says as he kisses his way down my neck and pushes my chin up with his thumb.

"Get over yourself. I was over you the moment you walked out."

"I only left because I didn't know you were my mate. I

should have felt it from the first time we met. I didn't want to hurt your feelings when my true mate arrived.

"I also thought you were only a human. If you were, not much could've happened between us. I would have torn you apart," he says as he nuzzles my neck and inhales.

"Mate? What the hell are you talking about?"

"Everything you're feeling is because you're my mate. You will be able to handle me because you were made for me. I'll never walk away from you again."

He's driving me crazy with his sensual kisses against my neck. I stifle a moan as my body reacts to him. Frustrated with myself, I push at his shoulders, but he brings his face to mine and takes my lips.

All my fight fades as he devours me. In one swift motion, he has me wrapped around his waist as he holds me tightly in his arms. My pussy begins to pulse for him.

As he swirls his tongue in my mouth, I whimper and lock my fingers in the top of his hair. His mouth is cool and tastes of cool mint.

I don't know what I was expecting, but his kisses are making my toes curl. I get lost in the kiss and begin to grind against him.

The more he kisses me, the more I begin to feel complete. However, I force myself to pull away. His blue eyes seem to glow as he looks back into mine.

"Wait, this is moving too fast. I don't even understand what's going on. What are you? How am I not human?"

"From what I've learned, your father is human. However, you're something else entirely. We haven't figured that part out yet. Your scent is familiar, yet it's not. Each of you has this slight variation.

"I'm not sure if it's because you're part human or if it's just unique to each of you as individuals. It's odd but alluring. Almost intoxicating," he says.

"Ardan, what are you rambling about? Each of who?"

"Your sisters. Two of my brothers have found their mates in your sisters, Ray and Taylor."

"You've met my sisters?"

"Yes."

"Hold on, wait," I say and slide down his front.

I push at him to get some space to think clearly. It's no use. I need him near to subside the racing of my heart and this nauseous feeling. As soon as I put space between us, my stomach pitches and I groan as I begin to feel faint.

As if knowing just what I need, Ardan wraps his arms around my waist from behind and tugs me back into him. I don't miss the bulge digging into me as he rains kisses down my neck once again.

"I can't think while you're doing that. Can you please stop?"

"We should seal the bond. It will help you feel better," he groans as he palms one of my breasts.

"Listen, buddy. I have no idea what you're talking about. I'm not sealing anything until I know what's going on," I bite out.

He reaches around me to tilt my head back, then brings his lips to mine. I squeeze my thighs together, trying to stem off the throbbing happening between my legs. I don't know whether to be happy or frustrated when he doesn't connect our lips.

"You are my mate. You feel the fever as much as I do. This need to be inside you, to have me inside you. It's only going to increase until we accept the bond and seal it.

"I am a demigod, and you were chosen for me. I've lived a very long time waiting for you. I want to bend you over right here and take you now, but I can sense your nerves.

"I never want to harm you, Billy. Everything I do will be to protect and pleasure you. I know we will be perfect

together, like water and ice. One can be rough the other can be soothing, but they will come together as one in the end.

"Allow me to show you how we flow together. I'll taste you first to let you get used to the idea that you're mine and only mine," he breathes against my lips, then flicks his tongue out to lick them.

I whimper and shiver in his hold, my knees nearly giving out. I'm so wet right now, I bet there's a stain on my jeans. He growls.

"Ardan, please," I whisper, not sure which I'm pleading for more—answers or for him to put out this need building inside me.

"Billy, I will answer all of your questions once I've fucked and claimed you. I promise, baby girl."

His words come out strained and tight, as if he's doing all he can to get them out without demanding. I turn in his hold and look up into his eyes. They're still glowing.

"How do I know you're not using some type of magic to trick me into sleeping with you?"

"If I go down on you, it will curb the lust for now. We can go back to the clubhouse and your sisters will confirm what I've told you. They have sealed their bonds already," he says with a pained expression.

There is a knock at the door, and I know for sure it's Carson this time as he croons out my name. I look up at Ardan with wide eyes.

"You have to go. That's my brother. He won't understand any of this."

"I'm good at explaining away situations to humans. Or I can make him forget," he says with a grin.

I think back to when Ricci tried to have my memory erased. Could that really have been Ardan? He did just say he's lived a long time.

I shake the thought off as something else to ask later.

Right now, I need him out of here. My gut keeps telling me that him and Carson meeting is not going to fly.

"No, you need to go."

Carson knocks again. I begin to panic. All he needs to do is test the knob and he'll find the door unlocked.

"Billy, if I leave, you're going to be in pain. The closer I am, the better you will feel."

I groan. "Then make yourself invisible or something. You can do that, right?"

He scoffs. "Yeah, but—"

"No buts, be gone. I'll get rid of him and then we can talk or whatever."

He rolls his eyes at me and vanishes before my face. I heave a sigh of relief and turn to answer the door. A growl fills the air, and my jeans change to a black pair of sweats instead of the light blue jeans I had on.

"Thanks," I whisper and shake my head.

I need him gone, not just invisible, but I like that he doesn't want to leave me in pain. My mind is reeling as I run the last ten minutes through my head.

I have so many questions for Ardan. I don't know whether to feel crazier than ever or to feel relieved because I've found a source for some answers.

Ardan

My Mate

I move to lean against the wall as Billy goes to answer the door. There's no way I'm leaving here without her after she was attacked.

I reach to adjust myself as need pulses through me. I want my mate so bad it hurts. A grin comes to my lips.

It's her. I'm so fucking happy it is. I don't know if I'll be able to reel it in. As I cross my arms and lean against the wall, her ass comes into view and her jeans are soaked through.

I growl and use my magic to change the ruined garments. I change her underwear too, as I pocket the soaked pair. I wouldn't dare to inhale them because I know all restraint will be lost.

Watching closely, I pick up on her nerves as she opens the door. A guy comes into view, looking anxious. However, it's the look of lust that comes to his eyes that makes me stand up straight.

"Why aren't you answering my texts or calls?" he says quickly.

"I was getting ready. I didn't have my phone with me."

"Well, aren't you going to let me in?"

"We should go. I'm starving."

I glance around at the mess from the fight and then down at the floor where the puddles of water lay from her banishing those three. Those guys smelled just like the hunters who were after Ray. Assuming she won't allow him in because of the mess, I use my magic to clean it up without her noticing.

"You know, maybe it's not a good idea to talk in my car. Let me in, we can order in, or I can cook for you."

"I'm already dressed. Let's head out like we planned."

"Why are you being weirder than usual? If you're hungry, I can whip you up something quick. Then we can talk."

"I don't have much here … You know what, let's just rain check this."

"We need to get our stories straight. If my captain figures out I did this because I want you—" he cuts off.

"What?"

I release my arms to my sides and ball my fists. She said this was her brother. He doesn't sound like a brother to me.

"Nothing. We need to clear this up. The fact that you're my sister alone could be a problem."

"I understand how big a problem this could be for you, for me, and for Mack. Our relationship never needs to come up because there're no real records of our adoption.

"Mack pulled some big favors to protect us as kids. When he was finally able to send us to school as Salvados, he took a big risk. Trust me, Carson, I'm going to do everything I can to protect him and you," Billy says pleadingly.

"You want me to trust you, but you won't even allow me

to come into your place. Do you have some guy in there or something?"

"Carson—"

"Baby, where are the towels?" I call, using my magic to throw my voice from deeper in the apartment by the bathroom.

I stifle a chuckle as Billy stiffens. She turns her head and glares in my direction. I know she can't see me, but I feel as if she's looking me in the eyes.

"Who the fuck is that?" Carson growls.

I don't like his tone. I'm tempted to flood his body with water until it comes from every orifice of his being. If Billy didn't seem like she cares about him, I would.

"That is none of your business. I'm a grown woman. I don't have to explain anything happening behind this door," she says as she turns back to him.

"You gave your virginity away to some stranger? Who the fuck is this asshole?"

"None of your business. I will call you later, Car," she bites out.

She goes to close the door, but he sticks his foot in the way. My anger rises. I flash to the hallway of the bath and return with a towel wrapped around my waist and my hair damp.

"Never mind. I found them," I say as I step into the room.

Billy spins around with her mouth open. She takes me in from head to toe. I can smell her sweet arousal from where I stand. She winces and I know it's because of the fever.

"Who the fuck are you?" The asshole says as he pushes his way into the apartment behind Billy. She whips around toward him and folds her arms over her chest.

"I'm her old man. Who are you?"

"Ardan, please," Billy sighs.

I walk up behind her and wrap my arms around her

waist. She melts right into me, bringing a smile to my lips. I dip my head to kiss the top of hers.

"I know you from somewhere," he says and narrows his eyes at me.

"He's my neighbor."

"The biker?" Carson says incredulously.

"The one and only."

"Ardan, this is my brother, Carson."

I note his wince as she calls him her brother. She may see him that way, but it's clear he has some other idea. I can read the jealousy all over him.

"Good to meet you, *brother*," I say, reminding him of his place.

"You're unbelievable, Billy. You're pushing me away for this guy? Eddy told me I was wasting my time. I just thought … it's always been you."

"I'm sorry I don't feel that way for you. Car, this really isn't a good time to do this."

"Right, clearly, you're busy. Don't worry about me. Maybe it's time I had a change of scenery anyway," Carson says and turns to leave.

"Carson, don't be like that. I'll fix it. I promise."

"Don't make promises you can't keep. There's no way for you to truly fix what's been broken."

"Carson, Carson, wait," she pleads.

"Let him go," I say into her ear.

He's not going to listen to anything she has to say. I can see it on his face. She turns on me with anger in her eyes. Carson walks out and slams the door behind him.

"Why the hell would you do that? I asked you to disappear for a reason. I never wanted to hurt him like that."

"I'm not going to apologize for being possessive over my mate. What business of his is your virtue?"

"Ardan, I had it handled. He's my brother. I know how to deal with him. I didn't need you to come to my rescue."

"Your brother," I snort. "Your brother sounds a lot like he wanted to be the one to take what's mine."

"I'm not yours," she growls and stomps her foot.

"You keep telling yourself that. You're cute when you're defiant."

"Why didn't you erase my memory all those years ago?" she blurts out.

"What?" I say as I halt.

I was about to tug her to me for a kiss. We need to seal this bond before I lose my fucking mind. However, her words bring me to a dead stop.

"You saved my life. About thirteen years ago, Candido had planned to kill me. You stepped in and he told you to erase my memory if you weren't going to allow him to kill me. Why?"

Speechless, I stand studying her face. I knew there was something familiar about her. I remember that night.

"I was pissed off at Candido as it was. I didn't want to be involved in his nonsense, but we had no choice."

"What do you mean you had no choice?"

"The Ricci family somehow found out about a curse on my mother's people that allows humans to make us their slaves. We have served four generations of Riccis so far. Candido now has the power to summon us.

"That night, I had to appear when he called. However, because he wanted me to harm you, an innocent. I was able to refuse, thank the gods," I explain.

"But why didn't you erase my memory fully?"

"I thought I did. Apparently, the gods have been at play for longer than we thought," I murmur almost to myself.

"Shit," she says and pushes a hand into her hair.

"What? What's going on?"

"I thought you were connected to Candido and his dirt. I've been investigating you guys. I might have mentioned your club in the reports I just turned in.

"Candido tried to kill a woman in a vision I saw. I started to investigate the warehouse where I knew it was going to go down. I saw you there and made the connection.

"I mean, I was already suspicious of your club. When you first moved in, I began to remember parts of that night from thirteen years ago. Seeing you at the warehouse linked you to Candido and I added you and your club to my reports," she says.

"This is what you two are disagreeing about?"

"Yes."

"Don't worry. I'll be sure to tell my brothers what's going on, but we'll make it go away for us. Ricci can fuck off."

"But don't you have to answer to him?"

"No. Not anymore. Once we seal our bond and my youngest brother finds his mate, we'll never have to answer to him or his family again."

"In that case, I'd let you fuck the shit out of me just to make sure Ricci rots under the jail."

I crush my lips to hers before she can get the words all the way out. I love the taste of her lips. I should slow down, but I've waited so long to find her and have her in my arms.

Billy reaches for my towel and snatches it from my waist. I don't think twice before I make her clothes vanish. In the next thought, I have her legs wrapped around me as I flash us to her bedroom.

"God, I hope nothing interrupts this. I want you so much," she pants as I move my lips to her throat.

"There isn't anything that's going to keep me from claiming you," I growl.

"Wait, I need to go lock the door. What if those bastards come back?"

"They're not coming back. I just locked the door and added a force field to keep anyone out. You're not going anywhere, my little kitten. Not until I've fucked you thoroughly."

"Ardan, yes, please. God, yes."

I grab one of her breasts in my palms and knead it as I kiss my way to her little tight nipple. Her full breast fits into my palm perfectly. I'm going to savor this sexy body as much as I can before it's too much.

She cries out my name as I move farther down her body. When I settle between her legs, her lips are glistening. The scent coming from her mound is intoxicating.

"Ardan, please," she moans as I allow my breath to tease her but make no move to seal the deal.

Her arousal has my mouth watering. I want to give myself time to reign in my restraint. Our verbal sparring already has me hard as fuck.

There is no way I'm going to rush this and embarrass myself. Imagine that, me, a demigod who can't last more than a few seconds. However, as I remember her brother saying she's a virgin, I think I might just come now.

I will be the first to claim this sweet, warm body. My mate has never known another man. While pissed that her brother knew this fact, I'm turned on to make her mine and seal our bond.

"Oh shit," she cries and bucks up off the bed.

I eat her pussy like I'm deep diving for treasure. My face is deep in her core, making her juices rain for me. I hum and groan as the most delicious flavor I've ever tasted in my life fills my mouth.

"Oh my God, I can't breathe. Damn, holy shit," she cries, bringing a chuckle from my lips.

I'm going to love fucking her if this is her reaction from a

little head. I'll be sure to go down on her every chance I get as well, just to hear her cries of ecstasy.

Locking my palms over her thighs, I push in deeper. I'm rewarded by her screams of pleasure. Gliding one palm to her belly, I claw at her soft skin, then flatten my hand over it.

Billy reaches to lock her fingers with mine as she rides my face. The way she's rolling her hips is driving me crazy. Her legs begin to shake, and she gushes into my mouth once again.

"So fucking delicious," I croon as I lift from my belly and start to crawl up her sated body.

I settle between her legs with my forearms on either side of her head. She looks up at me with a dazed expression. Slowly, I lean in and take her lips to allow her to taste herself on my mouth.

As I kiss her passionately, she glides her hands down my back and palms my ass, tugging me into her. I release a laugh and lift enough to palm my length and guide it to her entrance.

Teasing her lips with the tip, I stare into her eyes as if asking for permission to enter. She glares at me as if not willing to beg me for what she needs. I nip at her lips, then move to her neck to inhale her sweet scent and suck her skin into my mouth.

"Ardan, what are you wait—"

Her words cut off as I slide into her. I'm only about an inch or two in when she begins to run away.

"Oh no, baby. You said I could fuck the shit out of you. That's just the tip. Come here," I groan as I pin her waist to the mattress.

BILLY

"*OH FUCK*," I scream as Ardan thrusts into me.

I dig my nails into his ass as tears sting the backs of my eyes. He stills and drops kisses all over my face. He has taken over my insides.

"That will be the one and only time I will ever hurt you," he says into my ear.

Then as if in apology, he takes my lips in a searing kiss. I drag my nails from his ass to his back and that seems to egg him on. He begins to rock into me, rolling his hips with the in-and-out motion.

He's so hard and long, not to mention thick. I'm crazy wet, but I feel him stretching my insides with his big fat dick. My eyes roll into the back of my head as he begins to pound into me in earnest.

"You've been right under my nose for a year. Shit, you're perfect. I've never wanted anyone more than I want you," he says gruffly.

"You feel so good. Am I supposed to be this wet?"

He laughs at me and kisses me hard. "Yes and no," he groans.

"What?"

"Because of my powers, you will always be wetter than normal for me and only me."

"Oh," I moan. "Okay. Ardan?"

"Yes, baby."

"I think I'm going to come again. We might need to change the sheets," I whimper.

He responds with more laughter. "I have you. Just enjoy the ride. I'll handle the rest."

I begin to quake and come all over him. He lifts my legs onto his forearms and begins to dance in my pussy like he's

competing for a championship. I call out a bunch of nonsense as he rocks my world.

When I have enough wits about me, I look up into his face. He has a sexy grin on his lips as he stares down at me. I look down my body to see he's watching my breasts as they jiggle with his thrusts.

I bite my lip and reach to squeeze my breasts. Lifting my gaze back to his, I find so much lust and heat in his eyes. Feeling a little naughty, I reach for his soaked length as it moves in and out of me and allow my juices to coat my fingers.

Then I bring my fingers to my chest and wipe the juices first on one nipple and then the other. Ardan growls and dips his head to quickly pull my peak into his mouth. He takes a deep pull of the hard tip, causing me to buck off the bed with the motion.

"Yes," I whimper. "God, yes."

Reaching for my hand, he kisses my fingers that have my essence on them. I smile at him and stick my fingers into his mouth. He shifts a bit and begins to thrust from his new position. He's tapping my insides at a new angle that feels like he's about to come through my belly.

The wicked smile he gives me around my fingers is everything. The sheets beneath me should be soaked, but I know he's taking care of that like he said he would. So when I feel like I'm about to squirt all over the place, I think nothing of it.

"*Ardan*," I sing like a prayer.

However, this man doesn't stop. He keeps fucking me like a machine built to force pleasure from my body. I reach over my head to grab for anything to keep my soul inside my body, but I don't know if it's any use.

He allows my fingers to pop free from his mouth and reaches to palm one of my breasts. It's crazy, but I think he's

growing harder. When he lifts my hips and starts to thrust down into me, I know he is.

I wrap my legs tightly around him and link my ankles together. However, he pries my legs free and holds me open for him to move freely, which drives me fucking nuts.

"You're killing me," I cry.

"*Fuck*, Billy. I can't stop fucking you. It's too good. Tell me you're ready to seal our bond. I need you," he grunts.

"Ardan, I want. I need."

"You need to say yes. I'll take care of the rest, baby. I promise."

"Yes," I whimper and nod frantically.

There's something fierce building up in me. I can feel it coming from my toes like a geyser rushing through me. It's going to explode any second now.

I knew fucking him would be hot, but this shit is next level. I can't even see straight at this point. All I feel is him and his dick. And still, I want so much more.

"Billy, I have never in my entire existence felt anything like this," he growls.

Then he leans in and takes my lips. Before I know what's going on, my mouth fills with the taste of peppermint. It's so cool and refreshing, but I'm left feeling confused.

When he pulls back and condensation pours from both our mouths like we're standing out in the cold, I know it's something he has done. I lift to capture his lips so he can do it again.

He allows the kiss and the flavor bursts in my mouth, causing me to grin. I nip at his bottom lip and tug. A laugh bursts from my lips as another mist cloud comes from his mouth and nose this time.

"That's so cool," I breathe.

"That is something I can only share with you. My true mate. It's my true breath."

I place a hand behind his head and groan as he shifts to his knees and lifts me into his lap to sit upright. He places his forehead to mine.

"Ready?"

"Yes," I moan and nod.

"Good girl. Repeat after me."

I still have a million questions, but my gut is screaming for me to trust him and flow with this. Although he has owned my body, I still feel like there should be more between us. I lock my hands in the top of his hair and hold on for whatever comes next.

I'm ready. I don't know if I can turn back, but I'm good with that. Ardan feels right, righter than anything has ever felt in my life. My heart is telling me he is safe. If ever there is a person in my life I can trust, it's him.

I'm supposed to be here with him. This is who I've been waiting for. As I have the thought, he begins to speak.

"I, Ardan, Third-born son of Tanrı, bond my heart, body, mind, and soul to you, Billy Ann Salvado. My water is your water. My ice is your ice. My essence is your essence. I am your mate and you are mine."

"I, Billy Ann Salvado, bond my heart, body, mind, and soul to you, Ardan, third-born son of Tanrı. My water is your water. My ice is your ice. My essence is your essence. I am your mate and you are mine."

He closes his eyes and growls. My mouth falls open as I watch his skin glow. When he opens his eyes and looks into mine, I can see what looks like ocean waves rolling and crashing within them.

He palms my ass and begins to drop me up and down on his hard-as-fuck dick. The look on his face is so intense. I palm his cheeks and kiss his lips.

For a moment we just breathe each other in. I feel him

swelling even more inside me, causing me to bite my lip. He feels so good.

He bands his arms around me and holds me against his chest as he begins to thrust up into me. I'm still so wet for him.

My pussy begins to clench around him and my heart feels like it's going to race out of my chest.

"I need you to come with me. Once I come inside you, you will be mine forever. Our bond will be sealed and make us complete," he breathes against my mouth.

I should hop my ass up off him, but an overwhelming rush of emotions washes over me, and I don't want to be away from him for a second. When I feel his hot seed inside me, it comes with a sigh of relief from my lips.

"I am finally whole," he says into my hair as he holds me tightly.

I inhale as the same feeling comes over me. I feel complete for the first time in my life.

Billy

What's Going On?

"This doesn't make any sense," I say as I sit in Ardan's lap while looking down at my phone. This is the third time I've tried and failed to log into the chat my sisters and I have been using to talk to each other.

"I know. Something is wrong. Could it be something blocking the Wi-Fi signal here or something?" Ray asks.

"No. You shouldn't have any interference. Our system is high tech. Our human brothers made sure of it for their needs whenever they're here. We also protect it with magic so it's impenetrable," Reilly replies.

I shake my head and try again but get the same results. When I look up, Ray and Taylor have similar looks on their faces as they, too, try to log in with no success. I frown.

"I never log out. I don't know what's going on," Taylor says.

"Same here. This is crazy," Ray murmurs as she stares down at her phone.

"Don't worry about it. I'll find her and then we'll know if she's Charlie or not," Reilly says dejectedly and gets up to walk off.

I watch after him. I'm even more determined to help him now that I know who Charlie could be to him—or should I say Lee?

I get the feeling she is one and the same. It only makes sense. I want Reilly to find her more than anything so Candido will lose all his cards to play.

"Thank you for wanting to help my brother," Ardan says into my ear.

I turn to look back at him over my shoulder. After showering together, he felt it would be best if I came back here to the clubhouse with him. Since he cleaned up my place for me, I figured, why not?

All I needed to do was get dressed and brush my hair into a ponytail after the mess he made of it during our session. Thank God for the supernatural healing thing.

If I weren't supernatural, I'm sure I wouldn't be walking for another three weeks. Man, Ardan is hung like a motherfucker. If I had seen what I saw in that shower before we had sex, I would have run.

"Taylor and I are heading up for the night. It was nice meeting you, Billy. I look forward to getting to know more about you," Bradan, Ardan's twin, says.

"It was nice meeting you too. Taylor, I can't wait to hang out when I have some time," I say and smile at my sister.

"Me too. I have work and school tomorrow, but I hope to get some free time to spend with both of you," Taylor says to me and Ray.

She seems a bit shy, but I like her. She's much smaller than Ray and me. I've been wondering what our birth order is. I don't know why Ray feels like the oldest. Taylor and I seem to be a toss-up for the youngest.

"Don't drown her on the first night," Bradan teases Ardan.

I look up into his eyes as he stands and tucks Taylor into his side. I search his face, wondering how much of that is a joke. He winks back at me with a playful smile on his lips.

I recognize him as the other biker from the warehouse that day. If not for the hair and the eyes, they would look just alike. Both of my sisters look so happy here.

I guess Ardan was telling me the truth about everything. I'm still trying to wrap my head around it. I have so much to digest.

"I think we're going to call it a night as well," Kendrick says as he stands and helps Ray get up from her seat.

"Can I have one more hug?" Ray says to me with a hopeful smile.

I stand and pull her into me, hugging her as tightly as her baby bump will allow. She squeezes me back. Oddly enough, it feels like a hug I've needed for a long time. Not being a hugger, there's this connection I wasn't expecting to find.

"I look forward to spending time with you. I'm so happy to finally have met you. I've always wanted siblings. Now I have three," Ray says happily.

"You'll be tired of me in a week," I tease.

"Doubt it," she says and kisses my cheek.

Yup, the older sister. I chide myself for feeling like I'm about to burst into tears. When Ray pulls away and looks into my eyes, I see the tears building up in hers.

I give her a nod as I fight back my own. It's been a long day. I'm sure she's just as overwhelmed as I am. Then there's the baby.

Releasing her, I take a step back, only to have Ardan tug me back into his lap. Ray smiles and places a hand on her belly. I shake my head as I think of the fact that she's pregnant with a baby from the past.

I feel like I've been dropped into the twilight zone. None

of this should be real. My thoughts go back to the brothers' earlier conversation.

Reilly mentioned something about iron. I want to know more about that and what it all means. I'll have to remember to ask Ardan about it later.

"Or you could ask me now."

I jump as Ardan's voice plays in my head, clear as day. However, I know he didn't speak because his lips were on my neck, and I had those thoughts to myself. I know I didn't speak them out loud.

"How did—"

"I've been waiting for your thoughts to become clear to me. Your mind is as stubborn as you are."

"What the fuck? I'm losing my damn mind. I know you're not in my head," I scold.

"Oh, but baby, I am."

"Oh no, you're not. Ardan, I didn't sign up for this. I'm a damn detective. I don't need or want you in my thoughts. I'm not even supposed to talk to you about my work.

"Are you telling me you'll be able to see the details of the cases I'm working on? This is crazy. Make it stop. Now."

"You have the ability to block me out. I don't like it, but because of the nature of your job, I understand. I hope someday you will be comfortable with our bond and you will choose to let me in," he says aloud.

"How do I close you out?"

He sighs and nuzzles my neck. I squirm in his hold. I need to keep my wits about me, and I can't do that with him on me like this. I think that's his point.

"It's not. I just can't keep my hands off you. It's simple.

"To close me out, you need to find the door in your mind. Pull it closed and I won't be able to see into or hear your thoughts. We can still communicate like this, but your thoughts will be limited to me until you open the door again.

"I will only know what you chose to let me into," he replies to my thoughts.

I quickly search my mind for this door and pull it shut. Ardan chuckles into my ear. A shiver runs through me as his breath tickles my skin.

"We should head upstairs too," he breathes against my neck.

"What? I need to head back to my place."

"I thought we could stay here tonight. I don't want you in your place alone."

"I have work tomorrow and none of my things are here. I need my workbag," I protest.

"Not a problem," he croons as my bag appears in my lap.

"My service weapon and my badge," I say.

"Look inside."

I open the bag and peek inside. Sure enough, both are in there. I shake my head. I'm going to have to get used to this magic stuff.

"Okay, fine. I'll stay, but only because I have questions."

"All of which I plan to answer after I've taken you again," he says with a wicked grin.

"Tour first, I'll think about the rest."

He rumbles with laughter and lifts to stand while holding me close. Ardan takes my bag and slings it over his shoulder. I listen intently as he points out different areas and the species occupying them.

"You will be presented to everyone as my mate tomorrow," he says, interrupting my thoughts.

"Tomorrow? I have work," I say in confusion.

"As you have said. I will call a town hall meeting for the afternoon before we leave."

Stopping in front of an elevator, I then turn to face him. "We?"

"You can handle yourself with humans, but you got lucky

earlier. I'm not going to chance them sending others who are more skilled and more powerful.

"I will be with you when you're not here. Wherever you need to go, I will be there," he says so matter-of-factly.

"Okay, back up a little. I have an entire life outside of you, outside of this. Whatever this is. As I'm sure you have obligations outside of me. What are you talking about?"

"This I understand. However, I will adjust to your life. My sole purpose will be to ensure you're safe. I will maintain my obligations to the club as well. This is nonnegotiable, Billy."

"Excuse me?"

The elevator opens and he stalks toward me, causing me to back into it. I look up into his eyes and see the unyielding determination in his gaze. I stumble backward a step. He shoots his hand out to steady me.

"I know you understood what I said. None of that attitude is going to work with me, Billy. You can reel that right on in. I don't have to interfere with your life or your career, but I will be there to protect you."

My protest is cut off as he delivers a passionate kiss that ends the conversation. I run my fingers through the short sides of his hair as he devours my mouth. When I get to the longer hair in the back, I thread my fingers in it and lift onto my toes.

Ardan groans into my mouth and palms my ass in his large hands. This man is going to be problematic. I don't even remember what it was I was going to say.

"My job is important to me," I breathe when he breaks the kiss.

Lifting his hand to run his thumb against my bottom lip, he nods. "I know this. I promise you won't notice I'm there. If you want, I'll allow you to wear me around your neck."

I wrinkle my brows as the elevator opens and he takes my hand to walk me out. As we walk down the long corridor, he

rubs his thumb back and forth across my knuckles. It's like he's placing me in a trance.

Once at the end of the hall, he turns left and opens the second door we come to. I step into the room and come to a stop as a gasp leaves my lips. This isn't what I thought I would find behind that door.

This is a very nice clubhouse for what it is, but this is above and beyond what I was expecting. I thought we would walk into a dorm-type space or something. A bed, a dresser —the basics.

However, we've just walked into one of the most opulent bedrooms I have ever seen. The walls are a cool blue and there's something so calming about the space. There is a bed lifted up on what looks like a raised platform in the center of the room.

The platform is surrounded by a pool that looks deep enough to swim laps in, although concrete floors surround the perimeter of the room and encase the bed and pool. From this end, the pool looks to have an infinity edge that drops down into a lit space that emits a blue glow.

There are clear stairs that float over the pool and lead up onto the platform the bed is on. The bed is huge, but there seems to be enough room to walk around the bed on the sides. I'm thinking the bed is a California king, if not a custom-made king for him.

On the back wall behind the bed is a fireplace with blue glass inside. However, what takes my breath away about the fireplace is the crest above it. It's like the crown with the sword running sideways through it and the chain draping them are coming out of the wall and looks to be made of glass or ice.

"Wow," I say as I take it all in.

"Still thinking about your apartment?" Ardan says teasingly.

"No, I'm wondering why you ever lived there," I murmur.

"I bought the building a year ago after feeling drawn to it and then moved in. Now I know what the draw was."

"You own the building?"

I turn to look up at him. He has a mischievous smile on his lips. He shrugs as he studies my face.

"I do. I own quite a few properties."

"I will keep that in mind. This room is nice. Not at all what I thought would be in this clubhouse."

"We all designed our spaces to our own needs and personalities. That door over there leads to my private kitchen," he says, pointing to the left. "Over there, if you walk through the bathroom, you will find the walk-in closet. That can be yours. If you want more space, I can create it."

"I should be fine. I don't need a lot of room for a spend-the-night bag."

"I don't need to read your thoughts to know you think this is one night. Don't fool yourself. Welcome home, baby. Make yourself comfortable."

"There is so much I still need to process. Look at this place. It's like a luxury hotel suite or something. We just walked through a warehouse-like structure. Where the heck docs this fit in?

"Do I really have my own magic? What did you mean, allow me to wear you around my neck? I'm not committing to calling this my home until I have some realistic answers. Not that any of this seems realistic," I say and palm my fore-head, turning to look at the bed longingly.

I'm starting to feel the exhaustion from the day's events hitting me. Maybe once I go to sleep, I'll wake up and this will all be some crazy dream. Ardan moves to wrap his arms around my waist, and I sink back into him.

If it weren't for the fact that he makes me feel so relaxed, I

would probably be out. This is all so crazy. I sigh and try to reel in my wayward thoughts.

"This necklace will serve as a talisman. I will be able to fit into it while you are working. If I'm needed, I will be able to force my way out. It is only one of our options," he says.

I look down at the necklace now around my neck. I lift the pendant and smile at the pretty crystal wave. The thought of this huge man fitting inside this wave that rests between my breasts is unfathomable.

"I would like to hear the other options. You're a lot of man; this doesn't seem right to force you into."

"You're not forcing me into anything. We can talk about those other options later. Right now, I want to take you to *our* bed," he replies, placing emphasis on *our*.

ARDAN

"THAT WAS SO INTENSE," Billy pants as she lies on top of my chest. "I had no idea I could see your thoughts as well."

She's right. Our session was intense. As I took her sweet body, I began to show her my thoughts of what I wanted to do to her. How much better it would be when I took her to her limits.

I have no doubt Billy loved what she saw. I'm now looking forward to turning things up. Especially with the use of an ice cock. That one seemed to rile her up.

I rumble low with laughter. "I enjoyed showing you that you can."

She lifts her head and stares back at me. Reaching up, she

palms my cheek and runs her thumb down the bridge of my nose. I can't help smiling back at her.

"Like what you see?"

"Maybe. I was just thinking. I never registered all your piercings before. I mean, of course I caught this one in your nose, but I never thought about the fact that your ears are full of them.

"I was a bit preoccupied earlier today, but I noticed your dick is pretty loaded with them as well. I feel like there's some story there," she says as she searches my gaze.

I hold her gaze and give her the answers she's seeking. In fact, I give her answers to all the questions I believe she has from the brief time I spent in her thoughts before she shut me out.

"Thank you."

"For what?" I ask.

"Answering so many of my questions by showing me. You're intentionally letting me in. I'm not ready to give you free rein of my thoughts, but I see the gesture," she says.

"I will wait for as long as you need. I'm not going to force you to do anything you don't want to."

She snorts. "Yet, here I am in your bed, and you're insistent on following me to work."

I begin to run my fingertips up and down her back. She melts into me and nearly purrs with the gesture. I bite back a laugh.

"Something tells me you don't mind either."

"I don't know if I do. Not yet at least."

"Good. Keep that in mind. I'm going to make things go away for you and Carson. That's nonnegotiable as well. I know that's on your mind. I want to take it off."

"Is that something you saw before I shut you out, or are you creeping back in? Something also tells me you could take my thoughts if you wanted, whether I want you to or not."

"It was and I could."

The room falls silent for a few beats, and I think my little human has finally fallen asleep. I'm not tired, so I lie staring up at the ceiling, savoring the feel of my mate in my arms. I don't know why our mates have appeared now, but I'm not complaining.

"Ardan, don't change your mind," Billy whispers and then the door to her thoughts comes open.

My heart begins to ache as I'm thrown right into the time when she was a little frightened girl running away to save her own life. Then I'm taken back to how people repeatedly let her down.

The more time I spend in her thoughts, the more I begin to understand her. I stiffen when I come to the bond she has with Carson, Mack—the man who raised her—and Eddy—the one she truly bonds with as an older brother.

I know she has fallen asleep when her thoughts become more open than I think she means for them to be. I stop and slowly back out. I would never take advantage of this gift.

Gratitude fills me as I have a deeper understanding of my mate. The abandonment, anger, the need to be independent —it all makes sense now. I think I will travel with her within the pendant.

That way, I can show her I'm there for her whenever she needs me, but I'm not there to take her power away. Billy needs that sense of control, and I won't shatter that. It's going to be a challenge, but I'm willing to bend for her. Only her.

"I will never change my mind. You're stuck with me," I murmur and lean in to kiss the top of her head.

Billy

Daily Blessings

I groan and as I'm woken out of my sleep by an annoying sound. Reaching out toward the sound, I slap my hand toward it. Lifting my head, I find my phone on a clear glass, floating shelf. Something like an end table.

"That wasn't there last night," I mutter as I sit up.

Looking down at my phone, I huff. It's after noon already. I didn't mean to sleep in that long. As images of last night fill my head, I rub my thighs together and remember why my body needed the rest.

"Hello," I say as I answer my phone that's begun to ring again.

"Billy Ann Salvado?" the caller asks.

"This is she."

"I am Sergeant Beckett Turner with IAB. I've been trying to reach you all morning," he says.

"I'm sorry. My phone was on do not disturb for my day off. I must have forgotten to turn it off. How can I help you?"

"I have a few more questions for you. I was wondering if you could … come down," he begins to say distractedly. "Um … do you mind holding on?"

"Yes, of course," I say, hoping I manage to keep the nervousness out of my voice.

Reaching for the sheet, I pull it up over my chest as if Detective Turner can see me through the phone. I chew on my lip as I look around the room. It takes my breath away just as it did last night.

I knit my brows as I wonder where Ardan took off to. I was expecting him to be here when I woke. I'm guessing the clubhouse is a safe place in his mind.

"Sorry about that, Detective Salvado. Are you there?"

"Yes, I'm here. Do you need me to come in?"

"Actually, no. So sorry to have wasted your time. That will be all. I'm closing this investigation and clearing you and Detective Ramirez," he says and clears his throat.

I blow out a breath. Carson changed his last name back to his family name when he entered the academy. Mack didn't let on that he had been hurt by that, but I saw he was.

"Thank you for your time," Detective Turner says and ends the call.

I drop the phone in my lap and stare down at it. What the fuck was that? Last night begins to come back to me. I had been half-asleep when Ardan said he would make this go away for me and Carson.

"Did he do this?" I gasp to myself. "No fucking way."

I jump up out of bed and carefully make my way across the little landing over the pool and then down the stairs. With my hands on my hips, I look from left to right trying to figure out which way he pointed to for the bathroom.

Okay, magic. If I have you, please help me not pee on myself. Show me the bathroom, please.

A pulsing starts in my belly. I grab hold of the feeling and

repeat my chant, hoping to God I don't piss myself. I fist-pump when the door pops open and the light comes on in the room to my right. I rush for the door and step into a bathroom that's just as jaw-dropping as the bedroom. Ardan has good taste.

I pull a face and bob my head as I look around. When I note the water closet, I rush in and sit on the toilet. My eyes cross as I relieve myself.

I palm my forehead as the events of the last month run through my mind. Maybe I should talk to Ardan about those visions. I can't help but wonder if they have something to do with my magic.

"My magic. Ain't that some shit?" I snort.

I finish my business and go to wash my hands and see if he has any toothpaste. A smile comes to my lips when I find a little care package waiting for me with a note.

GOOD MORNING, baby girl,

I wanted you to sleep as long as you wanted. I thought of some things a human mate might need. I'm not sure if you know much about using your magic for these things. Something I want to help you with when you're ready. For now, here's everything I could think of. I'll be in my office or in the main hall. Come find me when you're ready. Remember you can call for me if you need help. Although I know you won't.

Your Mate,
Ardan

I smile and shake my head. I think to call for him just to prove him wrong. Instead, I begin to dig through the basket. I pull out a new toothbrush and a tube of toothpaste.

I lift a brow when I find my brand of deodorant and bodywash. A laugh bursts from my lips when I find my signature long T-shirt and jeans at the bottom of the basket.

"Okay, Ardan, I see you," I murmur and nod as I get to work cleaning myself up and getting dressed.

I love this bathroom. The shower is a godsend as the warm spray rains down on me, loosening my muscles. I find myself singing in the shower and shaking my hips.

"I could get used to this."

I jump and turn to find Ardan standing in the doorway of the shower. He's staring at me with a heated gaze. I love the way he stands with his legs wide and his arms folded across his chest.

Talk about things to get used to; I could get used to this view. I bite my lip and cover my breasts and my lower parts. He laughs and shakes his head, pushing off the glass he's leaning on to walk into the shower.

I lift a brow at him when his clothes vanish. This time, I get to take him in naked from head to toe. Man, his body is amazing.

"What happened to me coming to find you?" I ask as he stalks toward me.

"You were taking too long. I've missed you."

"I was taking a shower before I came to look for you. I have some questions for you."

He stops before me and grasps my face, then crushes my lips with a heated kiss. I moan into his mouth and lift on my toes to get closer to him. He smiles into the kiss before he pulls away.

"What do you need to know, my pretty mate?"

"What did you mean when you said you would make things go away for me and Carson? What did you do?"

"The Immortal Iron Brothers have a long reach. You'd be

surprised to know who is among our ranks. If that weren't an option, I would have used magic to fix it.

"Don't worry. This won't come back to either of you."

"Thank you again. I'll be done in a minute. I know you want to introduce me before I head out to work."

"Before *we* head out."

I roll my eyes. "We. I know you're coming with me."

"I thought some rest would cause you to see things my way," he says with humor in his voice.

"Don't make me change my mind."

He turns me back toward the spray and begins to rinse me off. I bite my lip and squeeze my thighs together as he lathers more soap onto my breasts, then runs his soapy hand down my front to cup my sex.

"I can't have you starting your day without a proper send-off," he says next to my ear.

"What?"

"Call it your daily blessing."

"Ah," I cry out as he shoves his fingers into me.

I lift onto my toes and reach behind me to grasp his neck. He drops kisses across my shoulder as he continues to thrust in and out of me. I can feel his length poking into me as he bands his free arm around me to keep me from tipping over.

"Ardan," I whimper.

"That's my name, baby. What can I do for you?"

"*Fuck*," I cry.

I begin to convulse from the husky sound of his voice in my ear. I fall forward and throw my arms out to catch myself against the wall. As I cry out for more, he pulls his hand from my pussy and shoves his fingers into my mouth.

I'm hoping he's going to replace his fingers with that long, thick thing between his legs, but I'm left pulsing for him as he kisses his way down my back. I look over my shoulder as he takes a bite of my ass.

He looks up into my eyes as he inhales deeply. The next thing I know, he buries his face in my pussy and begins to eat me like it's a profession.

When he adds his fingers to the mix, I roll my eyes into the back of my head. This is insane, but I'm not about to stop him from devouring me like this.

Instead, I lift onto my toes and stick my hips out to give him more access. He takes the offering and pushes his fingers in deeper. I cry out and start to rock against his face greedily.

"Ardan, yes. Oh yes," I whimper.

In no time, he has me on my toes. I'm trying and failing to get away as my legs begin to shake. His hands on my waist are keeping my ass in his face as he hums in pleasure. That deep rumble vibrates through me and settles in my belly.

When he rubs my clit then presses down on it, I'm done for. I cry out so loud I'm surprised when the walls don't shake.

"Ardan," I scream louder and shake my head in disbelief. "Wow."

I come so hard my legs buckle. Ardan catches me and stands, tossing me in the air a little before catching me to settle into his hold. I wrap my arms around his neck and bury my face there.

"Was it that good?" he chuckles.

"Yes," I pant as my cheeks heat.

He kisses the side of my face. A smile plays on his lips as they meet my skin. I melt inside from the gesture as my skin tingles.

He walks us out of the bathroom into the bedroom. I hold my breath as he climbs the stairs and carries me to the bed. For a split second, I'm expecting him to slip and fall into the pool. Then it hits me that this isn't an ordinary man—he's not human but a demigod.

He places me on the bed and pecks my lips. I look up into

his eyes and my breath hitches. I tear my eyes away quickly, not wanting to read too much into what I see there.

"Next time, I'll take my time blessing you. Right now, the community is waiting to meet my new queen," he says, with a handsome smile on his face.

His mustache is still glistening, wet from my juices. I reach to brush it clean. He takes my hand in his and pulls my fingers into his mouth, then kisses my palm.

"Delicious. I'm proud to wear your essence and will spend the day trying to inhale it as often and as much as I can," he croons with a smile.

In this moment, I hate my job, and I don't want to meet anyone. I want to lie back on this bed and allow him to bless me over and over again. Frowning at my thoughts, I take the clothes that appear in his hand and set them aside as he begins to dry me off with the towel that appears in the other.

I clear my throat and ask the first thing that comes to mind. "So let me get this straight. I will be considered a queen here, but you guys don't have one queen or king?

"No, there is not one. Our mother's people were all considered kings and queens."

"So now you and all three of your brothers are considered kings?"

"Yes, our community holds us in that regard," he replies.

"Okay, I'm starting to grasp it all. I think. Ray and Taylor are considered queens as well, right?"

"Yes, as Reilly's mate will be when she arrives."

"Does that mean we actually rule over anyone, or is it in name only?"

"Here, we divide our people by element."

"Element?"

"Yes, we each wield an element. Kendrick, however, can pull from and wield all our elements. Well, he's never tapped into Reilly's power."

"Why not?"

"Reilly's power is complicated. It can't be locked down completely by blessed iron. I think Kendrick has always feared killing his own power by pulling Reilly's."

"Well, what kind of power does he have?"

"Reilly has the power to give life or death. He can strip the power of other beings or hand it back."

"I get why Kendrick wouldn't want to pull from that. That's some deep shit. Okay, okay. This is all so fascinating. I'll stop interrupting. Back to the people and your element."

"You are fine. It's a lot to take in. The fire folk all follow Bradan's rule. Water folk are our people. Because of Reilly's connection to life and death, he rules the earth folk. Kendrick rules over us all."

"Water folk?"

"Merpeople, nymphs, water fairies, sea fairies, sirens—"

"Wait, wait, wait. I thought mermaids, sirens and nymphs were all one and the same."

He gives me a smile. "They are not. However, we decided a long time ago to make it seem as such. There are differences. Some species are more harmful than others.

"Oh, okay. Go on. I'm sorry."

He shakes his head. "Good question. I will help you learn of them all. We also rule over the water dragons and several others we don't speak of aloud."

At the mention of water dragons, my heart begins to race. I feel the blood drain from my face. Ardan tilts his head and studies me closely.

"What just happened?" he asks with concern in his voice.

"It's nothing. I was just going to ask you about something. I … um."

"Shit, can you hold that thought. We've been summoned to the main hall. The community has gathered. They are waiting."

I look to the clothes still sitting beside me. I guess my crazy thoughts and visions can wait. Ardan follows my gaze.

"Let me help you with that," he says and then I'm fully dressed.

"You have to show me that one," I say and laugh nervously.

I had been using my questions to avoid this for as long as I could. I still want to know what's expected of me. What will these water folk need from me?

I guess I'm about to find out.

ARDAN

THIS IS GOING WELL. I want Billy to feel welcome by all. I can sense this isn't easy for her. Although I can't hear or see her thoughts, I can sense her emotions.

They are all over the place, but the most consistent is her nervousness and desire to fit in. I'm not surprised by that after being in her thoughts last night. While Billy has forced herself to be independent, I came across memories of her wanting to be a part of things only to be left out.

My little mate is strong, but my love will make her stronger. Billy will know she belongs with me, and I will always be here for her. Water beings can be emotional and intuitive, so she will always know how our people feel about her. Their vibes will be easy to catch.

"Who are they?" Billy asks as she points to my little friends peeking around Rock.

They are waving up at the dais, hoping to get my atten-

tion. I give them a wave and they begin to bounce in place happily. With a grin, I give the signal for them to skip the line and come forward. The two come running and jump right into my lap, causing me to laugh.

"King Ardan. We were so excited to hear we could come see you."

"Can you make us a water slide?"

"Will you play with us?"

"Boys, I want you to meet someone special. This is Queen Billy, my mate," I chuckle.

"Hi," Beck says and waves.

Bourne blushes and waves but remains silent. Billy gives them both a bright smile. "Hello there. It's so nice to meet you," she coos.

Bourne gasps and looks up at me. "She sounds like a siren. Is she safe?"

Sirens were partially responsible for the deaths of the boys' parents. They led them to the monster who took their lives. I put the sirens responsible to death, but the boys have been wary of sirens ever since. It took a long time to get them to trust anyone.

I noticed the enchantment of Billy's voice last night. It has always been alluring to me, but it took on a new pull last night. It is a lot like a siren's call.

"Not every siren is bad. I've told you this before. And yes, she's safe. Billy would never do anything to hurt you," I reply.

"You're pretty," Beck says. "Will you play with us? We always have so much fun with King Ardan."

"I would love to play with you guys, but I have to leave soon. But if it's okay with your mom, I'd like to play with you some other time."

"Oh," Beck says and climbs off my lap with a long face.

What just happened? What did I do wrong? Billy says in a panic through our link.

"Their parents were led to slaughter. They don't have a mother, and they don't live here. Coming to headquarters was a treat for them today."

"I'm so sorry. I ... I"

"You didn't know. It will be fine."

Billy gets up from her throne chair and squats in front of Beck. He looks at her then looks at me as if asking if it's okay for him to engage her. I give him a nod.

"What's your name?" Billy asks softly.

"I'm Beck and that's my brother Bourne. We are water titans. Our dad was a sea guard. One day, we'll be big and strong, and we'll take his place."

"Quiet, Beck. No one is to know that," Bourne chides his brother and scowls.

"Your secret is safe with me. I'll protect it with my life," Billy says and winks at Bourne.

She then reaches to run her hand over Beck's curly blond hair. Beck's entire face lights up. He's always the first to warm up to people. He's also the most lethal of the two boys.

"Bourne is right, I shouldn't have told you that." He looks at me. "I'm sorry. I will do better."

"You are fine. Your queen is here to keep you safe. You shouldn't tell anyone else, but this once you are forgiven."

"How old are you guys?" Billy asks.

"We're five," Bourne replies.

"Oh, you're tall boys. Maybe we can play another time. I should be free this weekend or the one after that. Ardan can bring me to you. You don't have to come here," Billy says.

"Really?" Beck says with hope in his eyes.

"I will bring you to a meeting place. We will play together then," I reply.

"Oh, no. I made another mistake, didn't I?"

"No worries, pretty one. I will tell you all you need to know about them and anything else you need to catch up on. We can't go

to where they live because it's guarded heavily for their sake and everyone else's.

"There are others who would love to take them and have control of their powers. They may be children, but they are both very powerful and will be forces when they grow up. For now, I keep them safe somewhere known to few and accessible to fewer," I explain.

"Is King Bradan here? Can he play with us before we have to return?" Bourne asks as he looks up at me with his big bright-blue eyes.

"He is not, but I will let him know you asked for him," I say.

Bourne slides down off my lap and goes to wrap his arms around Billy's neck. She embraces him and holds him tight. When he releases her, he looks into her eyes.

"You don't mean us harm, but you can cause us pain. Don't get close to us if you don't want us. I won't allow my brother to lose another," Bourne says then walks off the dais without a look back.

Billy watches after him with her brows drawn. Beck throws himself into her arms and kisses her cheek. I'm too stunned to reply.

I've never seen Bourne like this. Although he does tend to be protective of his younger twin as Bradan is with me. I narrow my eyes as he finds a corner and sits in it with his arms across his chest.

"What just happened?" Billy says after Beck runs off after his brother.

"I'm not sure. Water folk can have the gift of sight. Bourne may have seen something to make him react that way." I shrug, still not sure what that was about.

I'll have a talk with him next time. I allowed the brothers to come to this meeting because I haven't seen them this month and I thought they would like to meet Billy. Maybe

it's time I spend some real time with them and see what's been going on with them.

Water titans can become dangerous. I would hate for it to come to that with either boy. They can never learn what truly happened to their parents; otherwise, I'm afraid they will be lost to us.

Once a water titan's heart runs cold, a different being is created. That I can't allow to happen. It's my duty to prevent that and I will.

"You have a lot on your shoulders with your people. Are you sure you have time to follow me around? I don't know how you do all you do as it is," Billy says with concern.

"I will always have time for you. They have been excited today. Many didn't really need me. They just wanted to talk," I reply.

I don't tell her I've mastered splitting myself in two. It's not something I've shared with many. Not even Bradan knows.

"Oh, okay. I would love to help."

"We can talk about that later. Let's finish up so you can eat, and we can head out for your shift."

Billy

Work Life

"Jenkins, I'm getting tired of seeing your face," I say as I walk onto the crime scene.

I've been called to a restaurant downtown. It's a nice place. Not somewhere I would think I'd be called to for a murder investigation. Yet here I am.

"I could say the same about you, Salvado, but yours is a lot prettier than mine," he retorts.

I pat him on the shoulder and get serious. This is my last call of the night, hopefully. It's the third crime scene of the shift.

"What do we have?"

"Male, gunshot wound to the head. Left dead in the freezer. Looks like he was dragged in there.

"The crew came in for prep. Halfway through service, one of them finds him in the icebox, chilling. No pun intended.

"Ha, ha. Have we got an ID?"

"James Clarence. Thirty-two. The head chef. Brother-in-law of the owner."

"Have we spoken to this brother-in-law?"

"Not yet. He's on his way down."

"No one found it odd that the head chef was MIA?"

"They said it's nothing new. He had a habit of coming and going throughout the night. Sous-chef says he ran this place and one other uptown."

"Got you."

I move toward the freezer as I tug on a pair of gloves. I can already feel the cool air coming from the box. I only take two steps inside before finding the vic sitting with his eyes open.

He already looks frozen solid. His green eyes are lifeless but seem as if they're staring right at me. I take a few more steps and squat before him.

"Damn, buddy. Who did you piss off?" I murmur.

Suddenly, I'm thrown into a vision. It's like I'm stood back up and turned around, then placed back outside the door.

Instantly, I reach for the door in my mind to open it for Ardan to see my thoughts. I figure this would be easier than trying to explain later.

Though I'm in the vision, I can feel the pendant around my neck warming against my skin. Ardan's agitation is also taking over my feelings. Something I didn't know could happen.

I force myself to focus on the vision to see what I will learn about what happened here. At least, that's what I hope will happen. I stand and watch as men in suits enter the kitchen as if they belong.

I know right away they don't, as Candido and Pauly Ricci appear among the men, I get a bitter taste in my mouth. I think I can already tell what happened here.

"Oh boy, here we go. I'm telling you for the last time, Candido. I can't move any more product for you through the restaurants. My brother-in-law found out and he's ready to can my ass. If it weren't for my sister, he would have," the guy in the chef's coat says.

I know it's the vic from the freezer. He has the same dark hair and mohawk. He's a tall guy with a broad build.

"Now see, that's not going to work for me. I'm having trouble with distribution as it is. I can't have my transport guys reneging on me too. Pauly, how do you think we should deal with this?

"I came for the box of clams you promised me. Not to do business," Pauly says.

"That's funny. I'm always doing business while you're always stuffing your face. Bardo, let's see if our friend understands the terms and conditions of our agreement," Candido says as he waves forward a big blond dude.

The blond comes forward and rolls his neck from side to side then cracks his knuckles. He's one big motherfucker. I'm taken aback when the chef knuckles up like he's ready to take this dude on.

The blond swings, but the chef ducks and comes up with a right hook. He lands it, but the blond doesn't even flinch.

I wince when the sound of his hand breaking reaches my ears. The blond grins as if he's unfazed. The chef dances back as he cradles his hand to his chest.

"Damn," I breathe.

"Ah, fuck it," Candido says and pulls a gun, putting a bullet in the head of the chef.

"What the fuck, Candido?" Pauly growls. "What the fuck are you thinking? You can't keep doing shit like this right now."

"At least I'm doing something. What have you done since this bullshit started? Huh?"

"Whatever," Pauly says shaking his head as he pulls a handkerchief from his pocket and dabs at his upper lip. "You're losing

control. We need to fix the real problem. I'm sure if you speak with them, there's a solution.

"Fuck outa here. Are you listening to the shit coming out of your mouth? You have our only option. Now make sure she does what needs to be done," Candido seethes.

"So I'm not getting those clams, huh?"

"If you don't get the fuck out of my face," Candido snaps. "Clean this shit up and find me someone to handle the shipments."

"Boss, should we call the bikers to handle it?" one of the other guys says.

"Would I be here doing this shit if the bikers were an option right now? No, you fucking moron. I want you to clean this shit up," Candido snarls.

"You all right, Detective Salvado?"

I come out of the vision and look up at the photographer standing over me. He's looking back at me with concern in his eyes. I shake my head clear and stand to my full height.

"I'm fine," I say after clearing my throat.

"We need to talk. That was a super I've been looking for," Ardan growls in my head.

"Is he one of the brothers?"

"No, not anymore. He made his choice," he says angrily.

"Why is he helping Candido?"

"That's what I want to know. He shouldn't be alive, let alone in this realm. When I find him, I'm putting him to ground where he should be."

"I didn't hear that."

"He's from my world. My world, my rules," he says curtly.

"Well, what did he do?"

"That's the boys' uncle. He killed their parents."

"Oh, in that case. Let's find that bastard and nail Candido."

ARDAN

"DAMN, it's been a long day. Although, I'll admit that wasn't so bad," Billy says as we ride up in the elevator from the club-house garage.

I've just emerged from the pendant. I haven't been that cramped up in years. I'm already cramping myself into this human form. However, being in that pendant is a hell of a lot more restricting.

"You have an interesting work life, for sure. Why homicide?"

"Ricci tried to kill me, remember? I thought if he was willing to do it once, he would be willing to do it again and eventually I'd catch him in the act," she says and pulls a face.

Candido is the last person I want to talk about. Once that ring returns from his finger, I'm going to kill him myself. I crowd her space, backing her into the corner of the elevator.

"When you're here with me, none of that out there matters. It's my job to make you forget," I say as I grasp her throat and tip her head back with my thumb.

Her eyes fill with lust as she licks her lips. I dip my head and ghost my lips over hers. As I breathe her in, my groin tightens.

She shivers and leans into me. I take her lips as I've been wanting to since the last time I had a chance. She places her hand on my waist and lifts onto her toes.

"Fuck this," I groan and teleport us from the elevator to our bedroom.

I now have her back pressed against the wall just inside

the doorway. As she pants, I deliver hungry kisses down her neck and snake my hand beneath her shirt to cup her breast.

Returning my mouth to hers, I then deliver a searing kiss and allow my true breath to fill her mouth. Billy releases a throaty moan as she hops onto my waist and begins to grind into me. The second I think of making our clothes disappear so I can take her to bed, a mind link comes through.

"I feel you have returned, brother. We should talk. Taylor and Bradan were attacked earlier," Kendrick says, sounding exhausted which doesn't happen often for us.

The last few days have taken a toll. I curse and pull away from Billy. She looks at me with such longing and want I almost tell Kendrick I'm busy.

"Are you in your office? I'll be there in a moment."

"I will be there by the time you arrive," he says.

"Shit, I've drawn you a bath. Kendrick needs to see me. Go relax, I will return as soon as I can," I say and peck her lips.

I don't miss the disappointment that appears on her face. I feel the same way. However, I need to know what's going on.

"Don't take too long. I might fall asleep on you," she says with a little grin.

I peck her lips again as I think of how I plan to wake her if she does. I want to get back before she finishes her bath and has time to fall asleep.

I have plans to lotion and massage her skin before I put her to bed myself. Her skin always looks so silky and soft. I want to become a part of the routine that keeps it that way.

I grow harder as I think of ways to add my lips and tongue to the process. Shaking the thoughts away, I leave before I don't make it out of the room. I already know one more kiss will make it nearly impossible to part ways.

"What happened?" I ask Kendrick as we appear in his office at the same time.

"The hunters were at Taylor's workplace. She wasn't harmed, but we believe we should begin to train the women in combat along with their magic."

"Did Bradan kill them?"

"No, getting Taylor to safety was his priority."

"Makes sense." I nod.

"Listen, I wanted to ask you something."

Kendrick moves behind his desk and props his feet up. I move to take one of the chairs before it. Once I'm seated, he nods for me to continue.

"Have you noticed anything siren-like about Ray?"

"Yes, Reilly, Bradan, and I pointed it out yesterday. Why?"

"The little titans pointed it out and it clicked that Billy's voice has the appeal of a siren. I'm noticing that while similar, each of our mates are unique. I'm just paying attention to what's different and what's alike." I shrug.

"Not a bad idea."

"The boys seemed to like her even after sensing she might be some type of siren. I found that interesting."

"I heard they were here. How are they? Have there been any incidents?"

"None lately. Speaking of which. Billy had a vision while at a crime scene. She let me in to view it with her. Bardo was with Ricci," I say the last few words tightly.

"You're fucking kidding me, right?"

"No. Saw it with my own eyes. Seems like Candido is using him for muscle."

"How the fuck did that happen when we couldn't even locate the bastard for the last year?"

"I had the same question. I'm gonna put him to ground when I get my hands on him."

"You'll get no pushback from me. Anything else you need me to know?"

"Nothing I don't have under control. I sent Kai with the boys for now. Rock has been at the warehouse helping Ocean.

"Amadeus is away, so I haven't been able to get in touch with him yet. Other than that, the books are sovereign. All dues are in order and earnings have been high."

"I'm not going to hold you, brother. I know you want to get back to your mate as much as I do. Let me know what you need to finally nail Bardo down, if anything.

"He shouldn't be running loose. If I were you, I'd start with the assassin's network. See if Kenji can give you any information.

"If Bardo is dealing with Ricci, that's most likely where they met up. I want to deal with whoever made that connection happen," Kendrick says.

"Should we go see Ricci about this?"

"I will kill Ricci if I see him again. He is barking up all the wrong trees. I say we allow him to hang himself on one."

I snort and nod, although I want to be the one doing the hanging. However, Kendrick is right. At this rate, Candido is going to get himself killed.

There are reasons we bridged the gap between him and our world. We had to do his bidding and couldn't harm him. All others, especially those in the underworld, will have no such obligation or hesitance when it comes to taking his life.

His problem, not ours.

"Good night, brother."

"Good night, Ardan."

We both vanish from his office to head our separate ways. I step into the bathroom of my room at the clubhouse to find my mate sitting in the bathtub. She has her head back and EarPods in her ears.

She looks so peaceful and gorgeous. This is how I've imagined her after work. In my tub, soaking as she allows the day to wash away.

I make my clothes disappear from my body and saunter toward the tub. Billy opens her eyes as I get to the edge of the sunken tub and enter. She bites back a smile and allows her gaze to roll over me.

I hold my arms out to my sides as if presenting myself. A crooked grin takes over my lips. Billy throws her head back as she laughs and it's the most beautiful thing I've ever seen.

"You think a lot of yourself, don't you?"

"Have I disappointed yet?"

"No, you haven't."

She reaches behind her to drop her EarPods outside the tub. I sink into the water to sit. Reaching for her legs, I lift them to drape them over mine, then drag her to me by the back of her thighs.

Billy cups my face and brings her lips to mine as I turn my face up. As we settle into place, I take her mouth in a passionate kiss. Right as I get ready to bring her down on my length so she can sink down, I get another mind link.

"Ardan, you have to get here quick," Kai says through the link.

"What's going on?"

"We don't know. The boys were sleeping and then—"

"Kai, Kai," I shout through the link and receive no answer.

"What is it?" Billy asks as she searches my face.

"I have to go. Something is going on with Beck and Bourne."

"Reilly, I need you to come with me to the oasis. Something is happening with the boys." I mind-link my brother, knowing I might need his help.

Lifting Billy from my lap, I place her beside me and go to

stand. She reaches for my forearm causing me to look down at her. She has concern written all over her face.

"I want to come with you. Maybe I can help."

"I don't think so. You have no idea what we're dealing with here. You're safer staying behind."

"Please," she says with pleading in her eyes.

I sigh and give a curt nod. If she's going to be my queen, she will need to know the going ons of our people. I can feel her heart and that she only wants to make sure the boys are safe.

"Fine. Let's move."

We both climb from the bath, and I dress us. Grabbing her hand once we're dressed, I teleport us to the main hall where Reilly is waiting for us. Together the three of us go through the portal I open up.

"Remember, they are children, but they are powerful. They will not appear as the little boys you saw. Stay behind me," I warn Billy before we step through the other side.

When we step through to the oasis, my mouth falls open. Kai is lying on her side, bleeding out. Aalto has a sword drawn as he fights off an angry water titan.

"Fuck," I growl.

The last thing I want to do is hurt the boys, but this has gotten out of hand. It's not their fault. We haven't figured out what's causing these episodes.

"Billy, no," I call out as she runs around me, headed for Kai to help her as she stirs and lifts her head.

Both boys turn their attention to her. Billy freezes in her tracks but she's already out of my reach and in the line of their sight. They both go to throw water bolts right at Billy as they swiftly surround her.

"*Ben kralım*," I roar.

Billy

Just Children

I'm not even sure what I'm looking at. This can't be the cute little five-year-olds I met this afternoon. As I look up, the two are looking down at me with glowing blue eyes.

They're huge and look more like men than two small boys. They are looming over me by about five feet. The name water titan makes sense in this moment as they move like they're surfing on water instead of moving on legs.

"What the hell?" I murmur to myself.

The sound of water rushing fills my ears as I stand frozen, trying to process what I'm looking at. The guy with the sword looks like he's going to attack now that the boys have their attention on me. Without thinking, I throw up a shield of ice between them and the man.

I look at my hands in surprise, wondering how I made that happen. I don't want any harm to come to these boys. I

may not understand what's happening, but these are two cute, innocent little boys. I can't allow them to be hurt.

"Ben kralım," Ardan roars behind me, causing me to look back up at the boys as they surround me.

They each have a bolt of water in their hands and are aiming them at me to throw. I throw my arms up to shield myself. However, nothing happens.

After a few beats, I peek around my arms to find what looks to be water knights. They are surrounding me and covering me with shields. They are the only reason I wasn't struck.

"I command you, titans. Stand down, now. This is over," Ardan booms.

Instead of obeying, one of the titans produces a sword and jabs it at the soldiers shielding me. I watch with wide eyes as Reilly jumps into the air and touches the forehead of one titan. Then, faster than the speed of light, he appears before the other and does the same.

Right before my eyes, the adorable little boys from earlier appear. They look around with wide eyes before falling to their knees in tears. I turn to look at Ardan and stumble back.

He's standing, glaring at me angrily, but that's not what throws me. Behind him stands what looks like a holographic version of him. It's taller than the boys were. Much taller.

Both the figure and Ardan have a crown on their heads. Water flows through and around the crown as ice forms around the base. The figure has his arms across its chest as he wears the same angry look on its face while glaring down at me.

The soldiers straighten and they all line up in front of me. The sheer weight of all of this causes me to drop to my knees in the puddle of water surrounding me. The water soldiers rush forward to surround me once again. I look up and see

they have expressions of concern on their flowing faces. Two of them grab me beneath the arms and help me to my feet.

I look back and forth between the two, trying to process what's going on. Before I can gather my thoughts, they move back to where they were standing with the others. All the soldiers place a hand over their hearts and drop to one knee, then bow their heads to me. I don't know what to do.

I can only stand with my jaw flapping. I turn my gaze back to Ardan and he still looks pissed. That's when Kai groans and I turn to look in her direction. Reilly is with her, and he seems to be healing her.

"What happened here?" Ardan barks out.

"We don't know. They were asleep. I heard a commotion and went to check on them. I found them in titan form," Kai says.

"What is triggering this?" Ardan says in frustration.

"How was any of that possible?" I breathe.

Ardan cuts his gaze to me sharply. I force myself not to cower. Although the look he gives me makes me want to piss myself.

"I will deal with you later," he says.

I frown, but I can't argue as he moves to sit on the wet floor and beckons the boys to him. They both scramble into his lap and wrap themselves around him.

"It will be okay. This will pass. We will figure out what's going on."

"I feel funny," Bourne says.

"Me too. I'm so cold," Beck says.

I don't miss the look that passes between Ardan and Reilly. I look around and know I'm in over my head, but I want to be here to help. I need to learn so I can help.

Feeling bad, I try to talk to Ardan through our bond. *"I'm sorry, but it's in my nature to protect. I didn't mean—"*

He sighs in my head, cutting me off. *"My anger is not with*

you. It's with the fact that you could have been hurt. I think we're moving too fast. I need to do better. This is my fault. Go back with Reilly. I will see you when I return."

"You're not coming back?"

"Not tonight. I need to remain here with them. They are frightened and confused."

"I understand."

Billy

Lost Communication

I've been in my feelings all day. I thought Ardan would return before I had to leave for my shift, but he didn't. I understand I fucked up. When I saw the woman from the warehouse bleeding out on the floor, I snapped into action.

If there was a chance I could save her, I wanted to. I wanted to find out who she was and ask her questions about Candido and that night he tried to kill her.

By the time I realized I had thrown myself in the middle of the problem, it was too late. I don't regret helping the boys to keep them from being harmed. Although I'm still not sure how I even managed that.

"What a long day," I groan as I step into the bedroom at the clubhouse and kick my shoes off.

I don't know what made me come here. It's like I've been moving on autopilot. My body brought me back here, not my mind.

I stand with my hands on my hips, not knowing what to do with myself. Ardan hasn't said a word to me all day, which has me pulling further into my shell. I felt the moment he entered the necklace this afternoon as I stepped into my car to head to work.

I wasn't expecting to feel this hurt from his silence. It's grating my nerves that I miss talking to him. At this point, I just want to forget about everything and decompress.

"What are you thinking, little mate?" Ardan says, startling me as he wraps his arms around my waist from behind.

"About what I plan to do before I go to bed."

"I'm going to make you something to eat," he says.

"You cook?"

"Yes, I can feel you are hungry, and cooking relaxes me. Go relax. We can talk later."

I turn in his arms and look up at him. "Why won't you talk to me now?"

He looks at me with his brows furrowed. Then he reaches to brush his thumb across my cheek. I want to know what he's thinking so I open my thoughts for him to see mine.

After a few beats, he grunts and pulls a frown. "You think I'm upset with you? I'm not."

"But you haven't spoken to me all day. You didn't return until I had to leave for work, and you said nothing as you entered the pendant."

"I lost track of time while in the oasis realm. I had to hurry back to make sure I left with you. The boys were struggling with what happened.

"They never want to hurt anyone and were very upset they attacked you. When I returned, I could feel you shutting down. I knew we needed to talk, but I didn't want to distract you from work.

"This isn't a quick conversation we need to have. When

you're in the human world, you need your focus. I would never place you in danger by rambling in your head.

"You were also surrounded by people and situations today. There was never a free moment for us to talk," he explains.

"I'm sorry. This is all so new for me. All of it. Not just your world but dating too. I feel like a fish out of water."

He cups my face and leans in to kiss me. All the sadness and frustration melt away as his soft lips touch mine. I begin to wonder if I can close off compartments of my thoughts to allow him in more.

"Yes, you can. The more you work at it, the more skilled you will become," he murmurs against my lips in response to my thoughts. "This is on me. I should be helping you to understand more."

"I could have reached out to you today as well. It's my fault too. I did shut down."

"Because you felt like you weren't needed or wanted. Billy, I want you wherever I am. Last night, I was angry with myself. You could have been hurt and that would have destroyed me."

"What exactly happened last night? Who was that woman? She's the one from my vision."

"You mean Kai? She works for our mercaptain. He's out of town and Candido tried to press her to find him. That is what you saw in your vision."

"She's a mermaid?" I ask as I see her in his thoughts.

"Yes, she is. As for the boys, water titans are born in pairs. Bardo, the being you saw with Candido at the restaurant, was their father's twin.

"When a water titan's heart turns cold, so do they. They become ice titans. They are vicious and care about nothing but themselves."

"What happened to turn their uncle cold?"

"His mate killed herself. No one knows why, but he found her body. After that, he was broken and inconsolable. He disappeared sometime after that, and then the sirens lured Brodny and Marina to him."

"And he killed them? Brodny and Marina are the boys' parents, right?"

"Yes, they were. That's when I found out Bardo had become an ice titan. He tried to take the boys, but I had already stepped in and taken them," he says.

I nod my understanding. This is much bigger than I understood. My heart goes out to the boys.

"So what was that about last night?"

"I believe that Bardo is somehow controlling the boys, trying to turn them. When they lose control, they can't see who they are harming. It's not them.

"It's whatever or whoever he has taking over their minds. I think he's trying to break them because he knows I won't accept an ice titan among the fold," he says.

"Oh my God, that's terrible. How do we stop him?"

He gives me a grin. I can feel the flood of warmth in his emotions. Suddenly, I have access to his thoughts.

"Of course I want to help them. I wish someone cared to help me when I was their age. Not having someone when you're that small is enough to make you jaded."

"When we find Bardo, we will find our answers. He's been eluding me for this very reason. Sea guards are important to both our worlds. Bardo has thrown the balance off and it will be years before Beck and Bourne can take their rightful places.

"I have substitutions in their place, but who knows how long I'll be able to keep that up. However, if he breaks them … if he can manage to harden just one of their hearts, we face dire repercussions."

"Is there something I can do while we try to find him?"

"Bardo didn't just kill his brother to get him out of the way. He killed his sister-in-law because that's the key to keeping young water titans safe and happy. Their mother. She guards their hearts. It's the warmth of her love and care.

"The boys haven't trusted many since losing their parents. I'm having a hard time finding the right female to care for them and nurture that good and peace within them.

"I do the best I can, but it's not enough. Reilly has been helping as much as he can, but we can't keep stripping their powers like that. We don't know the lasting effects it will have."

I gasp. "That's what he did to them? He stripped their powers?"

"Enough to get them to return to their natural forms. I'm not even sure how they are taking on titan forms. They shouldn't mature to that level until they're about sixteen.

"They certainly shouldn't be able to attack with such skill. It takes most titans years after maturity to be able to wield their powers."

I look down as my thoughts race with this new information. I can't help feeling like this is my task to take on. I need to help the boys, and I need to find their uncle to keep him from harming those sweet little ones.

Ardan grasps hold of my throat and tips my head up. I focus my gaze on him as he breathes me in. In the next motion, he lifts me onto his waist.

"Now I've made you two promises, and I've broken them both. I never break a promise. I'm always a man of my word, which means I need to make some shit up to you," he says against my lips.

I wrinkle my brows. "What?"

"I didn't make it back in time for your morning blessing and I didn't take your mind off work. You're thinking about finding Bardo and locking up Candido. I can't let

either of those things slide," he rumbles, then crushes my lips.

I grasp the sides of his head and allow him to devour me. No matter what, somehow, he also makes me feel whole. I think it's the bond between us.

I groan and whimper as my stomach growls loudly, interrupting our kiss. Ardan releases me to slide down his front. He kisses my forehead and then pecks my lips.

"Shower while I make you something to eat."

"Can you feed me with magic?" I pout.

"I could, but I want to do something romantic for you. It will all be ready by the time you're done. Then I will make good on my debts for the rest of the night. Now, that's a promise I plan to keep. No matter what," he says then kisses my lips once more.

"Fine," I say and turn for the bathroom. "What's the point of magic if you're not going to use it?"

Ardan rumbles with laughter. I look over my shoulder and stick my tongue out at him. He gives me this bright smile that makes his eyes twinkle.

"Man, I feel stupid," I mutter to myself as I enter the bathroom.

I should have talked to him from the beginning. I guess this is what Mack is always talking about, but can I really outgrow the habit now? I'm almost thirty.

"You can only try," I say to my reflection as I look into the mirror.

And try, I will. I'm going to do my best to make this work because, for the first time ever, I have someone who feels like home.

I wonder when Bourne and Beck last felt like they were home. I'm going to nail that son-of-a-bitch uncle of theirs and help them to feel safe again.

ARDAN

I WANT to follow Billy into the bathroom to make good on my promises, but I want to give her time to sort her feelings. Here I stand in my kitchen preparing a meal for our first date. I truly do enjoy cooking.

It has been a pastime of mine for centuries. I have learned to prepare cuisines from all around the world. For tonight, I've made lamb over rice and samosas with Pakistani flavors.

The spices and tastes are sure to hit the spot for Billy. I think she's going to love it. I get the nano ready and go to make a refreshing drink to go with the meal. However, I receive a mind link.

"I have one of yours down here in the main hall making a scene, brother," Brass says.

I groan and roll my eyes. I didn't used to mind when my folks would act out. I would head down there and straighten them out.

I have a mate now. Billy needs me as much as my people do. This is meant to be a night for her.

"I'll be there in a minute," I mind-link him back.

"Baby, I need to head down to the main hall. Our date and your food will be waiting when you're done. I'll be back as soon as I can."

"Okay. I'll wait for you."

"If you're hungry, don't wait for me. Go on and eat."

Billy

Not Expected

I decide to try my hand at magic once again. My instincts have been helping me out a lot, so I go with that to try to dress myself for our date. I stand in the mirror, looking at my naked body, wondering what to wear.

I get that we're staying in and it's late, but I feel like jeans and a T-shirt aren't right for this occasion. I've been on dates before, but for some reason, this feels like my first date ever.

I chew on my lip. I can't go wrong with pajamas, but what if I spice things up? I grin when I find myself dressed in a sexy two-piece with a garter belt and thigh-highs. It's a cute lacy bralette that holds up my firm breasts and panties that ride low on my hips.

"This could work," I murmur to myself. I turn around and look over my shoulder. "Oh yeah, this can definitely work. Maybe..."

I change the color from black to red then blue. I frown

and try one more time. This time, I find myself in a bright yellow. It works nicely with my skin.

"This is it."

Maybe this will make up for me shutting down on him. I go to walk out of the bathroom and, at the last minute, decide to add a robe to my outfit and a pair of clear stripper heels.

I smile to myself as the sound of my heels clicking fills the air. Once I step out of the bathroom, I stop in my tracks and gasp. The room has been totally transformed.

As I look up, there's a see-through floor above the original room. A clear staircase now leads to that level. In the center is a table set for two with candlelight. There are blue flowers decorating the upper loft and a soft blue glow lights the entire area.

He made a space just for our date. My heart melts and I wish he were here so I could thank him. Instead, I hurry up the stairs and sit at the table.

There's even music playing softly in the background. This is perfect. The only thing missing is the man himself.

My stomach growls the moment I sit down. Something smells delicious. I lift the dome over the plate before me and my mouth begins to water.

I close my eyes and inhale deeply. Placing the dome aside, I rub my hands together like a menace because I'm about to devour this food. I take my first bite and groan.

My eyes roll back in my head. I sag in my seat and savor the next bite. This is heaven. The nano is so soft and fluffy and the lamb and rice have so much flavor.

He put his foot in this. I sit eating and humming happily to myself. All thoughts of eating slowly to give him a chance to join me have gone out of the window. This food is too good to slow down.

Reaching for the fruity-looking drink in my glass, I take a

deep gulp. Oh my God, he's trying to make me marry him. If I came home from work to this every night, I'd need to triple my workouts.

I'm pissed he's been around all my life and I'm just finding him. By the time I clean my plate, he's still not back. I sit, fighting to keep my eyes open, but the music is lulling me to sleep.

"That was so good," I laugh to myself and pat my belly.

Slipping my robe off, I sit back in my seat and widen my eyes as if that will help me to stay awake. It doesn't help at all. I feel myself fading.

ARDAN

ONCE I HANDLE the asshole stirring up shit in the main hall, I teleport right to my room for our date. A smile comes to my lips when I find Billy fast asleep before a clean plate. I allow my gaze to roam over her lazily as I take her in.

I should go kick Eric's ass again. The yellow lingerie she has on has my groin painfully tight. She dressed up for me.

I move to scoop her up and flash us down to the bed. By the time I lay her down, I have turned the room back to the way it was before I set our date up. Climbing in bed beside her, I look down into her face and watch as she sleeps peacefully. I waver between waking her to make good on my promise or allowing her to sleep.

She moves to snuggle closer to me and sighs, causing me to decide on the latter—for now. I wrap my arm around her and savor her soft breaths.

"Sleep now, I will bless you later," I whisper.

BILLY

I WAKE with a gasp and cry out. It takes a second for me to register what's going on. I look down my body to find Ardan devouring my core. Grabbing the sheets at my sides, I try to relax the tension from my body.

Ardan hums as he locks eyes with me. He's working his fingers and mouth to bring my body to life. I don't even remember going to sleep, but boy, what a way to wake up.

"Ardan, please," I cry out.

He groans and keeps going. My legs begin to shake around his head, but he doesn't let up. I come, screaming and shaking, feeling like I might pass out.

He climbs my body to take my lips in a searing kiss. I take my fill of my flavor all over his mouth. He enters me and groans deeply.

I wrap my arms around him and hold on tight as he makes my toes curl. I would think I was dreaming if not for the hard slapping of his hips into mine.

"Fuck," I pant.

"That's what I'm talking about," he growls into my ear.

I clench around him just from the sound of his voice. He sucks on my neck and lifts my hips to squeeze my ass. If everything else could be this easy, I'd never want to leave his side.

I cling to him as he brings us both to climax sometime later. I do my best to catch my breath as he turns me onto my

side and wraps me in his arms as he pulls me into his chest. He kisses my shoulder, then nuzzles my neck.

"If I could gift you anything, what would you want?" he says into my ear.

I take a moment to think the question over. I don't normally like taking things from people. I go to tell him there's nothing I want, but in my mind, I think of how I've always wanted to be gifted a library like Bella from *Beauty and the Beast*.

"You will have to learn to let me spoil you, my pretty one. Nothing is too much," he says when I don't answer.

I try to remember if I've closed the door to my thoughts because I know he'll see how badly I would love to have that library. I groan to myself when I find the door sitting open.

Ardan chuckles and kisses my shoulder. "Too late now. I know your true desire. I will give you what you want, baby girl. Now, sleep so I can have you again."

The Bishop

Be Prepared

I enter the old run-down building and the first thing I note is the subzero temperature. This place feels like an ice box. I know, without a doubt, I'm in the right place.

It isn't often you come across an ice titan. However, they can be valuable when you do. I personally had a hand in creating this one. First, my lord filled his wife's mind with sadness and self-doubt.

When she became with child, I took over whispering words of despair as she would come to my confessional. We knew her suicide would break the titan, but the loss of his wife and unborn children was just what we needed to send him spiraling like a madman.

A few favors called in from some sirens who are on the outside of the brothers' good graces and our plan ran smooth as silk. He still has no idea I am the cause of his wife taking her own life.

She hadn't told him about the children before she carried it through. That was by design. It had a greater impact when the time came. I've been playing him since.

"Why are you back here? You have not given me what you promised. Don't you know I plan to kill you for your failure?" the titan says as I find him in one of the upper rooms.

"You must learn the art of patience. Your nephews are young. It is not as easy as you think to break their hearts. As long as they remain water titans, we will not have access to them. It is once they become like you, I will be able to hand them over to you," I say drily, not fazed by his threat.

He may be powerful, but I've regained enough of my powers over time to take him where he stands without breaking a sweat. Ice titan or not, he's no match for me. I believe he knows this as well.

He rumbles with laughter. "You assume I care for my life. I have lost everything. I have nothing else to live for. You may best me, but I will take you with me. Leave, I have nothing else to say to you."

"I am a man of my word. I promised you you would not walk alone. I will bring you your family. It will be done."

"There's something I never asked you," he says as he pins me with his cold blue gaze.

It's almost as cold as mine. His eyes have become vacant. There is a chance I could be losing my window to use him for the purpose I have in mind.

I tilt my head to the side and study him. "What is that?"

"What do you want in return? You came to me in my time of grief. You convinced me taking my brother's children from him would make things right.

"My mind wasn't right. I believed you. Why shouldn't I kill you where you stand and what the fuck do you want from me in the first place?"

"I believe I have another way to get you what you want. I

intend to find our mutual enemy, and when I do, you can take what belongs to you. No tricks, no tiptoeing around," I say.

He scoffs then throws his head back and laughs. I stand glaring at him as I try to hold my temper in. If I didn't need him for this plan, I'd dispose of him now.

Suddenly, his laughter ceases and he's across the room in a flash. I shouldn't have let my guard down around him. He has me by the throat with my back against the wall as he holds a blade of ice against my neck.

"He is my enemy because of you. What makes you think you can take any of them? Let alone Ardan, the king of water and ice. He will show neither of us mercy.

"I have been hiding in shadows, in places I once loathed. My honor is gone. I'm left to take jobs from scum. No, I want nothing more to do with you.

"Leave the boys alone. They are better off without me. I can be no father to them," he seethes in my face.

"Release him and I won't run you through," Ben says from behind him.

I grin at the ice titan. He couldn't have thought I'd come here alone. I am never without one of my hunters.

Bardo pulls his blade away from my neck. I reach to touch the place where he held the blade. When I pull my fingers away, they are covered in blood.

I frown. He will pay for this when all is said and done. Twin ice titans who I have raised from their youth will benefit me more than this one will anyway.

Bardo sighs heavily. "If we are to be slaughtered, I would rather fight and go down like a man. Leave my nephews alone and I will follow you as you wish."

"Good decision. I will be in touch. Be prepared for my call," I say with a grin and turn to leave.

I have no intention of leaving his nephews alone, but he

doesn't need to know that. It looks as if by the time I need to put him in play he won't know the difference anyway. He's already losing his mind.

Soon he will be a mindless weapon. He won't know or care who those boys are. They were always the end goal.

Billy

Just for You

"Ugh, shut up," I groan and shut off the ringer to my phone.

It's my day off. I had every intension of sleeping in. I stretch as I wake up fully to the scent of mint and coffee.

A smile comes to my face. Ardan has plans for us today. My curiosity from last night returns.

He wouldn't tell me what exactly we'll be doing. He has already used his magic to move my things here to the clubhouse. Each day I find a new room or area he has built to make me feel more at home. The room now has three levels.

I didn't want him to change anything about the bedroom because I love it so much. However, it's no longer the first thing you walk into when you enter the room. I'll admit, I love the place.

Although a part of me wants to slow things down and go back to my apartment. Yet, I haven't been able to bring

myself to do so. I think it's the bond thing holding me back. Besides, Ardan isn't having it.

In all honesty, whenever I think I'm going to put my foot down and head to my apartment for the night, my heart aches and the thought feels wrong. I tried to leave and go home last night.

Ardan made sure I forgot all about that idea. That's why I have such a big smile on my face this morning. I can still feel his mouth and hands everywhere on my body.

"You're awake. Get dressed and come out for breakfast. I have a surprise for you," Ardan says into my thoughts.

"Give me a sec," I reply as my phone goes off again.

It's Mack calling. I want to make sure everything is okay since I haven't spoken to him in a minute. I've been skipping my weekly visits to the gym, not sure what to expect when I run into Carson.

There is also the fact that Ardan doesn't allow me out of his sight. I sigh, knowing I need to deal with this sooner rather than later.

"Hey, Papi," I say as I answer the call.

"Billy, thank God. I thought something happened to you. What's going on? I haven't seen you in a week and Carson growls like a beast each time I ask him about you."

"I'm fine. I've just been busy. Carson and I are having a little disagreement. That's all."

"That's fine, but I'll feel better once I see you with my own eyes. I'm making chili tonight. You should come by."

I palm my forehead and look up at the ceiling. I feel bad for blowing him off, but what am I supposed to do? This is all so complicated.

"Papi, I already have plans. Can I get a rain check?"

"As long as I see your face next week."

I bite my lip. I'm going to have to figure this out. No

matter how independent I've tried to be all my life. Mack has never let go.

Even once I became eighteen and thought for sure he would put me out, he didn't. Mack was right there to help me figure out college and then the academy.

He was the one to find my apartment and gave me my deposit no matter how much I protested. He was so mad at me when I returned the money to his account.

He takes being my father to heart. However, I've never been able to accept that he's not going to fail me next. I'd rather do things for myself and not have to feel the pain of someone I tried to trust letting me down.

"I'll do my best," I say after a few beats.

I get out of bed and use my magic to dress in a pair of running shorts and a sports bra. I want to take a run after breakfast. After I'm dressed, I pad out to the main area barefoot.

"*Mi hija*," Mack sighs into the phone. "I worry about you. I only want to see you safe and happy. You won't even go out on a date with a nice young man. If it's a nice young woman you're looking for, I'm fine with that too."

I can't help but laugh at him. I mean, I give a full belly laugh. If he knew the things I allowed Ardan to do to me last night, he'd know that I'm definitely into men.

I know he means well, but I can hear the nerves in his voice. I have no doubt he would support me no matter what, but I can tell he's holding his breath.

"Papi, I like men. You can relax," I say and shake my head.

Ardan turns to look at me with amusement on his lips as he takes me in. I give him an appreciative once-over as well. He's dressed in a pair of low-hanging jeans, a fitted T-shirt, and his cut. His feet are bare as well.

As I stop in front of him, he places a hand on my waist

and tugs me to him to peck my lips. Without prying into his thoughts, I know exactly what he's going to do next.

"Good morning, baby girl. I've been waiting for you to get up," he says in that strong, rumbling voice of his.

I purse my lips and glare at him. He has the audacity to wink at me before he pecks my lips once again. I swat at his shoulder and shake my head.

"Billy, who was that?" Mack asks.

"That was my boyfriend," I say through my teeth as I watch Ardan's face light up.

"Your boyfriend?"

"Yes, my boyfriend. I'm seeing someone."

"When will I get to meet him?"

"It's new. I don't know if we're ready for that," I say and look away from Ardan.

"Is that your father? I'm looking forward to meeting him," Ardan says with a slick-ass smile on his face.

"Oh my God," I whisper-yell as I cover the phone.

"Were your plans tonight with him? Bring him by for chili," Mack says excitedly.

"Papi, I will find time to come by. Just not tonight. Okay?"

"All right, all right, but I want to meet him soon."

"I'll call you later," I say and end the call.

"I can't believe you just did that shit. What the f—"

Ardan places a finger over my lips to silence me as he chuckles. I turn to look over my shoulder to see with he's looking at. I'm met with two tiny little faces staring back at me from around a corner in the living area.

I knit my brows. That corner wasn't there yesterday. When both the boys smile and wave back at me, I can't help but lose all my anger.

"Where did you two come from?" I say with a smile.

"You promised to play with us. King Ardan sent for us," Beck says excitedly.

"They've been upset about attacking you. I wanted them to see for themselves that you're fine and you're not angry with them," Ardan says in my head.

"That was almost a week ago. They're still worried about that?"

"Yes, they are still five, after all. And their nature makes them more emotional than other beings."

I squat down and open my arms to them. Both boys come running and wrap themselves around me. Bourne surprisingly holds me the tightest.

I give them a good squeeze back. I don't know why, but I get the feeling this is exactly what they've been needing. I kiss the top of each of their heads.

"Have you eaten?"

"No, we were waiting for you," Beck replies.

"Well, then. Let's eat."

"You're not going to come see your surprise?" Bourne asks.

"It can wait," Ardan says.

I turn to look up at him. He gives me a mischievous smile, causing me to lift a brow at him as I shake my head. I can only imagine what he has added to our little apartment this time.

Our apartment. When did I start thinking of it as that? My heart swells as I wonder if the surprise is a bedroom for the boys to come live with us.

"What are you thinking, pretty one?"

I haven't opened my mind to him this morning, so he looks at me curiously as my emotions must reach him through our link. I bite my lip and shake my head.

"I might tell you later," I reply.

He smiles back at me and kisses me on the lips. The boys start to make noises of disgust before taking off for the dining room table. I stand watching them and their excitement.

I'm still trying to find their dirtbag uncle, but I've come up empty. Ardan hasn't had any luck either. He actually told me to stop digging and allow him to handle it.

If I have it my way. I'm going to find him and then Ardan can do whatever he wants with him. As the boys' laughter fills the space, I double down on that promise.

ARDAN

THE LITTLE TITANS have passed out for a nap on our couch after Billy and I have played with them for most of the afternoon. I'll be sending them back to the oasis realm when they wake.

"Do they have to go back?" Billy asks as if reading my thoughts.

I take a seat in the accent chair and tug her into my lap. I love how she snuggles into me. She's becoming more open to me with each day.

There's no way I'm allowing her to spend a night away from me. I almost lost it last night when she tried to go back to her old place. I've been working to make this our home.

I come out of my thoughts to answer her question as she settles in my hold. "Yes, that realm helps to contain them. What you saw would have been much worse if it happened here. Like I told you, we don't know the lasting effects Reilly stripping their magic will have."

"I hope it isn't causing any real damage."

"You're not alone. Reilly will be able to heal them to some

degree, but if it's bad enough, there would only be so much he could do," I say in frustration.

"That makes me sad. They're so cute and seem so lonely. I want to visit them more often. You know, wake up earlier and spend mornings with them or something."

"My queen already wants to take care of her people." I nod and kiss her forehead. "I think they would like that, but I'm sending them away to stay with a friend for a little bit. I think it's best now that I know Bardo is still alive and could be the one behind causing the problems."

"Will that be safe?"

"I'm sending them to live with trained assassins and one of the most powerful immortals I know. Kai will be traveling with them. They will be safer than ever."

She opens her mouth as if she's going to say something, then closes it and shakes her head. "I don't want to know. Supernatural shit. Not my business or jurisdiction."

I laugh and tighten my arms around her. "I will take you there someday and you will see they are needed in this world. Not at all what you're thinking."

"Not my business," she sings.

She rolls her shoulders and sighs. I reach to massage her neck. It's hard not to always want to touch her.

"That better?" I ask.

"Yes, that's perfect. For five-year-olds, they throw a mean water balloon. I think I'm going to have bruising."

I search her face as she snickers. Reaching to trace her hairline, I admire her beauty. No makeup, a ponytail, and that gorgeous smile, that's all it takes to take my breath away each time I look at her.

"Show me where it hurts. I'll ice it for you," I murmur against her temple.

"Look at you, always wanting to take care of me."

"You have no idea. All you have to do is allow me."

There's so much I want to do for her. I'm doing my best to pace myself when all I want is to shower her with love. No man could ever cherish her the way I plan to for centuries to come.

"*Mm*. What happened to my surprise?"

I chuckle. It took long enough for her to ask. Once the boys started that water fight after breakfast, her surprise was forgotten.

"It is still waiting for you."

"It's around that corner over there, isn't it? You think I didn't notice you used magic to block it off while we were playing with the boys?"

"I was hoping you didn't."

"Come on, what is it? What are you hiding?"

"Go see her yourself."

I don't have to tell her twice. She pops up out of my lap and races toward the barrier I have up. I'm taken aback as she causes the barrier to vanish.

Not for the first time, I note that she's coming into her magic on her own. I've wanted to help her along, but in true Billy fashion, she's been finding her way by herself. I'm starting to admire that about her.

"*Oh my God. You built my library,*" she squeals in my head. "*Babe, there's a window in here and a window seat with sunlight coming in. Like, what the fuck? How?*"

"*Do you like it?*" I ask as I flash to stand behind her and wrap my arms around her waist.

"Yes," she whispers aloud. "It's exactly like I always imagined."

She steps forward and spins around to take it all in. She stops and covers her mouth with her hand. I break into a huge smile as she squats to take in the surprise the boys left for her.

"Are those their little handprints?"

"They are."

"Wait, these are all children's books," she says as she fingers the books on the shelves next to the boys' handprints.

She looks back up at me with questions in her eyes. I move closer and squat down behind her. I can't help leaning in to take her lips.

I break the kiss and look into her eyes. "They asked to have books here for you to read to them. I didn't think you would mind."

"I don't. Not at all. I'm honored."

I search her face with my gaze. My heart aches to make this little being happy. She has already brought so much joy into my life in such a short time.

"I can't believe I've lost so much time with you. The gods have been cruel to keep you from me, but they have made up for it in making you so perfect for me."

"You know you were already getting some for the library, right? You don't need all the pretty words."

I laugh then take her lips and kiss her hard. I'd build her a new library each day just to see the twinkle she has in her eyes right now. She kisses along my jaw.

"Thank you. I love it so much."

I get ready to tell her I love her, but I'm not sure it's the right time with Billy. I might scare her away. I hold my tongue and take her to our bedroom instead.

It's time for her daily blessing.

Billy

At Peace

Two weeks later ...

I pad from the bedroom to my library just as I have every morning for the last two weeks. There's something about the feel of the cool floors beneath my feet that makes me feel alive. As I enter the alcove the library is in, A huge smile comes to my face as it does each time I come in here.

"How is this my life?" I sigh.

The space is perfect. I love the blue light the comes on as I step inside. It gives the area a warm glow. The room is wrapped with white bookshelves that are filled with books by color, giving a gorgeous rainbow aesthetic.

I can't help myself, every time I come in here, I have to run my fingers across the spines of the books just to make sure this is real. I inhale deeply and the scent of books fills my nose. This has become my happy place.

A face-splitting smile comes to my lips as I look at the bench seat and find my e-reader waiting for me. I had left it in my workbag last night. On the round table by the bench sits a cup of coffee and a plate with toast and fruit. There's also a bouquet of fresh roses in a gorgeous vase.

I move to sit and pick up the note resting on top of the e-reader. My face hurts from smiling so hard. I didn't know I could feel this way about anyone, but Ardan has made his way under my skin.

I'm falling hard and fast. I live for my morning blessings and our dates at night. No matter what's going on with the clubhouse, he always makes sure to spend time with me before I go to bed. Or he'll wake me to put me back to sleep if he has to handle club business when we come in from my shift.

There's something comforting about knowing I always have him with me. Even now, he was gone by the time I got out of bed this morning, but this surprise makes me feel like he's here to wrap me in his strong arms.

GOOD MORNING, pretty one,

I thought I'd leave your space ready for you. I had some business to take care of but you're on my mind and I wanted to make you smile. I'll be back before your shift. Enjoy your alone time.

Your Mate,
Ardan

I SIGH and lean my head against the window. I love that the light and weather from outside comes through every morn-

ing. Although, I've been learning to use my magic to change the view to suit my mood like a mood ring.

I know it annoys Ardan that I won't allow him to help me with my magic. However, I want to figure it out on my own. It just feels right.

"Thank you," I mind-link him.

I furrow my brows when he doesn't answer me back right away. Normally, he responds as soon as I open the link to talk to him. I open my thoughts to him to see if he'll respond.

"Billy, are you here?" Someone calls through the apartment.

I rush into the foyer and find Dracon with his head stuck in the door. His eyes light up and a warm smile comes to his face. I've noticed that Ardan trusts few alone with me, and Dracon is one of the few.

"Good, you're decent. May I enter?" he says.

"Yeah, come in. What can I do for you?"

He steps in and closes the door behind him. I note that he stands before me like a soldier ready to take his station. I get the feeling Ardan has been sending him around to watch over me when he's busy with club business.

"King Ardan asked that I come sit with you. He had to take off on a mission," he says, proving my point.

I roll my eyes. However, my interest is piqued as his words sink in. I lift a brow as I study him.

"A mission? What kind of mission?"

"A water spirit has escaped from The Final Tides. King Ardan has gone to handle the situation."

"The Final Tides?"

"Yeah, it's like a purgatory for the souls of water beings. Darker souls that we don't want to return and all that. It's where the water guards Brodny and Bardo used to protect."

"Is there anything I can do?"

"No, he would like for you to continue with your day. I

am here to spend the day and this evening with you until he can return. I have a charm bracelet the king would like me to travel in this evening when you start your shift. He has charmed it so I can enter and exit as he can," he looks a bit nervous about the last part.

"Have you spent time in a charm before?"

"No, I haven't. That's some genie shit. However, it's an honor to be given the power to do so.

"Don't worry. I'm a skilled warrior. You will be safe with me."

I laugh and give him a smile. I don't miss the disdain in his voice as he mentions the genies. I'm still in awe of all the beings that truly exist right under our noses.

"Relax, Dracon. Have a seat. I'm going back into my library to finish my breakfast and read a book. I'll let you know when I need to leave out. Would you like something to eat?" I say with a smile.

"No, thank you. I had something already."

I give him a wave as I turn and head back to the library. My mind is racing with thoughts. There's still so much for me to learn. Ardan has shared so much but I'm still learning new things with each day.

Bardo comes to mind. With Ardan away, I could follow the last lead I found on him. That might be my task for the day.

Ardan said to leave it to him, but he already has so much on his plate. I can take care of this one thing. Yup, that's what I'll do. Dracon will be with me. It will be fine.

That's a plan.

***

"QUEEN BILLY, I don't think we should be here. I know of this place. It's not safe for you," Dracon says.

I didn't force him into the bracelet. I'm not on the clock and I just didn't feel right forcing him to do something he's never done before. I'm sort of hoping Ardan returns before my shift starts.

It's clear Dracon is nervous about entering the charm and remaining there for hours. However, now that he's speaking up, I'm second-guessing my decision.

"I will be in and out. I just need to know if he's been here," I mutter as I continue to watch the building from my car before we enter.

"He who? Only the lowest of the low hang out here. Others who could never join the brotherhood or reap its benefits. Who would you know here?"

"I don't know him. I just need to find him."

"King Ardan will have my patch if something happens to you. This seems like a bad idea. I am one of the youngest, and yet the kings have promoted me time and again. Please, being your guard has been one of the highest promotions I've had yet."

"Lighten up, Dracon. I'm not helpless. I don't need you to guard me. If you are worried, stay here. You can tell Ardan I gave you the slip."

"He is not likely to believe that. There is a reason I was chosen."

"Fine … wait, that's him," I say as Bardo walks toward the building, looking around as he goes. "Got him."

"You are looking for the ice titan? Do you know how dangerous he is? Only ice creatures have clearance to hunt him.

"This is how he's been eluding King Ardan for so long. There haven't been enough hunters to confirm his death and

now there aren't enough to hunt him now that it's been confirmed he's alive.

"I'm sorry, My Queen. Neither of us should engage him. I will take my punishment for this. I cannot allow it," Dracon says firmly.

"Calm down. Get your drawers out of your ass. I'm not going in. I don't need to ask questions if I've seen him with my own eyes.

"I now have solid information for Ardan. Let's get lunch before my shift starts."

"Woman is going to be the death of me," Dracon murmurs under his breath.

"Or I just might toughen you up," I laugh.

"Running into burning buildings doesn't make you tough. Knowing when to sacrifice for the good of your team is as tough as it gets. To be tough is to know when to stand and when to stand down."

"I will keep that in mind."

ARDAN

I HAD to move quickly to get to The Final Tides. I barely had enough time to mind-link Dracon to give him instructions and leave the bracelet for him. I made sure he could be with Billy all in one thought.

The problem is. The shark-shifters who have been guarding The Final Tides in the titan's place can't mind-link from down at that sea level. One had to rush to the surface to

contact me. I knew by that time, the water spirit who escaped had too much time to get a lead on us.

There are traces of magic all over the outside of the cell the water spirit had been housed in. Yet, it has no distinct marker of who it belongs to.

"What water spirit was in this cell?" I ask before I walk inside to see what I can learn.

"It was İntikam," the shark-shifter whispers.

I roll my eyes. Beings have refused to say the name aloud for fear that the spirit would be released into the world again. It is already out. There's no need to whisper now.

"Leave," I ordered as I step into the center of the cell.

Once I'm sure they have left me alone, I go to release my powers so I can figure out how this spirit managed to break free. It's clear that it had help.

"*Ben kralım*," I say as I hold out my hands at my sides.

The water surrounding me begins to ripple, then it starts to spin counterclockwise, encircling me. The old spirit appears before me. It seems to be waiting for something. I tilt my head to study the spirit more closely.

That's when rustling happens outside the cell. I turn my attention to the barrier meant to seal this spirit in. However, instead of seeing who helped this creature escape, I'm blinded by light.

I inhale deeply and shake my head to clear it. "What the fuck was that?"

INTIKAM

. . .

I CAN FEEL my host awakening. She is powerful. Her powers are growing and rising to the surface. Her vengeance is growing, making room for me.

I have known that I needed to be free of this prison to take my place. Yet now that I have been freed, I know not how to get to her once I escape.

The force that broke my cell open gave no further help. I couldn't even sense who or what it was. My instincts told me to stay here, remain hidden.

Now, this being, with the presence of a god and the essence of the one the alpha once loved, is here. I settle into my hiding place to fully take him in. My aura begins to pulse.

He has been with her. He is aware of my host. Very aware of her.

"Ben kralım," he calls out and the water around him begins to swirl like a cyclone.

This is it. This is my chance to latch onto this being and follow him to my host. As his eyes glow blue and the cyclone continues to swirl, I take my chance.

As he inhales, I ride the intake of air and flow into his body to wait. He will take me to the one whose magic calls to me. He will get me to the one I belong with.

Ardan

Unhinged Desire

"*E*veryone, *keep your eyes and senses open,*" I say through the mind link as I step back into the human realm.

With no leads I can go off, I had to return and get to my mate. Billy is the only one who can calm this raging desire inside of me. I will find Intikam.

It is only a matter of time. Water spirits are driven off of emotions. Intikam has a specific emotion that will force the water spirit to surface enough for me to locate it.

If Reilly weren't already trying to find his mate and the hunters, I would ask for his help. However, he has enough on his plate. I will find this water spirit and return it back to the afterlife where it should remain.

"What are you doing here?" Billy asks as she climbs into her car.

I found the vehicle parked behind some buildings in the city. Feeling that the hood was still warm, I climbed inside to

wait. This desire coursing through me almost feels like the bond fever all over again.

"Have you not missed me, pretty one?"

"Maybe, but I didn't expect to find you sitting in my car. I thought you would meet back up with me at the clubhouse since Dracon is with me."

"Dracon, you can leave," I mind-link.

"How did things go? Did you find the water spirit or whatever it was?"

"I need you. Your shift is over. Let's go," I command.

"Ardan," she drags out.

"Don't argue, Billy. I can smell your arousal. You want exactly what I need to give you."

I don't wait for her to protest. Instead, I use magic to transport us to the garage of the clubhouse. She sits staring at me for a moment, then turns the engine off.

I climb from the vehicle and round it to open her door. Billy steps out and looks up at me with concern in her eyes. In such a short time, we have grown to understand each other so much.

I can hide my feelings from her, but she has still learned to read me and my moods. Her expression tells me she understands that it's been one of those days. Magic doesn't fix everything.

"Do you want to tell me why you have brought me here in such a rush? I've driven home any other night. What's the rush?" she asks as she stands before me.

I answer her by crushing my lips to hers in a hungry kiss. My head seems like it fogs over as I get lost in the kiss. I deepen it, desperate for more of her.

Losing patience, I teleport us to our room. She clings to my hair and returns the kiss eagerly. There is a pulsing within me as if I need to release the pressure building.

I break the kiss and shake my head to clear it. Billy shrugs

from her jacket and tosses it to the floor. I forget trying to figure out what's come over me and rush to cup her face and devour her again.

She tastes amazing. I groan into her mouth and stroke my tongue against hers. Because I know how much she likes it, I release my true breath as I grasp hold of her ass.

We are in the bedroom in the next thought. However, I don't take us to bed. Before I have time to get too lost in my thoughts, I cause our clothes to vanish. As I hold her to me, I fall back into the pool, not breaking the kiss.

BILLY

I'M SO CAUGHT up in the kiss, I don't register the falling feeling until we hit the water. However, I don't panic. Instead, I allow him to continue to consume me.

Ardan breaks the surface of the water as he stands in the pool and brings me to wrap around his waist. My back hits the wall of the pool and he growls as he moves his lips to my neck.

"Ardan," I gasp as he pushes into me.

He lifts his head to look me in the eyes. There is something different in his gaze. Something I've never sensed there.

He continues to thrust into me, causing my toes to curl. I cup his face and communicate with my eyes that I want him to turn so his back is facing the wall. He nods in understanding and shifts us.

I use my magic to create footholds in the wall of the pool

for leverage. Once I have my footing, I place my hands on his shoulders and go to town on his dick. I rock and roll my hips as I ride him.

Enjoying the ride, I throw my head back and open my mouth on a silent scream of pleasure. Water splashes around us as I continue to ride the shit out of him.

"*Fuck,*" he growls.

He has a tight hold on my ass as he tries to control my movements, but I'm not allowing him to take control. I drop my head to look in his face and the pleasure there is too great for me to stop now.

There's this coiling in my core that I've never felt before. This climax is going to be off the charts. Just as I start to convulse, Ardan shifts our position again.

He tosses my legs over his arms and pins me to the wall as he drills into me. I throw my head back in another silence scream. This time as my mouth is open, I feel like I take an involuntary breath.

My head is spinning as my orgasm rocks through me hard. So hard, my head hurts a bit. Ardan grabs my hair and tugs my head back gently. He then takes my mouth in a passionate kiss.

"I have never wanted you so much," he groans into my mouth. "I will take you for centuries and I will still never have enough of you."

I scoff. "Centuries? The dick is amazing, but I don't think it's going to extend my lifespan," I say breathlessly.

"Not the dick, my pretty mate, but the bond will. You will live a very long life. You are stuck with me eternally."

I'm too sex drunk to process his words. I bury my face into his neck and breathe him in. That ocean-and-clean-breeze scent has a hint of mint to it tonight. As I'm breathing him in, we land on our bed with a bounce, his weight settling between my legs.

As I clench around him, he begins to move his hips in a druggingly slow grind. I throw my head back into the pillow and cry out.

He nips at my lips as I claw my fingers up his back. Locking my legs around his waist, I hold on tight as he increases his pace. Ardan drags his palms up my outer thighs as he grunts and thrusts.

"Billy, baby. I … Fuck. I want all of you," he says in my ear.

I glide my hands down to his ass and dig my fingers in. I want all of him too, but the fear of him disappearing or hurting me haunts me. My heart is telling me not to fear him, but my mind isn't ready to let my guard down.

Not when this could all be some magic-induced feeling. What if the magic wears off? What happens then?

"Let me in, Billy. I will keep you safe. I can't live without you. I would never hurt you," he says as if I've allowed him into my thoughts.

"Give me time, Ardan. I'm getting there. I just need time."

He covers my mouth with his and pours a ton of emotion into the kiss. I cling to his shoulders as he makes love to me. I try my best to fight the stirring happening in me.

"I will be here," he breathes against my lips when he breaks the kiss.

Ardan

I Like Him

"Good morning," I say as I run my fingers up and down Billy's back as she lies across my chest.

Her skin is so soft. I look down into her eyes as she looks back at me with a sated grin. I've just finished blessing her for the day.

"Good morning," she says.

She searches my face with her gaze. I reach to brush a lock of hair from her face. She lifts a hand and palms my cheek.

"Uh-oh, what's wrong? You're mad at me about something," she says.

I want to kiss her for knowing me so well, but I'm fuming at the moment. If I hadn't promised her my tongue every morning, I wouldn't have woken her with pleasure this morning.

"Did you think Dracon wouldn't report to me?" I murmur, trying to hold back my ire.

She sits up and pulls the sheet up to cover her breasts. As pissed as it makes me, I still love the defiant look in her eyes. It's not that I don't think she can't handle herself.

I believe in time she will be a force. However, right now, she doesn't know enough about our world and she's placing herself at unnecessary risk. She could have gotten herself and Dracon hurt or worse.

"I figured he might, but I needed to make sure that was a legit lead. Ardan, it was. I saw him enter the building. Now you—"

"What would I have done if I lost you?" I bark, causing her to jerk her head back.

"I—"

"You didn't think of that, did you? Do you even know how dangerous that was? Dracon would have given his life for you to return to me, but if he had fallen before you got away, I would have lost you both.

"A warrior our people need and the love of my life. Finding Bardo is not worth losing you. Nothing is," I finish, my chest heaving.

Her eyes bounce around my face as she sits silent. I think over my words and realize what I've said. I close my eyes and drop my head back.

Billy moves to straddle my waist and cups my cheeks in her palms. When I open my eyes, she's a breath away from my lips. I place my hands on her waist and hold her tightly.

"You love me?"

"I do. I'm madly in love with you. I would cease to exist if I lost you. I've waited all my life for you. That's a long fucking time.

"Now that I have you, the fear of losing you is very real. With hunters on the loose, an ice titan in the shadows and now a missing water spirit, my fear isn't invalid.

"I know what it's like to have power and to watch power-

lessly as someone is taken away. I don't think I could handle that. As strong as I am, I promise you I'm not that strong."

"I … I."

"You don't have to say it yet. I feel it already. When the words are ready, they will come. I just need you safe. No more reckless missions. Promise me."

She pecks my lips. "I promise."

I grasp the back of her neck and take her lips. However, her phone rings, breaking into the moment. As she holds out her hand to call the phone to herself, I kiss a trail down her neck and make my way to her breast to pull her nipple into my mouth.

She moans and tries to wiggle away. I follow, laying her on her back and kiss my way down her body. I stop at her belly button to worship it.

"Hello, Papi. What's up?" she breathes into the phone.

I smirk against her skin as I continue to kiss the soft flesh. Goose bumps rise and she squirms beneath my touch. I watch as her stomach caves, then look up her body to lock eyes with her.

"I didn't forget. We've both been busy. I'll try to make some time to come by soon," she replies to what's said on the other end.

"I'm never going anywhere and he's not going anywhere anytime soon. You should just take me to meet him," I say in her thoughts.

While she is talking to her father, I trace the tip of my tongue across her belly, spelling my name. I groan deeply as the scent of her arousal begins to rise to my nose.

"Ardan, could you stop? I can't think straight."

"What is there to think about? Tell your father you will bring me by later today. Then I can reward you with a good fuck to start our day. Don't you want me to let you up so you can go read?"

I begin to suck her flesh into my mouth as I move lower

down her body. She tries to close her legs, but I pry them open and lick my way from her knee to the apex of her thigh.

"Oh my God, Papi, I need to go. I'll be there later," she pants into the phone and hangs up, dropping the phone to the bed.

I climb back up her body and take her lips. This kiss is different. I can feel her letting her guard down. It's like she's returning my words without speaking them aloud.

Just when I think I'm going to take control, she pushes me onto my back and straddles me. When I look into her eyes, I note so much has changed in such a short time.

I can't help feeling like so much more rests within my mate. Billy hasn't even scratched the surface of who she is. However, rushing her to come into her potential isn't something I want to do to her.

I would have lost my mind if she had to force her magic to survive Bardo. The last thing I want is for Billy's magic to corrupt her mind. As magical beings, we normally come into our magic gradually. When forced to mature in our gifts, some lose themselves.

"Focus on me, babe. You wanted my attention; now you have it," Billy says through our link as she sinks down on me.

I growl and sit up, then flip her onto her back. I toss her legs back and hold her waist as I drive into her. I'm taken aback when her eyes turn blue before going back to their reddish-brown color.

Her magic is truly awakening. It's happening with each day. I will be here to make sure it doesn't overtake her.

"I'm always focused on you," I say aloud.

BILLY

· · ·

I GUESS I can't avoid this any longer. It's time for Ardan to meet Mack. I could have kicked Ardan's ass for what he did this morning while I was on the phone with Papi.

If I hadn't been in my feelings already about him saying he loves me, I probably would have. That's why I invited him into the ring with me. I know he can't use magic in front of a bunch of humans so this should be fun.

"Do you always spar with males?" Ardan asks as he tapes my hands for me.

"Most of the time," I say as I smile up at him. "Sometimes there aren't any women around on my skill level. I have no choice but to spar with the guys."

"Billy, sport. It's good to see that face," Mack croons as he appears.

"Hey, Papi. I want you to meet Ardan. Ardan, this is my father, Mack," I say.

Ardan turns to look at Mack and Mack cranes his neck to look up at him. His mouth drops open and he knits his brows. Ardan holds his hand out and Mack slowly lifts his for him to take.

"It's nice to finally meet you. I've learned so much about you," Ardan says.

I roll my eyes. I allowed him into my memories of growing up with Mack before we arrived. I could feel how happy that made him.

"It's nice to meet you. Although I haven't learned much about you. She's allowing you to tape her hands for her. That means a lot. Billy doesn't allow anyone to do anything for her," Mack says as if he's in awe.

"That's not entirely true," I protest.

"It is," Ardan chuckles.

"Yes, it is," Mack says at the same time.

I fold my arms over my chest and glare at the two. "Are we getting in the ring or not?" I say, ignoring them both.

"Let's go."

Ardan makes quick work of taping his own hands as he chops it up with Mack. I relax as Mack seems to take to Ardan. My heart feels like it's going to come out of my chest as Ardan talks of human things and acts as if he's some normal guy.

I don't know why I'm so surprised he would do this for me. In the last three weeks, he has done so much for me just to make me happy.

We go to step into the ring, but Mack stops me before I get too far. I tense up, not sure what he's about to say. I look at him and he smiles back at me.

"I like him. He's tall as fuck, but he's a good guy. You look happy. I'm glad you've let someone in."

I cup his face and smile. "It has never been my intention to shut you out. I respect you, Papi, and it means a lot that you approve of him."

"He cares for you. I can tell from the way he looks at you. A biker," he snorts. "You are full of surprises."

"I guess I am."

I laugh and kiss him on the cheek then go to climb in the ring as Ardan holds the ropes open for me. Once in the ring, Mack calls for us to start the fight. I'm annoyed that Ardan is taking it easy as if I'm a fragile doll.

At least, it seems like he is. I'm shocked when I land two body shots. It happens so fast. I block Ardan's first punch, but the next one connects with my side and buckles me.

"Damn. Shake it off, Billy. You're doing great. You're moving more fluidly, but that's a damn good right he has," Mack says.

"Are you all right?" Ardan says in my head as I try to catch my breath.

"I'm fine. Don't baby me. I can't get better if you're not going to challenge me."

"Billy, I'm not holding back as much as you think. I've never seen you fight before, but I don't think you've ever performed like this. Maybe we should take a break. I can feel your power rising."

"Is that a bad thing? I feel great," I say as I circle him.

"There is something we call peaking. It's when our magic rises to a level that's greater than the normal level we naturally operate in. That isn't safe in this environment.

"Not to mention, you could reveal yourself. It is against the by-laws for you to reveal yourself in front of humans. For the safety of the humans here, I say we end this match," he replies.

I drop my hands and step back. Now that he mentions it, I do feel a little strange. I place my hands on my hips and take a few breaths.

I go to ask him a question out loud, but all the air is sucked out of the room. I follow Ardan's gaze and find Carson talking with Mack. Carson is giving Ardan a death glare.

"Oh boy," I mutter.

This is why I've been avoiding this. I should have known he would show up on the one day I decide to come through. I haven't spoken to him since that scene at my place.

"Looking good in there, Billy," Carson says and nods.

"Thanks," I murmur.

Ardan moves to my side and wraps an arm around my waist. Because my body doesn't know any better, it sags into Ardan of its own accord. He leans down to kiss the top of my head.

"Why do you have to taunt him?" I say through our mind link.

"I'm doing no such thing. I have told you before. I will not deny what's mine for another's comfort. He will do well to see you as a sister and not the object of his affection."

I sigh and shake my head. *"Will you let me talk to him?"*

"No."

"Really?"

"You will do it anyway. Just know if I don't like what I hear or feel coming from you, I will end the conversation. That I will not bend on."

I look up at him and smile. That's a lot more than I thought I would get. *See? We can compromise.*"

He grunts and walks off. I can't say I don't enjoy the view. He took his shirt off for our match and is only in a pair of gym shorts that are hugging his firm ass nicely.

I'm brought out of my thoughts by the strange feeling of being watched. I turn to find Carson's eyes on me. There's something off about his gaze. I can't put my finger on it, but something shifts in his eyes and sends a chill through me.

My hands begin to tingle with my magic, causing me to ball my fists. Ardan was right earlier. This isn't the place for me to lose control. I would hate to cause Mack to lose business.

I purse my lips and turn for the locker room to shower and change. Having a glaring match with Carson isn't doing much. We're going to need to have a real talk.

Billy

Taking Root

"Are you hungry?" Ardan asks as he sits on the floor next to me as I run my fingers through his hair.

We're in the library. I had some extra time this morning, so I ended up in here. Ardan came in a little while ago to sit with me.

"A little, but you don't have to get up. I want you right here with me," I reply.

"You said you like the food I cook better than the food I magic for you," he chuckles.

I laugh. "You have a point. It's not a crazy big difference, but just enough."

"I'll make something quick. This is the first time in days that I'm not being summoned for some bullshit with the others. I want to be by your side as much as you want me here," he says and stands to kiss my forehead before turning to leave.

I pout and sulk as I turn my attention back to my e-

reader. Ardan has grown on me. I feel like something is missing when he's not around. Even when he's in the necklace around my neck, I miss his physical presence beside me.

It's been a month since I've been living here at the clubhouse. I know I'm living in this bubble that Ardan and I have created for ourselves. It's been mornings of passion, me time in my library, then long talks as Ardan tests my magic at random—I have to keep on my toes around him.

Our routine has become so natural. In the afternoons, I spend my time getting to know the water folk who come and go. Since I don't go by the gym as much anymore, Ardan has been sparring with me a bit most afternoons before I have to get ready to go to work.

Work has been interesting. Candido's name has been coming up more. Although I haven't been brought in on the conversations, much to my annoyance. I know the most about the Ricci family.

I could help them build a real case. I would have them dead to rights in no time, but I'm being kept out of the loop on purpose. It's total bullshit if you ask me.

I knew the feds weren't going to pull me in on their case, but I thought the PD task force they started would rope me in. I have my theories, but I've been holding my tongue for now. That's going to end soon. I can feel it.

"Billy," Ardan barks through the apartment.

I look up as he appears in the opening of the alcove. He looks panicked. Something I'm not used to seeing on his face.

I drop my e-reader and stand. His eyes are glowing, and I know he's not looking at me. It's more like he's looking through me.

"What? What is it?" I breathe and rush to stand before him.

"Stay here. Don't come out of this room until I tell you it's

safe. It's Reilly. He's losing control. You don't need to be anywhere near him."

"Go. If you can help him. Go."

He nods and disappears.

I move back to the bench seat and sit. Blowing out a breath, I run a hand through my hair. Ardan has mentioned a few times that things have been a little strange around the clubhouse.

I can't imagine what has made Reilly lose it. He's always so calm and even-natured. Although I can see the frustration of not finding his mate, he has never seemed like the type to lose control.

My mind goes to Candido. If he hadn't separated us, Reilly would know if Lee was his mate and he would have found her by now. Candido is the root of all evil if you ask me.

I can't wait to take him down for all he's done. I get this strange feeling in the pit of my stomach. I've been feeling it more and more for the last few weeks. It's like something is taking root inside me.

"I guess my magic hates you too, Ricci," I snort to myself.

Not able to get back into my book, I go to get my things ready for my shift. I have two investigations to close out. I have no doubt that wife killed her husband.

I got lucky with that cold case. My magic actually closed that one. I had one of those visions for the first time since the murder of that chef.

I'm still not sure what triggers them. I believe it has something to do with water. Jenkins knocked over the bottle of water on my desk as he was handing the cold case file over to me for Captain Gates.

"He has found his mate," Ardan says from behind me as I strip from my clothes to jump in the shower.

I turn to find him looking at me with a heated gaze. I

smile and walk to him to wrap my arms around him. He palms my ass and dips his head to take my lips. I don't think I will ever get used to how my core floods from just his touch.

"Is it Lee?" I ask before I lose my train of thought.

"I don't know. You remember how the fever felt. He took off with her so they could seal the bond. We will know when they come up for air."

"Lucky girl," I tease.

Ardan lifts me onto his waist. "She doesn't have to be the only one. Let's take advantage of this time we have."

He takes my lips, then groans in frustration as he breaks the kiss he just started. I look into his face and know he's been mind-linked. Patting his chest, I slide down his front to get to my feet.

"I'll be waiting when you're done."

He cups the back of my neck and kisses my forehead then my lips. I'm curious when I feel him stiffen and he stops to search my eyes. I smile up at him.

He shakes his head. "I'll be back as soon as I straighten things out."

ARDAN

I SHOULD BE FOCUSED on what these mermaids are saying to me. Especially since I haven't been able to reach Amadeus. It's become my responsibility to watch over the merfolk.

However, I can't stop thinking about the current I felt coming off Billy. It was strange. Nothing like the magic I've felt from her in the past.

I've been keeping her on her toes as far as using her magic goes, but I've still been cautious. I can't help but feel like her powers are behind this wall that's ready to break. However, every time I think about breaking the wall down, something stops me.

Yet, that feeling earlier … that was something else entirely.

"King Ardan, can you help us?" River asks.

"Did you all really need me for this? You are both nearly two hundred years old. Can you act your age and not the one in the mirror?"

River blinks at me a few times as if she's shocked, while Brooks snorts and tries to cover it up. I'm done with this pettiness. I have no idea why everyone has been acting like children around here.

"Yes, My King. We will figure this out on our own," Brooks says.

"Thank you," I say and stand.

"Brother, before you go. Do you have a minute?" Brooks says, halting me.

I sigh but reclaim my seat. River glares daggers at Brooks before she storms out. I roll my eyes and shake my head.

"I'm sorry about that. It's my fault. We were in a relationship when we applied to open the business. I should have known better—"

I hold my hand up to cut him off. I don't want to hear this shit again. I approved the business in both their names. They each will have to pay their dues for the business, not just Brooks, as River wants.

In fact, all the funds can come from Brooks as long as it's the right amount, I don't care. The loan provided is the same, so the terms are as well. I will not be decreasing the repayment because River doesn't want to continue with the business.

"What is it you wanted to talk to me about?"

"Yes, sorry. It's about the ice titan. We've been monitoring the location you gave us. I can't help feeling like someone has been tipping him off.

"Not one sighting. Yet when it's my shift to watch for him, I can scent him in the air. I thought I should report this to you as I don't know who can be trusted," Brooks says.

I tighten my fists on my desk as I think through his words. I had a team put together to monitor the location Billy said she saw Bardo enter. I already felt like the results were taking too long to be reported. Each shift has an ice being who should be able to take Bardo on sight, or they should call for me.

"Thank you. I will look into this."

He nods and places a hand over his heart then bows. I haven't had any reports of the twins transforming since sending them away. I wonder what Bardo is up to.

"I think it's time to look in on Ricci," I murmur to myself.

Billy

Full of Surprises

"What are you up to?" I say as I find Ardan leaning up against my car when I walk out of the precinct at the end of my shift.

I look around to make sure no one saw him appear out of thin air. It's been a long night, the last thing I need is to have to deal with a noisy human. Not seeing anyone, I walk right into his waiting arms.

"That was brutal. I've never wanted to tear a human apart more in my life. I thought I'd do something special for you," he replies as he wraps me in his embrace.

"God, I thought he was going to force you out of the necklace. Gates was in a particularly nasty mood today," I groan.

Captain Gates tore into me like nobody's business. I think he went off on me for an hour. I didn't even do anything to warrant the blasting. It wasn't my case or investigation he ripped into me about.

The only reason he took it all out on me is because I asked about the Ricci investigation. I caught a few whispers that Candido is facing a RICO and his businesses are being audited.

Ardan had mentioned wanting to know if Bardo had been in contact with Candido since the murder of the chef. I thought I could ask the captain to fill me in, not tear me a new one.

"He almost did. If it wasn't against our laws, I would have really put him in his place."

"Wait, what's that supposed to mean? You did something, didn't you? What did you do, Ardan?"

He gives me a mischievous grin. "I may have turned his bowels to water. He'll have the runs for a day or two."

I gasp. "You didn't."

"You're not the only one who wants to stake out Candido. By the time he returns, we'll have the answers we want."

I can't help laughing. "I'll be more likely to be reprimanded for it too. He's only going to come back irritable."

"Not as irritable as his bowels." He shrugs.

"Oh to be a fly on the wall when that situation hits."

"He'll make it home if he doesn't make any stops before his *shituation* sets in. Now, it's time to forget about him. Get in. I'm driving," he says as he opens the passenger side door.

"This is new."

"I want you to sit back and relax. I can change the car for one of mine if that makes you more comfortable."

"How would you do that? Someone would see."

Before I finish my words, my city-issued sedan turns into a candy-blue Mercedes truck. Ardan stands laughing at me as my mouth sits open. I look around quickly to see if anyone is paying attention.

"Get in the vehicle, Billy. I know how to cloak my magic.

No one saw anything. Not even a super would have seen my actions."

"Well excuse me," I tease and hop into the passenger seat.

He closes the door and moves to get in behind the wheel. I don't know why I'm so excited. Probably because Ardan doesn't miss when it comes to his surprises.

I've felt so pampered in the last month. I may not know what sex with other guys is like, but I've dated enough to know Ardan is the exception when it comes to taking care of his woman. With each day, I know I'm getting closer to saying those words.

I don't think it's the bond forcing these feelings. It's Ardan's actions. He has made it safe for me to open up to him.

Because of him, I've gotten used to forgetting about work once I'm off the clock. I've come to appreciate the concept. With a smile on my lips, I sit back and close my eyes.

***

"COME ON, baby girl. We're here," Ardan rumbles in my ear.

I open my eyes to find his bright-blue eyes staring into mine. He's standing outside the car as he ducks inside to wake me, brushing a lock of hair out of my face. As I remember he has a surprise for me, I smile and come awake.

He backs out of the vehicle and holds his hand out for me to take. I take his hand and rush out of the car excitedly. Ardan gives me a bright smile and squeezes my hand.

"What are we doing here?" I ask as I look around.

I'm not really sure where we are, but excitement still fills me. It's around two in the morning, so I'm not really sure

where we're going or what could be open at this time of night.

"You said you've only ever been to one concert in your life. I've been to thousands." He shrugs. "I figured after the day you had, dinner and a private concert would be the perfect wind down."

"You're kidding, right? At this time of night, you're taking me to a private concert?"

"We can do something else if you don't want this," he says and looks down at me to search my face.

"No, please. I'm excited."

He gives a little chuckle and a wide smile. My heart swells when he wraps his arm around me and tugs me into his side. I allow my guard to fall a little more.

Ardan leads me into what looks like a garden. In the center is what looks like a stage in the middle of a fountain. I gasp when I read the name of the band on the drums.

"Are you freaking kidding me? Freezes Tides? How did you get them here this time of night?" I squeal.

"You do understand there's nothing I wouldn't do for you. It doesn't hurt that they are supernaturals. Water and sea fairies," he replies.

I was listening to this band this morning while reading. I think they're awesome and they put me in such a vibe for the book I was reading. Ardan came into the library and found me with a smile on my lips.

He mentioned it and I told him how much I enjoyed the band. That's when he asked if I had ever seen them live. I told him I had only been to one concert in my life. Now here we stand.

"This is awesome," I breathe.

"You haven't seen anything yet. Come sit. Dinner is waiting."

I give his hand a squeeze as he walks me to the table set

for two facing the stage and fountain. I find my second wind as we sit. I'm too excited to be exhausted.

"Ready?" he asks as he stares into my eyes.

I nod and food appears before us. In the next breath, the band appears on the stage, but that's not all. A light show starts within the fountain. As the band begins to play, a water show joins the lights and the music.

I sit in awe as the water and lights react to the sound of the music, changing colors from blue to yellow to red to purple back to blue. Water shoots into the air like mini geysers, randomly raising from various spots in the large square fountain.

"This is so romantic. You always create the perfect dates. I needed this more than you could know."

"I don't need to read your thoughts to know what you need. If you need something, it's my job to make sure you have it. I will always take care of your needs, Billy, and I will do so happily."

"Thanks."

I turn my attention to the plate in front of me and smile. A Philly cheesesteak and fries are on the plate, also something I've been craving. I may have thought about it when my thoughts were open to him earlier.

I tend to leave them open more often these days. It does help to strengthen our bond. He has been doing the same.

I take a bite of the cheesesteak and groan. This is hitting the spot. My thoughts go to the first time he fed me this meal.

"You used your magic that night. To get the food for me," I say.

It's a statement, not a question. I knew it was too good to be true that night. That joint I wanted the food from makes a killer cheesesteak, but never this good.

I look at Ardan and give him a rueful smile. Tilting his head, he studies me. He lifts a brow as I hold my smile.

"What?" he asks.

"I wonder if you'd be as good at this without magic at your disposal," I taunt.

"I'm even better when I have to rely on only human methods."

"This I have to see."

"We have centuries for you to learn all the ways I plan to love on you, my pretty one."

"There you go again. I still haven't had a chance for that to sink in. A month ago, I hadn't planned anything past the next day. Now you are speaking in centuries.

"What does that look like to you? I mean, will I age? I couldn't possibly keep my career if I'm not going to age."

"You won't age, but you can use your magic to make it seem like you have. It is my hope that you won't want to be an officer forever. Especially once we begin to have children of our own," he says.

I look down at my plate and allow my thoughts to race. Do I love my career? I love the idea of finally placing cuffs on Candido and seeing him behind bars.

Do I have it in me to give it all up once that's done? What would I do with my time? Children?

Feeling vulnerable at the thought of children, I allow Ardan into my thoughts. I allow him into my feelings as a child. I allow him to see why I've never thought about being a mom.

"My love, you will be a wonderful mother. You nor I will ever leave our little ones without us. They will be loved and protected. If you think my brothers would allow a child of mine to live without love and protection, you have lost your mind.

"Our community will also be there. If there is ever a

reason we can't be there, know, without a doubt, they will be covered."

"I get that, and I hear what you're saying, but they would be my kids, my responsibility, mine to protect. I don't ever want them to feel like I don't want them or I'm not there for them."

"In time, you will see how powerful you are and how long your life will be. You will have the power to protect and care for our offspring.

"I have seen your heart. It's not in you to abandon our children. Nor will I abandon them or you. You can put those fears to rest, Billy. Let me be your safe place."

Tears fill my eyes. I let my guard down a little more. I knew I was damaged, but I've never thought of how damaged I truly am.

That fucking Candido did a number on me. I'm terrified of failing as a mother. So much so, I've never thought of having children of my own.

In all honesty, I've avoided serious relationships because of it. I want Candido to feel what I felt as a small child. Then I might be able to heal.

The need to avenge my sisters and me grows stronger by the second. That feeling in the pit of my stomach comes to life and begins to pulse. Ardan gets this strange look on his face as the feeling grows.

"What?" I ask.

"How are you feeling? Are you okay?"

"I'm perfect. Thank you again, Ardan. Your words mean a lot to me. I have a lot to think about."

"Take your time. I'm not rushing you to make any decisions tonight."

I nod and turn back to the band as I allow my thoughts to work. Children? Can I be a good mom?

Amadeus

Training

"The greatest of our kind have mastered the arts of the trickster. You cannot be a true puppet master without understanding illusions," my grandfather says in my ear as he walks around me.

We have been at this since I arrived. He hasn't allowed me to contact anyone back home or to mind-link with Ardan or Kai. I have been frustrated, but I have committed to my training.

"Focus, Amadeus. It is in you. You will tap into great potential, my grandson. Trust me."

"I am trusting you. I have done all you have asked."

"You have, but you have not mastered the last task given."

I sigh and close my eyes. As a merman, I haven't used magic outside of the normal mermagic. What he is asking of me is outside of my scope of understanding.

I'm still working to harness this power he has asked me to

awaken. My grandfather has had millennia to perfect these skills. He is asking me to do the same in a matter of a few months.

"You are too focused on your limitations. Limitations others have set upon you. Dig within, Amadeus. Reach for your power.

"Forget what you have been told. Who you think you should be and what power you think you should wield. Go beyond the expected. Don't listen to what you've been told you can and can't do," he coaches.

I allow my body and mind to relax. He's right; I have been in my head about what I've been led to believe I can do. The powers of the merpeople.

I was made to feel like a freak when my other powers began to surface. It was drilled into my head that I shouldn't be able to do the things I had come to do.

Centering myself, I let all those stigmas go. How could someone without my power tell me how it should work or its limits? Suddenly, my entire being begins to hum. I'm tapping deeper into my powers.

"That's it, *Watashi no mago*. My grandson. This task you can achieve."

I can feel the transformation happen. When I open my eyes, pride fills my chest. I have done it.

"Very good. It is holding," my grandfather praises. "Come, take a walk with me through your creation."

I nod and begin to stroll with him. Where we were once standing in his meditation room, we are now walking through what looks like the underwater coral reef I grew up playing in. The gardens of the sea.

"You have questions about why you must master illusions," he says. It's not a question.

"Somewhat," I reply. "I get that I am needed for İntikam's

return, but I don't understand why we are so focused on my illusion abilities."

"I have lived a long existence. Been through many wars, watching the world change around me. Beings have come and many have gone. I've been hunted and I have been the hunter.

"I have been a geisha when needed and I have trained geisha as well. Anything to survive the time and era I've been in. They have come for this dojo, my temple, more times than I can count."

"Is that how the assassins started? The geisha?"

"Yes, I made myself useful. Since the time of our creation our beauty has been lusted after by male and female. I have used this to my advantage when needed.

"Geisha is art. Another illusion. Secrets are exposed in comfort. The geisha bring comfort. Not all comfort demands intimacy," he replies when I lift a brow at him.

He continues as I nod in understanding. "I may be the dominant force, but I became outnumbered with time. Everything is a cycle, Amadeus. All things must have balance.

"To leave a being like you and I unchecked could promote chaos. The gods measure our hearts every day. In Christianity, their text mentions dying daily.

"You and I do the same. We are reborn each day with a new heart. It is for us to decide if that heart will remain pure. The assassins are permitted because they serve a purpose."

"They keep the balance," I murmur the thought.

"Ah. Yes, you understand. By revealing to you your true power, I've made you one of the hunted. You too will learn to guard yourself within the confines of balance. Never destroy that which is fruitful.

"What you touch, you change, but only for the good of another. We take nothing in the name of our own desires.

This will challenge your heart each day of the rest of your existence," he says, almost sounding regretful.

"Then why do it?"

"The gods have need of our help. You were the one I thought best to handle this situation and all that will follow."

"The gods? Why can't they do whatever they need on their own? They are gods."

"That they are. You and I are manipulating loopholes from ancient times. They cannot be directly involved in changing Ardan's life and I cannot do this on my own.

"This needs to be done by a supreme being. Someone with higher magic—"

"*Sofu*, I am no supreme being," I cut him off.

"Ah, but yes, you are, *Watashi no mago*. You have reached and mastered the ninth level of our powers. Only two levels stand between you and what I am."

I stop and stare down at my hands. I've seen what my grandfather is capable of. How could I be anything like him?

"I would not ask you to do this if I didn't have faith in your abilities. Ardan would know the threads of my doing. He would see right through my illusions," he says, pulling me back from my thoughts.

"He'd be able to read the signature of your magic. I have known him a long time. Would he not be able to read mine?"

"No, we don't believe so. Where he will see through me right away, he's never seen your true power. He won't see through you, not right away. All we need is for you to buy us time."

"Time for what?"

"Time to awaken part of the answer and assist another." He pauses to look around. "Well done, my grandson. Your lesson is complete. I have guests for you to meet and someone you might want to be reacquainted with."

I nod and go to follow him. Suddenly, I get this over-whelming feeling. It's like nothing I've ever felt.

"Ah, yes. Your deed will not go unrewarded. You feel her, don't you?"

"This can't be. My mate?"

"Yes, you have been chosen to have a gods'-given mate. She was chosen by the goddess Güç herself. Su-Vaha has now revealed her for you. Come, you shall see for yourself."

Ardan

Shattered Mirrors

A month later ...

I step into the room of revelation and look around at the mess. No one has come in here to clean up since two months ago when Kendrick found Ray. The mirrors are all shattered to pieces.

I make quick work of restoring the room. I'm not going to be able to sleep without at least trying to locate my nephew. Maybe the mirrors will reveal him to me.

We all have our mates and as Bradan pointed out, they are more than what we think. I was floored to see Ray flash to Kendrick and get so close to his desk. In the month that Lee has been here, I've sensed that she's more powerful than a being who just came into their powers should be, even though Reilly treats her like a porcelain doll.

"What does any of this mean?" I mutter to myself.

I don't understand how a baby disappears from a womb.

I've been so excited for the arrival of Knox. My first nephew. I was counting on watching my brother with his family so I would know what to expect.

Hearing the pain in Kendrick's voice as he revealed to us what his mate had come to tell him made my chest ache. To have lost hope before it could reach its full potential—for beings like us, it's almost unfathomable. Not that it hasn't happened, just never like this.

I know I said I was going to my mate, but I can't bring myself to tell her this news. Not when one of her fears is not being able to protect and care for one of our own.

I lift my hands palms up and look up at the mirrors. *"Ben kralım."*

My iron releases and I stretch to my natural full height. The magic of the room allows it to expand to accommodate me. Although my crown is on my head, I have not released my avatar.

I gaze into the mirrors to see what they will reveal. I'm expecting to find a baby or little boy lost. However, what I find in the reflection before me are two boys.

The twin titans. I furrow my brows. It was just reported to me today that they are doing well. They ask after Billy and me a lot.

"Show your meaning in revealing this," I command of the room.

The images change and the boys are in full titan form. However, one is water, the other is ice. I nearly drop to my knees. This means I have failed them.

To lose one is to lose them both. Once they part from each other, they will always feel lost. Ice runs through my own veins and I drop to one knee.

"What have I done?"

That's when the image changes again. I knit my brows as I observe what's happening in the mirrors before me, like

watching a sports game on multiple screens that all make one image.

The titans are standing side by side, but that's not what stands out to me. It's the mischievous grins in the corners of their mouths. They reach their hands out toward me and that's when a pair of blue arms appear from behind them, placing a hand on each of their shoulders.

I narrow my eyes. I can't see the rest of the figure. From what I can tell, the hands look like claws. A nagging feeling in the back of my mind tells me I know more about this figure, but the pieces won't connect, or they are being held back from connecting.

The twins look back at the figure, then back toward me. As they turn their hands as if to catch something, each captures a triton. One of ice and gold, the other gold with water flowing around it. However, I'm confused because they are not holding the element of their being. The water titan is holding the ice triton, and the ice titan is holding the water.

Before I can ask the mirrors to reveal the truth behind this vision, it vanishes and the mirrors go black, leaving me with none of the answers that I came for and full of questions I didn't have when I came in here.

"I won't allow this. I will not fail you, sweet boys."

With a heavy heart, I leave the room of revelation. I don't understand why the mirrors chose to show what they did. The desire of my heart is to find the boy who is lost.

I shake my head to clear it. My thoughts turn to earlier. Bradan's words outside of Kendrick's office come back to me.

For her, it feels right. If she's anything like me. It's wiser to release the pressure cooker than to let it build.

My brother is right. Our mates are meant to be like us. However, I'm the opposite of Bradan. I know when my

emotions and temper run free, my powers can flood everything around me.

It is best not to release that chaos. Perhaps that's why I feel cautious about pushing Billy too hard and unlocking what I feel within her.

Where it's the right thing for Bradan to push Taylor, I know it's unwise for me to do the same. Nevertheless, I can't help feeling like Billy will need to take those steps sooner rather than later. Something is brewing.

Knox's disappearance feels like some type of marker of sorts. This is a pivotal change the gods clearly don't want us to understand. I'm not going to give up. There has to be an answer.

However, as I head to our apartment upstairs, I can't shake what the mirrors revealed. It's haunting me with each step I take.

This is just the beginning, brother. Get ready.

Billy

Seasoned Warriors

"**B**illy and I will train together," Lee says before anyone else can make assignments.

Ray and Taylor walk off together without asking any further questions, as they have already been in their own little bubble together. I roll my eyes at them and turn my attention back to Lee.

I look at her curiously. She has an unassuming look about her. I won't say she can kick my ass and I wouldn't say she can't.

In all honesty, I'm not sure I or any of my sisters truly know how to use our magic in battle, which is what this training session is about.

"I will bind you for now, but I still want you to be careful," Reilly says to Lee.

Ardan frowns. "No magic for today. Let them hone their combat skills. Let's see what comes naturally to them."

"Billy and I will display seasoned warrior skills," Lee says

and lifts her head. "But Ardan is right. She and I don't need to use magic today."

"How do you know I will have skills?" I pipe up.

"Trust me." She winks.

"Trust you? You are the only one who seems to remember we're related from a past life, and I've spent my entire life not trusting a damn soul. You're going to have to do better than that, sis," I say and pop my hip as I cross my arms over my chest.

"Good to know I'm not the only one who gets the cynicism at will," Ardan snorts.

I glare at him. He purses his lips and looks away while trying to hold in a laugh. I'll deal with him later.

"You know something, I'm going to ignore that because you've been like this since the beginning of time," Lee snorts.

"Stop talking like you know me, Lee. It's getting annoying."

"Fine, let's not talk. I'll show you I know you," she says as twin swords appear across her shoulders.

I hold my hands out on instinct and the same axe and shield from the first time I needed to protect myself appear. Lee looks me over and smirks. I glare back at her.

I don't know Lee well. We have only ever spoken online and a few times since she arrived. I've been cautious of her since she revealed she knew about our past lives.

I don't understand why she didn't find us sooner. If I had knowledge of my sisters all this time, I would have found them as soon as possible. So yeah, I'm giving her ass side-eye and a ton of attitude.

"I see you're still using those antiquated things. It's the twenty-first century, you might want to use something else for your go-to," she taunts.

"Thanks for the advice, but I think I can handle you with what I've got."

She shrugs and pulls her blades from their sheaths. They sing as she frees them then take a fight stance. I have to admit, this does feel really familiar. I don't have time to think much about it as she launches in for an attack.

"Tighten up, Billy. Don't underestimate her," Ardan coaches.

I duck out of Lee's reach and turn to bump her in the back with the shield. Not hard enough to hurt her, but a warning. She recovers quickly and comes at me swifter and with more accuracy as if she was just playing with me at first.

I adjust and treat the shield and axe as I would my fists in the boxing ring. Using my magic, I make it so the shield is transparent on my end. It helps, but Lee is skilled just as she said.

"You both need to use your battlefield more wisely. Take advantage of your surroundings," Reilly says from the sidelines.

"And your speed," Ardan adds.

Lee and I both adjust. As she boxes me in with her speed, I begin to move more quickly and keep out of the corner she's forcing me into. I hate to admit she's right.

This axe and shield aren't the best weapons. They are only affective in close range combat. Lee's swords allow her to keep a greater distance.

"What are you doing, Billy?" Ardan growls when I drop my guard and arms midattack.

"She will be fine. She's trusting her instincts," Lee says for me.

I hiss at her as I call two new weapons. Ninja stars appear in each hand. They are glowing blue and are cold to the touch as if made of ice. I begin to use the room as I run and circle Lee, throwing up a barrier to keep my attacks from harming anyone outside my opponent.

"I can feel your animosity toward me. It's fueling a part of

you. You want someone to blame, but it's not that simple," Lee calls after me.

"I thought we said no talking," I say and toss one of the stars at her.

She blocks it with one of her blades and does the flash thing I've seen Ardan and the others do. I wonder if I can move that fast. As I have the thought, Lee pokes me in the butt with one of her blades as she appears behind me.

"Got ya," she snickers.

I form another star to replace the one I threw and turn to toss the two I'm holding. Lee is fast, she disappears before either can nick her.

"She's playing with you and getting under your skin. Don't allow your emotions to give her the win. Make her earn your defeat. Use her overconfidence," Ardan says in my head.

"How is she doing that thing? How is she moving so fast?"

"You can do it as well. See yourself forward then leap. She is right, you need to trust your instincts as you already have with your magic."

I come out of my head and focus on using all I have learned. Lee does seem overconfident because she has knowledge I don't have. She is also using my emotions to keep me from thinking and besting her.

I shove all my feelings down and go at her with skill and technique. Feeling like I need to find another advantage, I try to flash like she did. My heart pumps with excitement as I go from one side of the room to the next in the blink of an eye.

"That's it, baby girl," Ardan croons with pride.

I throw two more stars but they turn to water and drop to the floor in puddles just before slicing her skin. I stop and look at her in confusion. I had aimed to nick her arms.

"He will never allow you to hurt his mate," Ardan says in my thoughts.

I huff and place my hands on my hips. Lee saunters over

to me and tugs me into a hug, holding me so tight I can't breathe. After the initial shock wears off, I return the hug.

"I couldn't come for any of you until now, but make no mistake, I've wanted to since I was old enough to understand how to travel. I am not your enemy. I have always loved you even though you don't remember me, I know you and I love you.

"I always have and always will and I'm willing to wait for you to learn to love me and let me in again. You are not alone, and no one will ever hurt you now that I'm here," she whispers into my ear.

I tear up and grasp her tighter. Her hug squeezes out all my warring thoughts and the mistrust I've been harboring toward her. Somehow, I find the same enthusiasm I had when I found out I had three sisters.

"I'm sorry," I murmur.

"You have nothing to be sorry for. I love you."

The words are stuck in my throat. They are so hard for me to tell anyone. She gives me a squeeze as if to say she understands. I squeeze her back and give her a nod instead.

ARDAN

"NEXT," I grumble as I sit back in my desk chair and slouch in my seat.

My thoughts go back to training earlier. I'm proud of Billy. She did well. Lee is amazing too. I sense that Taylor and Ray will catch up soon.

As I told my brothers we should—the night Knox disap-

peared—I've been watching my mate and my brothers' to see if anything else is changing about them. It's been two days, and I can't say anything has occurred to be alarmed about.

Although, I don't know my brothers' mates well enough to notice much, but I sense their increase in power. Billy, on the other hand, I know and there has been some subtle things that stood out while she was training.

I wish I were back in the training room instead of dealing with this. The craziness around here is only getting worse. I'm more frustrated than anything.

Some of this stuff shouldn't be brought to me. At this point, I'm mediating nonsense. However, I don't want this to fall on Kendrick so I need to weed out the foolishness that I can squash. I tune back in to the complaints as something catches my attention.

"Can you repeat that?" I speak up and sit up.

"There have been back-to-back typhoons over my nieces home. I would like to build a new sea complex for her family to come live here in New York," the sea fairy repeats.

I knit my brows. This is not the season for high typhoon activity. The water trolls who cause them are on vacation during this time.

"Your niece … she lives in Japan, I'm assuming?"

"Yes, born and raised. She has lost everything in this last storm. She has been staying with friends who were in safe zones."

"If I grant you this request to build this complex, you do know you can't start relocating sea folk from all over the world. It will throw off the balance."

"I am aware. Although respectfully, something is already throwing off the balance, My King. Those of us in the water can feel it."

The room begins to shake as my annoyance raises. It's not that I can't feel the problem. I am doing my best to create

place holders until the real solutions present themselves which will take time that's outside of my hands.

The vision of the twins comes to mind, and I bare my teeth and growl. I have to ensure both boys remain water titans. They will restore the balance.

I reel it in and focus on the task at hand. There is nothing I can do about the unbalance at the moment. That is a task I must put more thought into.

"I will grant your request. Have financials and designs for the complex to me by the end of the month and I will approve a community loan and repayment schedule," I say to the poor innocent fairy now shaking in front of me.

"Thank you and I apologize, My King. I spoke out of turn."

"You did not. There are things you are not aware of that are lending cause to the effects you see. I am dealing with it all."

"Heavy is the crown. I thank you for holding the weight of our burdens."

"I thank you for giving me your trust."

"Thank the gods for our queen. I know she will help you right all."

I smile. Billy has already done so much to bring joy to my life and grant me peace to think clearly. Our banter is just one of the things I wake to look forward to.

Billy

Returned Blessing

"*Y*ou just came from seeing dead bodies, how can you eat that?" Rafael, one of my CIs says as I scuff down a hotdog.

"I can't be seen with you in a five-star restaurant and a girl's got to eat, so street dogs it is. What you got for me? You said you had something I might be interested in."

"You know that guy Candido Ricci?"

My ears perk up. He has my full attention now. I polish off the second hot dog and wipe my mouth, then clean my hands and toss the napkin. I nod for Rafael to continue.

"Word on the street is he's trying to find entry to the headquarters of some biker gang. Iron Fists or Immortal Chain Brothers or something like that," he goes on.

"Immortal Iron Brothers," I correct him.

"Yeah, that's it. Shit like that usually doesn't grab my attention, but when I heard the amount he was willing to pay

to get into the place, I thought I'd mention it to you. Sounds like our buddy is up to something big."

"How much?"

"Forty grand."

I release a low whistle as Ardan growls in my head. I can feel that he's pissed. Candido has lost his mind trying to find the brothers in their home.

I don't think it's a wise idea, but who cares? If he gets himself killed, he gets himself killed. The thought makes me feel giddy.

"Thanks for the info, Rafael. Here's a couple of bucks. Stay out of trouble and stop lurking around my crime scenes. You have my number, call me next time," I say and hand over the cash.

Without another word, I walk off, shoving my hands in my pockets. I need to get back to the station to file some paperwork. Rafael stopped me before I jumped in my car to head back. Needing something to eat, I walked with him to find a street vendor.

I'm lost in my thoughts as I make the three-block trek back to my car and hop in. Ardan surfaces as I start the engine. I glance over at him.

"Do you have to report that information to your superiors?"

"No."

"Then don't. I will deal with Ricci."

"Cool, no problem."

As I drive, a large drink appears in the cup holder. I smile and grab it to suck it down. I forgot to order a drink with my dogs. I was more worried about a quick bite and getting the information Rafael had for me.

"Thanks."

Ardan grunts as if he's lost in his own thoughts, or he might

be mind-linking his brothers the information. I can't help but wonder why Ricci wants access to their headquarters. He has to be desperate if he's willing to pay forty grand to gain it.

"He is a fool. We have cut him off and have been ignoring him. This reeks of more than desperation. He's becoming a danger," Ardan says, causing to me to realize I've left my thoughts open.

"What do you plan to do?"

"He would never make it past Aravos. Whoever is selling Candido this promise, they're lying to him. Besides, since Lee's arrival, we've implemented coin access. If you don't have a coin, you can't get in."

I sigh. "Lee. I want to spend more time with her. You know, so I can build more trust and start to get to know her, but Reilly doesn't allow her to breathe. What's the deal with him smothering her?"

"Not my story to tell. He has his reasons. I didn't think it would manifest to this extent, but I understand."

My stomach growls as if I didn't just wolf down two loaded hot dogs. I've been eating more since we started training yesterday. I guess it's all the energy and magic I've been using.

Ardan laughs as he disappears once again as we pull up to the precinct. I don't know if I'll ever get used to him doing that. I park and make a mental note to order something once at my desk.

Climbing from the car, I get out and pull my phone out to check my emails. I'm waiting on a few test results to come in on a case. I bump into someone and almost drop my phone.

"Sorry," I murmur and look up. "Hey, Car, what are you doing here?"

"Only place I know to find you these days. You're never at your apartment, you don't come by the gym, you're never at dinner with Papi, so here I am," he says.

"In the middle of my shift?"

Ardan growls so loud in my head, it sends a shiver through me. I hate being cornered like this. Carson should know better. I try to remain even to keep from setting Ardan off, I can feel him ready to break free of the pendent.

"Since when is that a problem. You have shown up on me, and I used to drop by with dinner for you all the time. What changed?" Carson bites out.

"Where's dinner?" I challenge.

He purses his lips and rolls his eyes at me. I place my hands on my hips and glare back. I'm getting that weird vibe from him again.

Something is off and it goes beyond him being upset with me. It's like animosity is pulsing off him. I can almost taste it in the air.

My hands begin to tingle and that feeling in my gut begins to stir. However, what catches my attention is the feel of Ardan leaving the necklace. That's the last thing I wanted.

"I didn't bring dinner because I didn't know if I was wanted around anymore."

"Hey, baby girl."

I close my eyes and groan. As I inhale deeply, heat envelops my back. The feeling of being in a warm bath takes over me.

"I got your text about being hungry and picked you up something to tide you over," Ardan says.

I open my eyes and find him holding a bag of food up for me to see. My mouth waters and my stomach growls loudly. This man.

"Thanks," I say and take the bag.

"Yeah, I get it. Call me when you remember who you are, Billy," Car seethes and storms off.

I don't bother to call after him because I don't like the

feeling I get when he's around. I turn to face Ardan and he's glaring in the direction Carson just went.

"Calm down," I say, placing a hand on his chest.

"He smells odd. I want you to stay away from him. His human scent has been compromised. I don't know why yet, and I can't just confront him and reveal myself," Ardan says tightly.

"I don't know what you're smelling, but I do feel like something is off about him. Is there a way I could check?"

"No."

"There is, you just don't want me to know," I accuse.

He grunts and looks down into my eyes. "Finish your shift. We will talk when we get home."

"Ardan—"

"No."

Without another word, he vanishes. I know he's back in the necklace, as the weight of it makes itself known between my breasts. I sigh and head inside to eat and get to work. Hopefully, I won't be called out again tonight.

ARDAN

I'm still fuming from Carson's visit to Billy's station. I know I'm not crazy. Something was off about him. He smelled less like a human and more like one of my mother's kind.

I'm aware those hunters are still out there, but attacking him could be a trap. They could have placed their scent on him just to cause me to harm a human. I can feel that Billy

still cares about him, which is the other reason I didn't rip him apart as soon as I caught the scent.

"Ardan, you are causing the pool to stir with all your brooding," Billy says as she lies in bed beside me.

I focus on the room and realize she's right. The pool around the bed is troubled with my mood. I reel it in and turn onto my side to look down at her.

"Am I keeping you from sleeping?"

"No," she says, reaching up to cup my face. "I'm not tired at all. Maybe I can help you clear your mind."

I smile back at her. I had wanted to allow her to rest, but I want her more than anything. It occurs to me that I haven't revealed to her my latest addition to our place.

I place my hand over hers and bring the back to my lips. Her eyes fill with lust and my mind is made up. Before I can change my mind, I use my magic to move us to the room I added this morning.

All the walls in this room are made of glass. Behind three of the walls of glass are water and sea life. Schools of fish swim by as sharks float around as well.

The fourth wall holds shelves—some open-faced—others have mirrored soft-touch cabinet doors that sit flush to give the illusion of large panels.

"Ardan, this is beautiful. Where are we?"

"The third floor of our apartment. Our playroom, if you want a name for it."

She looks around in awe. Then she turns to me and places her hands on my waist. I lift a brow as she looks up at me from beneath her lashes as she bites her lower lip.

"What are you up to, my pretty one?"

She doesn't give me an answer. Instead, music begins to play throughout the room. "Slow" by Tank, that's what she told me the name was the last time she played it. I grin down at her and search her pretty face.

Billy lifts her right hand and snaps her fingers. The next thing I know, my arms are cuffed behind my back and I'm standing before her naked.

I tilt my head to the side as I look at her while the design of the room begins to change. At first, the walls begin to cover with condensation. Blue lighting wraps the room, rising from the floor and illuminating the glass panels.

Water begins to flow from the three walls the mirrors aren't on. The water gathers into grooves in the floor around the perimeter of the room. The sound and the visual changing the aesthetic to a calming one.

"Nice additions, but why have you cuffed me? Did you think I wouldn't welcome your changes?" I tease.

"Not at all. The cuffs are for you to receive a blessing for a change," she says and takes a step back.

She flips her wrist out in a gesture as if in offering and then snaps her fingers again. This time her clothes vanish and are replaced with a sexy shimmering blue lacy panty and bra set. Complete with thigh-highs, a garter, and strappy patent leather black heels.

I'm at full mast instantly. The way her breasts are spilling out of the bra have my mouth watering. I widen my stance and lift my head as if in challenge.

"Show me what you've got."

Billy licks her lips as she pulls her hair back in a high ponytail. Then she saunters over to me and drops to her knees. I groan and throw my head back.

"Billy," I hiss out as she bobs her head on my length.

I'm covered in her saliva in no time. She's using both hands and her mouth to work me. I look down my body as my lips part and place my tongue in the corner of my mouth.

Gods, her mouth is insane. She tilts her head to the side and runs her lips back and forth. How is it she's so beautiful while sucking my cock?

"Fuck, baby. You can do no wrong. *Yes*," I hiss the last part as she deep-throats me.

I start to pump my hips, wishing my hands were free to grasp her hair. She hums around me as she continues to work her mouth. Drool is running from the sides of her mouth, covering her chin.

"I'm going to fuck you so good. Not even your powers will heal you enough to walk straight," I growl.

I've been allowing this, not removing the cuffs because I wanted to give her a chance to do what she wants, but my restraint is breaking.

I cause a half sphere to rise from the floor and prepare restraints of my own for her. I come down her throat with a deep rumble emitting from my chest. If I were a human man, she would have brought me down to my knees.

"My turn," I breathe as I release the cuffs from my wrists.

Reaching under her arms, I lift her from her knees and wrap her around my waist. Then I take her lips and devour her mouth. Not breaking the kiss, I tear her panties off and toss the ruined fabric to the floor.

Lifting her arms, I cuff her wrists to the top of the sphere. I chuckle as she reaches for the restraints to hold her own weight up. Always my little defiant one.

"Trust me, Billy. I'm not going to allow anything to happen to you. Letting go is a part of the pleasure," I say just below her ear.

I then allow a piece of ice to form between my tongue and her skin. I roll the cube against her flesh, then grasp it between my teeth and drag it slowly down her neck, over her shoulder. She moans and shivers, bringing a smile to my lips.

Teasingly, I roll the ice across her collarbone, then back up her throat to her chin. When it has melted against her skin and dripped down the valley of her breasts, I begin to kiss my way to her breast and capture one of her nipples in

my mouth. She jerks against me and releases her tight grip on the chains.

I suck harder, and the tension in her body releases, allowing her body to hang free. I guide my way inside of her and groan. The way her pussy tightens around me feels so damn good. We lock eyes and the feeling intensifies.

"Oh shit, babe," she cries out as I bounce her up and down. She's so wet and tight.

I cup her ass in my palms and squeeze as I thrust into her. I take her lips and release my true breath, causing her to moan into my mouth. I pull back and watch as condensation pours from her nose.

She's smiling back at me as I rock into her. Her head lolls to one side as she keens and grinds her hips back into me. I cause mist to release from the sphere, cooling our bodies down.

"Yes, yes, yes," she moans.

I keep plowing away. When she begins to convulse, and I know she's about to come, I free her wrists and create a bed for us to land on.

We land on the bed with a bounce, causing me to drive deeper into her. "*Holy shit*," she drags out.

I grab her legs and pin them out at her sides as I work my hips, thrusting into her. One day she will be ready for me to place my seed in her womb, and I will fuck her deep like this to make sure she's carrying my son.

"Yes, yes, fuck yes," she screams, as if reading my thoughts.

Ardan

Hidden Truths

I slice through the water of the pool, needing to clear my thoughts. Billy is fast asleep in the bed. She had a long shift, and with all her feelings, it took a toll on her.

Whatever the night made her feel, she blocked that part of her thoughts off from me. It probably had something to do with the family that was murdered, including two small children.

Humans fear us, but we have more reason to fear them and the evil in their hearts. I know a part of it is because of my uncle's influence that seeps out even from his prison.

However, there is still a choice to be made in the heart and mind. Once you decide to be evil and cruel, you're accountable for all you have done. Sure, humans have become reliant on blaming any and everything outside of themselves, but the truth is, once the fingers are removed, it's all them.

"We are changing shifts. Hudson and Ren are taking over," Dracon mind-links me.

"Thank you. I will talk to you in the morning. I want to make sure the queen's guard is complete, and I can trust each member."

"It's an honor to serve. I will make sure everyone is in attendance."

"Thank you, Dracon."

"Get some rest, My King."

I grunt and continue to slice through the water. Kendrick and Bradan are creating courts for their mates. I know Billy enough to understand that's not her thing, so I'm forming a guard to be with her whenever I can't be.

I still have hope that, over time, she will open up and a court will be an option, but for now, Dracon and the others have built a camaraderie with her that she seems willing to accept.

My mind goes back to what has had me in the pool trying to release some of my frustration and energy. We still don't have any leads on Knox. Every time I try to locate his presence, I find visions of the twins.

They are still safe in Japan. I have no idea why their life forces continue to interfere with my meditation. The frustrating part is that I feel another life force pulsing behind theirs when I tap into the visions.

I have no idea if that's Knox or something or someone else. What I know for sure is that this isn't normal and has traces of the gods all over it.

"No, no," I hear Billy scream.

I flash from the pool to the bed in a single breath. When I get there, she's still asleep, thrashing and flailing about. Her skin is glowing as well with a blue light.

I look her over, not sure whether to touch her or not. She cries out in her sleep again and whimpers, causing me to

throw caution to the wind. I pull her body to me and rest my back against the glass headboard.

As I settle her between my legs, I place my hand against her forehead to cool her heated skin. The moment I do, I'm pulled into her mind.

Just like that, I'm falling through time. Confused and disoriented, I take a moment to catch my bearings. I know the time right away.

My brothers don't know that I didn't fully slumber when they did. Kendrick wasn't the only one who was restless. The time was boring, and humans were becoming a problem, so it was a good time to sleep, but I couldn't rest peacefully, so I would wake to explore from time to time.

To keep from being noticed, I learned to split my presence. I used other bodies as I had the power to do. I chose a water nymph who had an obsession with this stream that fed into a spring. I believe it was because of the young girl who frequented it.

She was a pretty girl, brown skin with full wild hair. I had found the nymph in good taste. When I spent time in his body, he would spend hours waiting for her to arrive and then watching her.

As the memory comes back to me, the young girl appears. I understand right away I'm seeing this through the nymph's eyes, as I'm in his body and not mine. Almost like I'm having one of his memories.

"Zander, we can't stay long. Kendrick will be upset if we're late for training," someone calls in the distance.

"I only want to cool off in the spring. Gods knows it's hot out here as it is. Kendrick is going to have us all sweaty and tired with all that fighting and carrying on. I need time to be a lady, not a warrior," she calls back.

"You say this as you strip down to jump into a spring," the other replies.

"You have your meaning of a lady, and I have mine."

I chuckle as she continues to grumble to herself—shaking her

neck spiritedly as if still in a disagreement—as she undresses and looks around mischievously. I tilt my head to study her. There's this strong feeling that she's not just here for a dip.

Once down to her sheath, she strolls her curvy body to the water and climbs in. To my surprise a dragon appears from beneath the water. Zander doesn't look surprised at all.

Instead, she reaches out to it as she speaks with the dragon. I can feel the anxiety of the water nymph. He's concerned for her and ready to protect her if she needs him.

However, Zander looks comfortable with the dragon. I would say they are friends. She splashes water at it playfully and even goes as far as embracing its neck.

I look more closely at the dragon and recognition hits. I have crossed paths with this being. I know the dragon well.

So many centuries have passed since I've encountered this being. Those were different times. I begin to wonder how the two have become acquainted.

This is no ordinary creature. In fact, this seems to be out of character for the being. I am taken aback as I watch their next interaction.

Zander kneels in the water and the dragon lifts it's hand to touch a claw to her forehead. A blue light begins to emit from the point of contact.

"He is blessing her," I murmur to myself.

I can feel the water nymph's confusion and panic. This is an ancient ritual the nymph wouldn't understand. The dragon has chosen Zander.

"No," I roar as the water nymph shoots an arrow at the dragon.

In the same instant, Zander has lifted from the water and now stands before the dragon, unknowingly stepping into the path of the arrow. The dragon knocks her out of the way just in time, but the arrow pierces its original mark.

I close my eyes as Zander's screams fill the air.

I'm brought back to the present as I'm struck in the jaw.

I'm startled by how much it stings. Now that I'm aware of my surroundings, I'm able to catch Billy's fist before it connects a second time.

There are conversations to be had and questions to be answered, but those will have to wait. My mate is in distress. I restrain her arms and rock her back and forth as I coo to calm her.

"You are safe, my love. You are in my arms, and I will keep you safe. Nothing will ever harm you. I am here."

BILLY

I'M DROWNING in pain and so much torment. I latch onto Ardan's voice and allow it to guide me away from all the chaos. Slowly, I open my eyes and look around.

I'm safe, I'm in our bedroom. Ardan has his strong arms around me as he rocks me from side to side. I close my eyes again and breathe him in, allowing his calming scent to fill my lungs.

"Do you want to talk about it?" he murmurs into my hair.

"No, I don't understand most of it."

"Then you can sleep in my arms. I will hold you and be here to protect you."

"Thank you," I say as I go to sit up.

He releases me reluctantly, probably thinking I intend to run away from him. Instead, I turn to straddle his hips and wrap my arms around him as I squeeze him tight and bury my face in his neck.

Lee giving me that hug the other day resonated deeply

with me. I don't often allow others to embrace me. Eddy has been the exception.

As I melt into Ardan, he tightens his arms, and I get the feeling he understands the depth of this gesture. I'm accepting him as my person. This isn't the bond leading me, this is my heart.

"Ardan, I ..."

"No need for words, my pretty mate," he says in my ear and pats a hand against my butt.

I'm filled with so many raw emotions. I know I need to decipher those dreams, but the pain and torment I felt while in them has left me bare and aching.

"Sleep, my little one. Sleep."

His deep, strong voice lulls me into comfort and my lids grow heavy. It's like I'm wrapped in a cocoon of safety and love. If I ever questioned Ardan's feelings before, I can't say I do now.

I believe he's allowing them to come through stronger than usual, so I push mine back. I may still have a hard time expressing the words, but my feelings are all in.

Candido

Backup Plan

I walk into the basement of the dive bar where I have my next meeting. Fixing my tie, I look around and snort. This is what I've had to resort to.

I'm still seething from the phone call that's led to this decision. I'm all out of options and everyone's looking the other way as if I'm the plague.

"Hello, it's about time you got back to me," answered the call.

"This will be our last conversation. I have what you asked for," she said.

"Well?"

"Maybe you should have kept a closer eye on them over the years. Neither girl is an option. They are twenty-nine going on thirty, for God's sake.

"Do you even want to know who they are now or what they do?" she hissed accusingly.

"You speak to me as if I'm a bad father. I was told to stay away. What does any of that matter to you anyway?"

"It doesn't but it sure as hell should matter to you. One is a cop and she's been hell-bent on taking you down. You made an enemy of your own child."

"Marone. Fanculo. You have to be shitting me. Just add her to the list."

"Yes, your list is long, but this foot is on your neck. You are closer to a cell than you think and if she has her way, she's going to make that happen sooner rather later."

I hung up right there. After I allowed them to take my three girls, I found a witch to look after the two I wouldn't get to see or know. I figured it couldn't hurt to have my own supernatural help.

I made her promise to tell me if anything ever happened to them that I should know about and I asked her to monitor if they remained pure. She has done none of that.

It's like I'm getting fucked in the ass left and right with no lube. *Marone.* So the other girls aren't an option and those fucking bikers still won't answer me.

This indictment is on my head, and they won't lift a finger to get me out of this situation. I still have my ring. How are they denying my summons?

"Candido, finally. We can't meet like this again. You're in some hot water and if I'm seen with you, I'm going down with the ship."

"Officer Gates, how you doing? Since when do we start off without pleasantries?"

"Cut the bullshit. You're usually the one entering the room rushing to be rid of me. My ass is on the line, and I have a detective who's on your ass.

"It hasn't been as easy to make shit go away for you. If I didn't know any better, I'd say someone higher up is pulling strings to reveal you. Salvado just got lucky."

Salvado, that's the name of my daughter. She's a cop and a decorated one. I never thought I'd be proud of a pig.

Yeah, I did a little digging after that phone call. Billy Ann Salvado is one of my little girls. She's not so little anymore and she's a knockout.

I made beautiful children. Marrying the four of them off would have been easy if I kept them all. I should have picked a better match for Ray. Maybe that's where I went wrong.

"Detective Salvado is the reason for this meeting. Name your price to have her suspended before the end of the week."

"Why would I do that? She's not on the task force gunning for you. I made sure of that," he says with a confused look on his face.

"Don't worry about why. I'm telling you she's a problem. I need her sat the fuck down before she exposes us both. I'm still working to get out of this mess.

"I have on good authority she'll fuck that all up. Which means, if I go down, you're coming with me," I say and smile.

"Fuck you, Ricci. I have two kids in college and one on the way next year. I'm still making alimony payments to that bitch who birthed the little ungrateful bastards.

"I'll put a bullet in your head myself before I allow you to make me lose my badge or my pension."

I think fast. I need him to do this so I can explore my other options. I have a meeting at the church in a few nights that should settle my problems.

"Killing me won't hide the truth. You think I would deal with a dirty cop and not cover my ass? I have enough recordings of our meetings to take you down, as well as every other motherfucker who was greedy enough to take my money for a favor," I bite out.

I don't, but it sounds good. I've been greasing pockets just in case of times like this for the last few years. I've had backup plans for my backup plans since realizing time might be running out on my hold on the bikers.

"Fine. I'll handle it, but you're covering tuitions and the next five years of alimony. She's a good cop, she doesn't deserve this.

"Tell me, what the fuck did you do to her anyway? I've always wanted to know why she hates your guts so much."

"Fuck if I know," I say as if I'm unbothered and turn to leave.

It's none of his damn business. My sweet little girls all hate me. I never thought it would come to this with Ray, but I can't blame the others.

I'm sorry, Billy. This isn't personal, kid.

Billy

On My Day Off

"Gods, I'll never get tired of you," Ardan growls as he pounds into me from behind.

I look over my shoulder to find him watching my ass with so much lust on his face. I squeeze my pussy around him and watch as his eyes flick to me.

He bites back a sexy smile and lifts a brow at me. I repeat the action, pulling a deep groan from him as he throws his head back and tightens his grip on my hips.

My thighs begin to shake. I end up on my toes as I try to lift away from him. It's no use as he grabs my hair and chases my pussy down to keep thrusting.

I end up face down with my ass half in the air as he pounds down into me. I'm so wet you can hear the sound of his strokes echoing through the room. As I try to crab crawl away from him, he grabs my thighs and pulls me back to him, holding my legs open like the handlebars to his bike as he continues to fuck the shit out of me.

"Ardan, holy shit, I'm coming," I scream into the mattress.

As if I'm not already wet enough and already quaking from my orgasm. He reaches beneath me to rub my clit and leans into my ear to growl, sending the vibration through me. My belly drops, I begin to squirt all over the place, and I can't help screaming nonsense.

"So good," Ardan groans and pulls out to tap his dick on my ass.

He leans over me to pepper kisses against my shoulder. Slowly, he turns me over and dips his head to take my sweaty breast into his mouth. He releases that one and moves to the other, licking his tongue across my mound before taking my nipple and a large part of my flesh into his mouth.

"Mm," I moan and run my hand through his sweat-soaked hair.

"Have you had enough? Can you take more?" He breathes against my lips after letting my breast pop free of his mouth.

It's my day off and we both decided to spend a lazy morning in bed. What started out as a playful conversation while we lay in each other's arms turned into a hot-as-fuck sex session.

I allow him into my thoughts because I can't speak coherent words just yet. I suck in a breath between my teeth as he sinks into me and reaches to lace our fingers together. My eyes roll back in my head.

"Does this answer your question? Can you see what your future looks like now?" he rumbles in my ear.

"Yes," I moan out.

I wrap my legs around his hips and start to circle mine. Clinging to his hands, I lift my face to his so we can kiss. My pussy jumps as the cool peppermint flavor bursts in my mouth.

"It's your day off. What the fuck do they want?" Ardan growls when my ringtone for work goes off.

I laugh although I was thinking the same thing. I go to free my hand to call the phone to me, but he tightens his hold on my fingers and begins to dive deeper into my wet pussy.

"Don't answer it," he says, looking me deeply in the eyes.

For a moment, I think not to. All the talk about me not having to work takes over. I think of Beck and Bourne. What if I had time to go see them? How are they?

I think of having my own children and that's when I come back to my senses. Ardan groans in defeat and drops his head to my shoulder. I think he's going to release me and allow me to answer, but he rolls onto his back as he remains inside me.

I look down at him and shake my head as he continues to guide my hips over him. Holding out my hand, I allow the phone to land in my palm. Right as I go to answer, Ardan hits my G-spot.

"Hello," I answer the call, then clear my throat. "Hello, this is Detective Salvado."

"Salvado, I want you in my office within the hour," Captain Gates barks and hangs up.

I pull the phone from my ear and look down at it with my brows knit. Ardan tightens his hold on my waist and begins to thrust up into me. I drop the phone and cover his hands on my hips with my hands.

"Oh my god. Ardan, we need to stop. I have to go," I plead.

"I'm not letting you go until you understand you can walk away and be happy."

"It will take me at least an hour to get across town at this hour."

"I'll get you there in seconds."

Stupid me, I think he's talking about my orgasm. I should have known better. I'm nearly delirious from sex by the time he allows me to get ready to head into the precinct.

Why do I feel like I'm about to get Craigged?

ARDAN

"THAT WAS TOTAL BULLSHIT," Billy growls as we step back into the clubhouse.

I took her to the station on the back of my bike using magic sense I didn't give her much time to get ready or to travel. I have no regrets.

She was glowing until that asshole suspended her for much of nothing. A fool could hear the bullshit spewing out of her captain's mouth. I can feel how pissed she is, and she has every right to be, but I can make a call to fix this.

"Don't worry about it. I'll have your badge and gun back by the morning. I can get you a transfer if you want. Just say the word," I say as I rub the back of her neck as we ride up in the elevator.

She blows out a frustrated breath. "You know, I know it's bullshit and I should fight it, but I can't say I really care. I mean, there should be more to life than trying to put Candido behind bars and hunting down real-life demons."

"Whoever told you demons aren't real?"

"You know what I mean." She wraps her arms around my waist. "Maybe you did convince me to be your nasty little bed doll. You can dress me up and fuck me whenever you want. No more hiding all night in my jewelry.

"You can push me up against any surface and have your way with me, day or night. We can put our playroom to use," she purrs and reaches to grab my throbbing cock.

You would think I didn't spend the morning inside her tight pussy. I twitch against her palm as she squeezes me.

"I love the way you think, but I know you wouldn't be happy, not like this. Let me fix this for you," I say as I look down into her eyes and run my finger down the side of her face.

Her eyes glaze over in thought. On one hand, I want to fix this for her. On the other, I want her to give it up and find something else she loves.

"Ardan, you are needed here in Japan," Kenji mind-links me.

"Why? What's going on?" I reply.

"It's the source stone. There was an attempt to take it."

"Was it successful?"

"No, they didn't stand a chance against my assassins. However, I don't think this will be the only attempt. They could have been testing the waters to see how far they could get. I believe you should be here the next time."

"I will be there soon. Thank you, old friend. There is much I need to discuss with you anyway."

"I will be waiting. It's been too long. I hear you have a mate. Congratulations. We will catch up when you arrive."

"What's wrong? What just happened?" Billy says with concern as she searches my face.

I open my mind for her to read my thoughts, not having time to explain it all and not wanting to alarm her. Then I wrap an arm around her waist to teleport us to Kendrick's room where I can feel him. I need to let him know what's going on and ask him to watch over my mate while I'm gone.

Billy gasps in my hold. "You want to leave me behind?"

"You have work. Dracon can watch over you while I'm gone."

"I'm suspended, remember?"

I race into Kendrick's room as I hear a commotion happening inside.

"Kendrick," I call.

My brother is in bed with his mate and the little light

fairy he and his mate were gifted. A sour look comes to Kendrick's face. I know right away he knows I don't have good news.

"What's going on?"

"I need to leave," I inform him as my thoughts race.

This isn't good. When we thought it was just Bradan's stone, that was one thing. Now to have mine targeted is a clear sign someone has knowledge of the sources of power, and they are after them.

"To go where?" Kendrick asks, pulling me from my thoughts.

"Japan."

I don't need to say more. He can read between the lines. I don't want to alarm Billy or the other two with more information than necessary.

"Is it gone?" Kendrick growls out, proving I'm right.

"No, Kenji and the assassins held firm. However, he doesn't believe this will be the only attempt."

To be honest, I agree. I wouldn't put it past the hunters to try again if this was indeed them. They haven't come after Billy again, but I am always with her. I can't say that would be the wisest thing to do.

"Go and take Billy with you," Kendrick says.

I open my mouth to protest, but I take the look Kendrick is giving me for what it is. It's a command, not a suggestion. Guilt from the one time in my life that I didn't listen to my brother consumes me.

"She is your mate. She belongs with you," he says.

I know he is absolutely right, only solidifying my guilt. We were enslaved because I didn't follow instructions and look where that got us. Kendrick has enough on his plate. It's not fair for me to ask him to watch over my mate while I go to Japan.

I close my mouth and nod. "Very well. She has been suspended from work, so it's doable."

"You didn't have to tell my business like that. Thanks," Billy says through our link.

She's been angry with me. I could feel it ever since she realized I hadn't intended to take her with me.

"Suspended?" Kendrick says.

"Long story and I don't have time. Rock can take my place helping Reilly with the hunters."

I've been literally splitting myself in two to help with the search. Rock is a good tracker, and he can give more of his undivided attention than I can.

"I will work on finding out who released Seraphina and how she was able to get away. Sounds like we might need to have a lockdown. No humans and no supers who aren't patched in. Old ladies only," he says.

"Wait, just wait a darn minute," Ray cuts in. "Everyone, slow down. I'm still stuck on Bradan walking in here with flaming hair and hands. Then my little sister runs in here looking like a little flame before returning to her cute little self.

"This is too much. Who the heck is Kenji and can I be a flame too?" Ray says.

She successfully lifts the tension from the room, bringing a smile to my lips. My interest is piqued. So Taylor can transform. I wonder what that means for Billy.

Bradan turns and leaves with Taylor under his arm. He pats me on the shoulder as he walks by. I'll have to ask him later what happened and how Taylor transformed. For now, I know him well enough to give him time and space.

"I will call you when we get there," Billy says to Ray.

I grab her by the hand to lead her from the room. We have a lot to talk about. Kenji's jodo will be a whole new world. I have my reasons for wanting to leave her behind.

Billy

We Need to Talk

"Billy, we should talk," Ardan says as he paces the pool.

I'm so confused and, to be honest, hurt. I can't believe Ardan had planned to leave me behind. We've been inseparable since he told me I was his mate. Why leave me behind now?

After this morning, after trying to convince me to give up my career, he's already ready to leave me behind at the first sign of trouble in his world.

As I sit on the side of the bed, I stare down into my hands, thinking. I'm trying to make it all fit together in my head. First, I was suspended for some shit that doesn't make sense—on my day off at that. Now this.

I don't know if I want to go with him after all. I blow out a breath and run my hands over my face.

The bed dips as Ardan sits down heavily beside me. He

wraps an arm around me and pulls me into his side. This is the coldest I've ever felt in his embrace.

"You are overthinking. I don't know what I'm walking into. The boys are with Kenji. You already know about the challenges with them.

"I didn't want to bring you along and get their hopes up, then have to leave them behind. In addition, Kenji has been guarding an important item for me, and there are a number of things I need to sort out before I feel comfortable with you in that space. Not to mention, there is Kenji. You know nothing about him."

"Okay, fine. I can understand that, but why can't you just tell me about him on the flight there? And don't you think it's time to address the situation with the boys? I want to help."

"First, baby. We're going to teleport to Japan. Not take a human flight," he says.

"Oh, I should have thought of that. Well, can't you show me in your mind?"

"No, that would leave things to interpretation. Kenji is more complicated than that."

"I thought he was a friend."

"He is one of my best and most trusted friends. Kenji is what we call a trickster. He means well, and at the heart of things, he's always doing what he feels is best for everyone. But sometimes the person on the receiving end doesn't always feel that way initially," he says.

"You think he would hurt me or something?"

"I don't think he would intentionally hurt you. But, Billy, you are my mate. I will always be more sensitive about your feelings and what's done to you.

"You have not seen the true results of my temper. I already have questions involving you and Kenji's antics. I don't want him playing his games with you."

"What sort of games? If I know, I can avoid them," I say as I get frustrated.

He gives a bit of a cynical chuckle. "That's the thing. This is what I'm trying to tell you. No one sees Kenji coming. He is a master manipulator. While he holds your focus here, he is giving you a life lesson over there." He points across the room.

"But you come out on the other side better for it, right?"

"Most of the time. Although, you'll want to kick his ass for it. He is a good friend and has always been there when I needed him. But I have watched him confuse wars and treat individuals like puppets for his use.

"I chose to send the boys to him for a reason. Kenji has been spinning illusions to keep them happy. It was my best solution to the problem until I can find a permanent one."

"What kind of being is he? Maybe I should stay behind."

Ardan laughs and kisses my forehead. "Kendrick is right. Your place is with me. I wouldn't be able to function without you.

"My source stone is very important. I must protect it at all costs. I left it with Kenji a long time ago so no one would be able to find it or take it," he replies.

"How do you know he's not tricking you now?"

"Because my stone isn't the only one that's been compromised. Bradan's has already been taken. We haven't informed anyone of this fact. The source stone is not a toy.

"Kenji would face severe consequences for its loss if he were to be responsible for its discovery. All of those we have trusted to guard them take the role with the utmost respect and regard."

"That's all you had to do, Ardan. I'm really not hard to deal with. I just don't like feeling like I'm the problem or like …"

He kisses my forehead again. "Or like you're not wanted. I

am very sorry I made you feel that way. I should have thought a little more carefully."

"No, I understand now. You always have a lot to deal with. If I do decide to resign from my job, I don't want to lie around all day doing nothing. That's not me.

"I want to help where I can and learn to use my magic for the good of our people. I'm sure I can use my detective skills in our world."

He gives me a grin. "I don't expect you to lie around and do nothing. I'm sure you will find something to take over once things settle. Come, we should go. Dracon and the others will meet us downstairs so we can transport together."

"Should I pack anything?"

"No, I will be able to get you anything you need once we're there. Or I can show you how."

Billy

Arrival

My stomach rolls and my head is still spinning even after we reach our destination. Ardan places his hands on my hips to steady me as he murmurs in my ear.

"Just breathe. The first time going long distances can be a little jarring. That's it. Breathe in, breathe out."

"Queen Billy," my name is sung as I try to catch my bearings.

I look up to find the little titans rushing toward me. They have gotten taller since I last saw them. Their hair is longer too. One has large blond curls that are bouncing as he runs at me. The other has his locks pulled back into a ponytail.

I squat down just before they reach me and hold my arms out. They throw their little bodies right into me. I squeeze them as hard as they are squeezing me.

I realize how much I've missed them as their ocean-

breeze scent fills my nose. One of them nuzzles my cheek and sighs deeply. I palm the back of his head.

"I've missed you," he whispers in my ear.

I pull away, thinking it's Beck, only to find it's Bourne. He's the one with the ponytail. His blue eyes sparkle as he looks back at me.

I cup his round cheek and lean in to kiss his forehead. He gives me the brightest smile ever. My heart melts.

"We have to tell you all about Master Kenji. He's the best. We have so much fun here. All the ladies help us with our training and the food is amazing," Beck says.

I look up at Ardan questioningly. He gives me a knowing smile. I go to mind-link him, but three others enter the room.

"Ah, you have arrived. Welcome. It is an honor to have you all here. I wish it were under different circumstances, but my home is your home," one of the men says as he looks around at our group.

I'm assuming he's Kenji, but he and the other man look as if they could be twins. Ardan mentioned Kenji's great-great-great grandson—or maybe a few more generations would be here as well. He's from New York too.

He looks around at the men who have come with us and gives a nod. Ardan has brought along six men. They were all waiting in the basement when we arrived to transport here— each carrying a small bag.

"Your things will be taken to your rooms. Ardan, my warriors will brief those you have brought with you to give them the lay of the land," Kenji says.

"Dracon, Hudson, you will run point. All of you follow them. Once you are briefed, return to me for your post assignments," Ardan commands.

The man who spoke looks me in the eyes and smiles. He then bows. I take him in, noting all the details about him.

Ardan mentioned before we left that Kenji takes many forms but upon meeting him, he would take one of two. He would either reveal himself as a smaller, meek old man. Or he would show his true self.

I believe this is his true self. He has long white hair—it looks to be flowing down his back—and a handsome face. He puts me in the mind of that Japanese Instagram model with the long hair and beard. I just can't think of his name right now.

To be a being as old as dirt, he doesn't look older than a thirtysomething. He's well-built and tall as well, maybe six-five, six-six.

He's wearing loose-fitting black pants and a black wifebeater tank top. It looks as if they just came from training or something. The other male has a bit of sweat dewing on his forehead.

When Kenji locks eyes with me, something in my stomach stirs to life. Not in a sexual way, but almost as if I've looked into the eyes of a kindred spirit. As if some part of me knows him.

"You must be Ardan's mate. I am Kenji. This is my grand-son, Amadeus. I believe you are already acquainted with Kai."

"Hello, it's nice to meet you all," I say.

"Yes, beautiful indeed. Kai has had only good things to say about you."

I look to Kai and smile. She returns the smile, but I note something is off about her. I don't know her well, but her vibe feels strange.

She's standing next to Amadeus, but it's as if she's trying not to acknowledge him. He's doing the same. I shrug it off as not my business and turn my attention back to Kenji.

"It's good to see you, old friend. Thank you for welcoming us in and for the heads-up. This is my mate, Billy."

"Welcome home, Billy," Kenji says.

As soon as the words leave his mouth, I feel strange. Something in the words seems to echo around me. Almost like they surround me and then reach into me.

Is this his powers? Is he trying to trick me? Ardan places a hand on the small of my back and moves closer to me.

I immediately relax. Although the feeling as if something has awakened inside me remains.

Kenji tilts his head at me and gives a mischievous smile. I narrow my eyes at him. He's not the innocent man he wants me to believe he is.

"Perfectly matched. The gods never make a mistake. It is we who alter and break their designs," he says ominously.

Amadeus begins to shift from foot to foot as if those words were to address him. I'm still mystified that so many generations are between the two. If I didn't know better, I would think the two were brothers.

Maybe a year or two removed. The only aging factor is the white hair, but I've learned that to be common among the merfolk. It's so beautiful and has such a shine to it.

"I look forward to getting to know more about you. Come, I bet you two want to freshen up," Kenji says.

"Can we show her the gifts you gave us?" Beck asks, looking to Kenji hopefully.

"No, he told us not to share them. You have to be more disciplined when given secrets," Bourne says.

"Patience, young Beck. All things come in time," Kenji says.

"He is in his true form. What does that mean?" I mind-link Ardan.

"Really? I wasn't expecting that."

"Wait, what do you mean? You're not seeing what I am?"

"As I said, he shows each individual what he wants them to see. I'm getting the old man today," he replies.

"What does that mean for me?"

"It's a show of respect."

"And for you?"

"He wants me to be at ease. He's giving me the appearance of dominance in the situation."

"Is that a good thing?"

He laughs in my head. *"This is Kenji. You will never know until he wants you to. This is normal. He has not started with his tricks yet."*

"What did Beck mean about the ladies?"

"You will meet them," he says with a smile in his voice.

ARDAN

"You are hostile toward me, brother. What has brought you here like this?"

"I fell into Billy's past. I found her in the presence of one of yours. She has been dragon-touched in a past life. You were working for my father back then.

"What is your role in all of this? Why is my mate reacting to you?"

"Is it your mate reacting to me? Or is it her spirit reacting to home? What you see is never what is happening. What you feel will confuse you more. It is what you know that will lead you to answers and none of us know anything," he replies.

I turn on him swiftly and grab him by his shirt. I throw him against the nearest wall. Thankfully they are all solid on this level. Otherwise, I would have thrown him through it.

"Don't give me your riddles. I am not one of your puppets to dance around. When it comes to my mate, you don't want to test me," I snarl.

"Dear old friend, you would think I were a nefarious character," he says as he reaches to pry my hand from his shirt. "I am an old man with too much time on his hands. I trust you to remember there was a long time when my familiar roamed freely.

"You would have to be more specific on the time. When was she touched? Are you absolutely sure it was my dragon? My brother, too, had dragons who roamed freely."

I narrow my eyes. My mind goes back to Billy's words. Would he really compromise the stone to play one of his games?

"Is this all a game? Did they truly come for the stone?"

"You and I both know the consequence of placing your stone in danger. I would do no such thing. I think we have been apart for too long. You are questioning my friendship, my loyalty, and my character."

I take a step back and pull a hand down my face. I think for a moment. Kenji still has access to step through to the gods.

Although he is my friend, I have always engaged him with caution. However, I know him well enough to know he would never compromise his position or access. He holds favor with them, but if my stone were taken because of his games, they would not hesitate to reprimand him, which could lead to his access being denied.

"Perhaps you are right. Forgive me. Billy is everything I've waited for. I know you mean well, but don't fuck with her. I have no tolerance for her being hurt. Not even for a second," I say.

"I am here to help, my friend. As this involves your feel-

ings, consider allowing her to train with my assassins. I can feel her powers are still somewhat locked.

"Training here will only ensure she's never hurt. Take this as my gift, old friend."

"I will think about it. Her training is being interrupted by our presence here," I muse.

"I am at your disposal. Now, about the boys."

"What about them? Have the transformations started again?"

"No, not that the perpetrator hasn't tried. They're just unable to get by me. I want you to consider this.

"One can be happy of mind but not of heart. My illusions are dealing with the mind. Those boys still need someone to attend to their hearts."

That figure in the visions comes to mind. What if whoever is trying to access the boys succeeds in getting by Kenji and taints their hearts because that's what I'm failing to address.

"When I am not guarding the stone, I will spend more time with them."

Kenji sighs. "You are already spending yourself thin. Besides, you and I both know the way of the water titans. It's a mother's love that cures their hearts. Why don't you allow Billy to do it?"

"She is not ready. Her fears will confuse them."

"Will they?" he asks and tilts his head to study me. "Or are your fears getting in the way? You can feel her love, but that's not enough. You fear the titans will reveal motherhood is unwanted."

I work my jaw as his words hit their mark. I will be as patient as I need to be with Billy, but I have not fooled myself into believing all her fears will be healed miraculously and she will want to have children of our own.

"I still know you well, my friend and I can see through

her. Her heart is not as fragile as you think it is. Nor is she as indifferent to love as you believe.

"She is capable of great love and compassion. It is no surprise she is the mate of Ardan. Ardan, the passionate one, the one of desire and enthusiasm for life.

"The high achiever. It is time you allow others to hold your burdens with you. She can't show you what you don't show her."

"What is it I'm not showing her?"

"Trust. You don't give trust, Ardan. You would rather do things all on your own than give your absolute trust. You have entrusted those boys' care to me, but you reach out more than a mother sending her cubs off to school for the first time.

"You do know I have work that needs to be done. If you want me to do something, allow me to do it," Kenji says and rolls his eyes.

He is right though. I have been placing my attention on everything. I may delegate tasks, but then I micromanage.

Billy is my mate. I'm supposed to share my burdens with her. She was designed to bring me balance. Allowing her to help me doesn't take away her independence. It does the exact opposite.

It also takes some of the pressure off all the things I have on my plate. A demigod can be overwhelmed too. I never complain because it's in my nature to just go with the flow.

But if I'm honest, since the boys came into the picture, I've been finding it harder to surf through my duties. Finding my mate has only added to my responsibilities, but I should let Billy help as she's been asking too from the beginning.

She put her life in danger for those boys. I can trust her with helping them. They already seem to have a bond with her.

257

"Ah, you know what I know now. You will make adjustments. This is good."

"I will consider what you have said. Not everything is as simple as you make it sound."

He waves me off. "It is. You will make adjustments. I am happy you are here. Come, you haven't seen the upgrades I have done. Time for tour."

Billy

Got It Wrong

"Good morning, My Queen. How did you sleep?" Dracon asks as I step into the hall where he's been waiting for me.

"You can call me Billy. I promise you it's not that serious."

"You say that now. Have you met your mate? He would have my head for the familiarity if not the disrespect."

"Well, when he's not around, I'm Billy. If he doesn't like it, he can take a dip. I've been Billy all my life.

"I'm not about to have people running around calling me queen all the time. I'm a cop. I lock up bad guys. I said what I said. Call me Billy, or don't call me at all."

Dracon chuckles at my rant. Clearly, to answer his earlier question, I didn't sleep well at all. I'm grumpy and irritable. I slept fitfully all night.

Ardan didn't seem too happy about that this morning. To be honest, he's been in a bit of a mood since he returned from his time with Kenji after our arrival.

Ardan doesn't usually wear his frustration or emotions, but it's clear he has a lot on his mind. I plan to do something about that this morning though.

Since I don't have my library to hide away in for my morning me time, I've decided to find Beck and Bourne so I can observe what their days are like.

"Where are we off to this morning? I made myself well acquainted with the layout of the entire property. Tell me where you want to go and I will lead you there, Officer Billy," Dracon says.

"Oh, you have jokes. You know Ren is quiet. I wonder if Ardan would switch you guys out if I request it," I taunt.

All the blood drains from his face and his smile falls. I can't help bursting into laughter. I'm laughing so hard I stop in my tracks to bend at the waist and hold my knees.

"I'm just fucking with you. I know how much your station means to you. Even if Ardan doesn't think I know all six of you are supposed to be my guards. Congrats on becoming first in command."

He looks at me as if he's in shock. I laugh and pat him on the back. "Like I said. I'm a detective. I pay attention to details. Now, about my plans for this morning. I want to find Beck and Bourne."

He gets this look on his face as if he's mind-linking. I wait patiently for him to get a location. He nods to whatever he is told and waves for me to follow him.

"They are in training," he says as we continue to walk.

"That seems to be a running theme here."

"It will be an honor to train here in the Ji Dojo during our stay. I'm most excited about it. Master Kenji and his assassins are legendary in our world.

"Each assassin is handpicked by Master Kenji himself and it's very rare that he'll pick a male. When he does it's an honor to that male's entire bloodline, even if another isn't

picked from that family. Other factions will recognize the status, and it leads to great opportunities," he says excitedly.

"Sounds like I might just lose you after all. I guess I can learn to live with the silent, broody type."

"Although it was once a dream to train within these walls to be one of the puppet master's assassins, I'm right where my fate intended. I would have you know Ren is quite talkative when you get to know him. He's still figuring out his place with you. We all are."

"I'll keep that in mind."

I'm beginning to realize I still have so much to learn about this world and the communities within it. There are so many moving parts.

I want to be a part, but I still don't know how to make that happen. This is totally outside my wheelhouse. Not just the supernatural world but wanting to be involved.

I mean, I'm trying. Ardan left after my morning blessing to guard the location of the stone. When I asked for a shift, I was told no, much to my annoyance.

However, Ardan did get this look in his eyes as if he wanted to say more, but he shook it off and changed the subject.

"This is the boys' training room. Hudson and Arledge are on their way. You can let us know if you need anything else," Dracon says, pulling me from my musings.

"Okay, thanks. Try to relax. I'm not going anywhere."

With a smile, I punch Dracon's arm playfully as I walk by to enter the little training room. The smile on my face grows as the boys come into view in their little gear with their wooden swords.

I look around to take it all in and freeze. I take in a sharp breath and narrow my eyes as I place my hands on my hips. Is this why he didn't want to bring me along?

"Well damn. This motherfucker."

ARDAN

"THANK YOU," I say as one of Kenji's servants brings me a cup of tea.

It is a part of his hospitality. My team will not go hungry or thirsty in his dojo. Everyone within these walls will be treated with respect and kindness as long as we are here.

"You are welcome, King Ardan. Is there anything else I can get you," the woman says as she bows slightly.

"No. We are fine."

I look around at everyone standing guard with me. Whoever thinks they can waltz in here and take my stone has to be powerful. As we took this into consideration, Kenji and I agreed we would split the shifts up between him, myself, and Amadeus.

We will each guard the stone with a team with us. This morning, I have Irving, Ford, and Ren from Billy's guard with me. As well as a few of the assassins since they know the dojo best.

Kenji has truly modernized the dojo from what I've seen, but there are still areas that remind me of old times as they have remained the same. I spent a lot of time here back when I was trying to find myself.

Not knowing if I should follow the plans my brothers were making for themselves, I spent time with Kenji. It didn't feel right to be away from them, but I was too restless to remain in one place all the time. Which is funny, considering how much time I spent here.

"Fuck me," I grunt and take a step back.

Everyone around me becomes alert. I hold up a hand to ward them off. This has nothing to do with intruders.

I feel the moment Billy's ire sets in. It hits me like a freight train and the door to her thoughts blasts open, sucking me in.

It would bring a smile to my face if she weren't so angry. I know I can't put this off, so I mind-link Amadeus and Kenji to see who can replace me.

Kenji appears and I vanish without a word. My mate's anger draws me right to where she is. When I enter the training room, she's standing with her back to me and her hands on her hips.

I walk up behind her and cage her into my arms. She stiffens and her thoughts continue to blast me as she curses me out in her head. I give her a squeeze and kiss the back of her neck.

"You can reel all that in. Tell me what you notice about them," I say into her ear.

"Other than the fact that they're fucking gorgeous and look like a bunch of brown anime characters whose breasts are about to pop out of their shirts?" she snaps at me.

I laugh and give her another squeeze. "Look more closely. Tell me what your supernatural eyes see."

She turns her head up to glare at me, then looks back at the women in the room. Kenji definitely has a type when it comes to his assassins. Her description is pretty accurate.

"Wait, what's wrong with their souls?" she says suddenly.

"Most of them don't have one. The others have particle souls. They function because Kenji causes them to live, breathe, and function. Once you accept this life, you're agreeing to hand over your soul to him.

"Assassins like these can't have a conscience. They can't have friends or families. They certainly don't have room for love or relationships.

"These women live to serve Kenji. They will fight and die to do so." I pause to drop a kiss against her neck. "I have no use for soulless women when I have you. They are not the reason I was going to leave you behind. I told you why."

"You said nothing about the army of gorgeous women living here."

"I didn't mention the gorgeous men either. There are a few males in the ranks. Each handsome enough to turn heads. I'm sure you will appreciate them when you see them. Kenji has good taste," I reply.

"Exactly how many women live here?"

"I'm not sure of the current occupancy, but Kenji used to keep anywhere from two hundred to two hundred and fifty assassins at any given time. This is a very large property. The dojo can house around six hundred behind its walls."

She thinks this over and knits her brows. "He can control two hundred and fifty assassins at once?" she says in awe.

"I'm quite sure he can handle more than that. Kenji is capable of great things."

"I see," she murmurs and turns back to Beck and Bourne, who are being trained by a group of five assassins.

"There isn't a single ugly one," she mumbles as three more enter the room.

I lean in to bite her ear. "You're fucking hot when you're jealous. Do you feel how hard you have me?"

"How do I know you're not lying to cover up how horny watching all these big-titty bitches are making you?"

Swiftly, I grasp the back of her hair and tug her head back. With my other hand, I pull her body back into mine with my palm splayed against her belly. Her ass is now sealed to my front.

"I can show you better than I can tell you. Do you need me to show you, Billy? Is that what you want? Do you want

me to remind you that your tight little hot pussy is the only one I want?"

"Don't you have someplace you should be?"

"Clearly, I'm needed here more. I will take Kenji's shift," I say and lick the shell of her ear, causing a shiver to run through her.

"Wait, I—"

Before she can come up with an excuse, I teleport us to the room we are sharing here at the dojo. I have made a few adjustments to suit my tastes and needs for the moment.

I make both of our clothes vanish and bend Billy over in front of a mirrored vanity. I want her to see what I'm about to do to her. She needs to see how much she turns me on.

"Because I took you as a virgin, I've been biding my time before I took you to the next level. I haven't fucked you my way yet. I've been toying with this little pussy," I say into her ear as I finger her with one hand and fondle her nipple with the other.

"Ardan."

"I love it when you say my name. Do you know how gorgeous you are? It would take a thousand of them to make one of you and I'd still only want you."

I pull my hand from her dripping-wet lips and hold it up where she can see in the mirror. Her eyes grow wide when an ice cock appears in my hand. I've formed it in the shape of mine. Big, fat, long, and veiny.

"You want that, don't you?" I croon in her ear. "You think that hot pussy can handle this?"

"Yes," she whimpers.

"Good, take this and place this condom on it for me, baby. Tie the open end closed. This will keep you safe and trap the water as that hot pussy melts it."

She takes the ice and places it in the rubber I provide her.

I watch impatiently as she ties it closed. With a big smile, she hands it back.

I grasp her throat and tilt her head back with my thumb. My lips are on hers in the next motion. I kiss her deeply and hungrily.

All the passion I have for this woman pours out of me. I would never give another woman a second thought even if there wasn't a bond between us.

I drop to my knees and palm her ass cheek as I tease her thigh with the ice sculpture in my grasp. I lean in and begin to feast on her.

"Ah," she keens and lifts onto her toes.

She looks back over her shoulder to watch me. I pull back and begin to run the barrier-covered ice through her wet lips. Holding her open by her ass cheek with one hand, I then push in with the ice dick.

It slips into her slick sheath with ease. As I push it in and out of her, I lean in and lick her ass, then bite it. Billy begins to gyrate her hips and push back greedily.

"Fuck, Ardan, baby, that feels so good."

"Does it, baby?"

I stand and allow my magic to move the dildo in and out of her to keep my hands free. Looking into the mirror, I palm her breasts and watch as her eyes roll and her face contorts with pleasure.

"Look at how beautiful you are. You're going to come for me, aren't you?"

She opens her eyes and looks into the mirror at me, then nods. The lust and desire in her eyes speaks volumes. We bite our bottom lips at the same time in the reflection of the mirror.

Before I can make my next move, she spins, gives me a push back, and drops to her knees. As I continue to magically fuck her with the dildo, she takes me into her mouth

and chokes me down. I love the savage way she's sucking me.

"Fuck, baby girl. Just like that."

She backs off to catch her breath. Her face is a mess from her saliva, but she has a smile on her lips. I shove a hand into her hair as she strokes me. When she looks up through her lashes to lock eyes with me, I jerk in her hands.

"You're my nasty little girl, Billy. I don't want or need anyone else. Now suck that shit and make me come so I can fuck the shit out of you," I growl.

"Say please," she says with a sexy grin.

"Please don't make me spank your ass for disobeying me," I chuckle darkly.

She pulls a face at me but throws her head back and cries out as I increase the pace of the ice dildo I'm still working inside of her. I get ready to tell her I'm waiting when she takes me deep once again. She bobs her head vigorously as she works me with her hands just as fiercely.

"Yes, baby, yes. Give me that mouth. Those pretty lips are so sexy on me. *Fuck*."

I come down her throat and pull out of her mouth to reach beneath her arms to lift her to her feet and turn her back toward the mirror. I pin her hands to the table with mine over hers.

Causing the dildo to vanish, I replace it by thrusting into her deep. She cries out and throws her head back against me. I pump my hips, pushing into her hard. The sound of my hips hitting her ass rings out around the room.

"Look at me," I command as I wrap my hand around her throat and give a slight squeeze.

She opens her eyes and looks into mine through our reflection. I pump harder and faster as we lock gazes. She lifts onto her toes, trying but failing to escape me.

I look down at her breasts in the mirror as they jiggle

from each thrust. She tries to reach back to hold me off, but I keep going. Reaching between her legs to rub her clit, I look her in the eyes once again.

"Do you want me to stop? Have you had too much?"

She shakes her head frantically. "No, please don't stop."

"Good answer because I'm nowhere near done."

I smile at her wickedly as I freeze my hand over as I hold my fingers against her clit and keep fucking her from behind.

"Holy fuck," she screams.

I lift the same iced-over hand to her breast and run it against her nipple. I'm so fucking hard inside her, with no signs of stopping anytime soon.

Grabbing hold of her hair, I tug her head back and lick up the side of her neck to her ear, making sure to cool my tongue against her heated skin. Her sweat tastes like candy. Not able to help myself, I pull out and turn her, lifting her onto the table before dropping to my knees again.

"Christ, baby, I get it," she calls out as I bury my face into her core and begin to eat her like the delicious snack she is.

She runs her fingers through my hair and tugs. I groan and hum as her juices flow into my mouth. With my hand, I rub her until she squirts.

"No, baby. I don't think you do, but you will."

Billy

Just Alike

"*P*api, I'm not in New York right now," I say into the phone.

"Since when?"

"I haven't been there for a few days. I think it's been about a week since we've been gone."

"We?"

I sigh and laugh. "Yes, Papi. We. Ardan and I are taking a vacation."

"I knew I liked that guy. I can't remember the last time you willingly took a vacation. You usually have to fall sick or something to sit your butt down and take off from work," Mack laughs into the phone.

"Yeah, I know. I'm looking to change that when I get back."

"I must be dreaming. I have to be. Does this mean I'm going to get to walk you down the aisle some day soon?"

"Phew, you're jumping that cart before the barrel. I would have to be proposed to in order to be planning a wedding. I don't think that's in my future."

"Why not?" Papi says into the phone while Ardan mind-links me the same.

I look at Ardan and shrug. He rolls his eyes and frowns at me then gets up to leave the room. I look after him with my mouth hanging open.

"Is marriage not a biker thing?" Mack asks, bringing me from my thoughts.

"I … Um. I've never asked."

"So, how do you know he wouldn't propose?"

"True story, Papi. I think I might be wrong. It's all so complicated."

"Can I give a little advice?"

"Yeah, I'm listening."

"Talk to him. Ask him his intentions and plans for your future. You may find he wants more than you think. I wish I communicated more when I had my opportunity."

"Thanks, Papi. I think you might be right."

As I listen to Mack continue to talk, Kenji walks into the lounge room I'm sitting in. He gives me a smile and takes a seat across from me. That feeling in the pit of my stomach awakens as it always does when he enters the room.

"Papi, I need to go. I'll call you when we get back to New York."

"Be good, sport. I miss you."

"I miss you too."

I hang up and stare back at Kenji. I'm still cautious of him even though he's been nothing but kind. He sits with such stillness and his gaze is razor sharp.

Suddenly, he moves his hands in a gesture as if he's placing a napkin in his lap, ready to eat. Then he places his hands on his knees. The action is slow and methodical.

I can't help feeling like he's just started some type of spell for one of his illusions. Telling myself to relax, I take a deep breath and remain quiet.

"You have no desire to train here at Ji Dojo?"

"I didn't know I could," I reply.

He purses his lips and shakes his head. He lifts one hand gracefully before placing it right back on his knee. I notice this time his pointer finger and thumb remain lifted.

"You are always welcome to train here. My assassins have skills that are unmatched. You will leave with the same skills."

"Thank you. It is kind of you to offer. I did have to interrupt my training to come here. I've been in mixed martial arts since I was little, so I didn't think much of the time off."

He lifts his hand again, this time holding it in the air as if calling for the check in a restaurant. When he lowers it, he holds it palm side up. One of the servants who's just as pretty as the assassins, walks in with a box.

I've learned you can tell the difference between the staff and the assassins by the uniforms they wear. All of the staff members wear beige as the assassins wear black or gray. I wasn't shocked to find out all servants behind these walls are as lethal as the assassins. Although, I believe the working staff all have their souls from what I can tell.

"Ardan and I have been friends for a very long time. He has known me in many forms and stations. There was once a time when I forged weapons for powerful beings," Kenji says as he waves for the large box to be placed in my lap.

I stare down at the box, not sure if I should open it. Ardan's cautionary warning rings in my ear. I could be opening Pandora's box with this guy.

"I, in fact, forged his. I believe in *Inyo*. Do you know what this is?" he asks.

"No, I'm not sure I do."

"You Americans know it as yin and yang—from the Chinese. The weapons I forged used to sing to me. They would tell me when they were meant to have a partner or counterpart if you will. I have held the partner to Ardan's weapon for a very long time. Many centuries, many moons, many tides."

"Are you saying that's what's in this box?"

"Ah, yes. You are following just fine. It has been singing since your arrival."

"I can't take this."

"Why not?"

"I'm just learning to use my magic. I wouldn't know what to do with this."

He lifts his left hand and makes a swiping motion from his right side to his left. The motion is so graceful and effortless. When he places his hand back on his knee, he again keeps his pointer finger and thumb lifted.

"You haven't opened the box to know what *this* is. How can you know you would not know what to do with it?"

I chew on my lip as I look down at the ornate box. I try to think of if I've ever seen Ardan's weapon. Although I've seen his avatar and knights, I can't remember ever seeing him wield a weapon.

Curiosity wins out. I flip the latches on the box and slowly lift the lid. My brows knit as the intricate metal comes into view. I'm not sure what it is at first.

It looks like an elaborate bow although there is no string to shoot an arrow. As I examine it further. I realize that although there are cutouts in the steel on each end, this is not necessarily a bow at all.

One end curves in one direction and the other end curves in the other. Each end is sharp and ornately carved as if the tips of a double sides blade. I've seen a lot of weapons, but I haven't seen anything like this one.

The engravings, the attention to detail. The artistry of the blades. I reach in and lift it by its ornate handle in the center. It fits nicely as the grip of a bow, but I see it for what it is as it's in my palm. I go with my instincts and push the little release that my thumb fits in as if made just for me.

Just as I thought, they come apart into two naginata blades. As I hold them in my palms they begin to glow, then a humming starts to come from them. I quickly secure them together as one weapon again and return them to the box as if they burned me.

"It knows it has found its home," Kenji says.

"Why are you giving this to me now?"

"This is a gift for your training. Your service weapon is of no use here or in the times to come. You will need something to match who you are," he explains.

"I'm going to stop you there. This … this is not me. I'd probably chop off a finger before I did any damage to anyone else. I'm good with my fists and gun. I always hit my target.

"As many Bruce Lee movies as I watched as a kid, I know I ain't him. Thank you, but you can take this back. It will only collect dust in the back of my closet if I take it with me. Give it to someone else who can put it to use," I say as I close the latches back. Then I mumble under my breath. "If you can find someone in this century."

This thing feels ancient. I'm no Samurai and I don't think I'm about to become one. I still don't know what made me use those ice ninja stars.

"This weapon will only respond to you and it's so much more than meets the eye. My assassins and I can show you how to use it. Join us just once and see how it feels."

"Can I think about it?"

He throws his head back and gives a throaty laugh. The sound is soothing and forces me to want to let my guard

down. However, he moves in that measured pace to lace his fingers together, not closing his palms.

My curiosity is piqued as laugh lines that weren't there before appear around his eyes making him look older and more relaxed. It softens his face, giving a gentler appearance.

"The two of you are just alike. Ardan can be stubborn too. He is used to being independent like you.

"My friend has never asked his brothers for help. He has learned to adapt to be everything to everyone—no matter the toll it has taken on himself.

"He will split himself in two to accomplish his goals, literally. Of the four brothers, he's the one who has mastered being in two places at one time.

"Why? Because he doesn't want to look weak to the others. He doesn't want to fail. I don't think he realizes the strength it takes to wield a dual presence," Kenji says.

"Why are you telling me this?"

"I see Ardan struggling. He wants to allow you to find your way to him in your own timing, but he needs you. He needs all of you."

I tilt my head and narrow my eyes at him. He gives me a bright smile. Folding my arms over my chest, I sit back in my seat and purse my lips.

"Okay, I hear what you're saying, but I'm catching what you're not. What is it you know about me that you're trying to spin?"

His smile grows so wide it looks unreal. I begin to feel as if I've just stepped into his trap. Ardan's warnings fill my head.

"Do you not feel it? You have been walking with it all this time." He pauses and tilts his head to mirror mine. "Has Ardan told you much about me?"

"He has shared some."

"You understand I have the power to manipulate and transfer spirits."

"I was told your assassins relinquish their souls to you," I reply.

"Ah, yes. They do, but I can give them back or place them in another vessel."

"Okay."

"Some spirits just need the right vessel to flourish in life. A pure heart with pure intention can make the difference when it comes to a moral compass.

"Vengeance looks different with the right heart. True power looks different in the hands of the right being."

"So the riddles have begun. He told me about those too. I'm a straight shooter, Kenji. I'd respect you more if you did the same with me."

It happens so fast, I'm not sure what's going on at first. He repeats all the movements with his hands, but in a much faster pace. Then he stands.

"İntikam, it is time. Speak," he says.

"Hello, young master. You have become so much stronger. Can you feel me now?" A voice says loudly in my head.

"What the hell?" I gasp and jump up from my seat, the box tumbling to the floor.

"Don't be alarmed. A blessing has been given," Kenji says.

"A voice in my head that's not mine or my mate's isn't what I consider a blessing."

"But this is your voice. You and İntikam are one. Like Ardan, you must learn you're not alone. You can rely on others. You need İntikam and İntikam needs you."

"He is right. We are stronger together. I will bring balance to you and you will bring balance to Ardan."

"Why do I need you?"

"It is the world who needs us."

"Kenji, with all due respect. I'm going to need you to explain why the fuck there's a voice in my head. What the hell did you just do?"

"You have felt İntikam inside you for quite some time now. From the moment you came into my presence, you began to feel the awakening. All I have done is seal the bond so you are one as it should be."

"You've got to be kidding me. I'm so stupid. I should have got up and left when you entered the room. Ardan warned me."

"Well, yes, I'm sure he did. I still have a question for you. Does it feel wrong?

"Can you say İntikam doesn't feel right? Like something you need to be apart from. Or do you feel like you have come home?"

I stand glaring at him as I take inventory of my person. Power is surging through me like never before. It's almost scary how powerful I feel.

My hands tingle as if needing an outlet to release some of this power I feel. The hum within is welcomed, that much I'm sure of. I shake my head to clear it.

"What does this mean?"

"You are now a dual being like your mate. You can learn to be here and there. We can train you to master this gift and that weapon for the time to come," he says.

"What's this time you keep talking about?"

"You will see. Train first, talk more later. We go now while Ardan licks his wounds."

"He's upset with me?" I ask softly.

"He is upset with himself. He doesn't know how to ask you for what he needs. He wars with what's good for you and what's right for everyone."

My shoulder sag as I feel guilty for my earlier words. I

didn't mean to intentionally hurt his feelings. I know something has been going on with him.

He's also keeping some of his thoughts from me. I didn't used to be able to tell when he was holding back but lately it's become clearer. That frustrates me because I've been leaving mine open more.

My mind goes to all he's had to endured alone for so long. Maybe I should try a different approach. We need to talk about whatever has had him in this mood.

I think it's time we do some heavy lifting. Not just talk, but meaningful conversations that lay out our real future, not hypothetically. Maybe it's time I treated him to a date instead of the other way around. If I want to start to show him I'm all in I need to put actions to it.

I snap my fingers as a thought comes to me. "I need a favor. I will train with you and your ladies, but you have to help me with something special for Ardan," I say.

"Name this thing you need, and it shall be done."

"I need you to tell me everything you know about Ardan. All the things he loves, times in his life he has enjoyed. Things like that. I'll take it from there," I reply.

"I can do this."

"Cool, but you can't tell Ardan. Deal?" I say as I hold out my hand.

"You should know never to offer a trickster your hand to seal a deal. We will always manipulate the ties and binds of that agreement," he says with a stern face, leaving my hand in the air. All traces of playfulness and warmth are gone.

He gives a bow and looks me in the eyes as he speaks again. "You have a deal, Billy. I will do anything for family."

ARDAN

"KING ARDAN," Beck and Bourne squeal as I step outside for some fresh air.

I give the boys a smile and dip to lift them up in my arms as they coming barreling toward me. They are all sweaty as they chatter a mile a minute. My frustration and anger melt away as I listen to them.

I'm not angry with Billy. I'm frustrated with myself. I want to give her time to process this new life without the pressure of its needs from her. However, at the same time, I need her.

"Where's Queen Billy?"

"She's making a few calls. What are you two up to?"

"We were playing. We did good in training today and Amadeus is rewarding us with playtime," Bourne says happily.

"Good job. I'm proud of you both," I croon and tighten my hold to embrace them.

They both make this little sound as they snuggle into me, causing me to think of how much they need this from a trusted female. The problem is Billy doesn't seem to be getting any closer to accepting us for who we are. I might be her mate and I'm satisfying her needs, but Billy holds me at arm's length at most times.

How can I ask her to be something I'm not sure she wants? Asking her to help me is like being a single father with two boys. She didn't sign up for this.

Yes, she has said she wants to help, but this isn't something she can flake on. Billy will break their hearts if she's not ready and changes her mind. She has a bond link with me, not with them.

Her rejection could be catastrophic for them. I will end up with two ice titans on my hands instead of the one from the visions. The balance will be lost and so will my solution for the problem.

"Will you come play with us? We have gotten fast, we can show you," Beck says.

I place them both on their feet and pat the tops of their heads. They look up at me with sparkling eyes. I'm thrown back in time to when Bradan and I were their size.

We looked at our father the same way, happy he had come to earth to see us. My heart pangs. I realize I'm committed to them for more reasons than being their king.

Their laughter fills the air as I form water guns for the three of us. I begin to chase after them as they take off. I take turns soaking the two as they try to get away.

"You've gotten fast, but not fast enough," I call after them.

"We'll show you," Beck laughs.

He goes to speed off, but trips and flies forward. The next thing I know he's sobbing on the ground. I groan and rush to his side.

"Hey, hey, it's just a little scrape. We'll get it cleaned up, little buddy."

"It hurts," he whimpers.

Before I can open my mouth, Billy appears. I look to her and knit my brows. However, her attention is solely on Beck.

"What happened?" she coos.

"I was trying to show King Ardan how fast I am, but I tripped and fell." Beck pouts and sniffles.

"Aw, you poor baby. Here, you eat this ice pop while I fix your boo-boo."

"Can I have one too?" Bourne asks.

"Of course you can. You can be my little helper too."

"What do you need me to do?" he asks excitedly.

"I need you to hold your brother's hand while I fix him up. Help him to be brave."

Bourne quickly reaches for his brother's hand with his free one. Both boys sit licking their ice pops while talking quietly to each other.

"Where did you come from?" I mind-link.

"I felt your panic."

"And you came running? Billy, I could have been—"

"Stop, I'm not a fragile bird. Can we talk about this later?"

"That we will."

"Here, have an ice pop. It's your favorite flavor, ocean candy."

I take the frozen treat as I frown at my mate. Quickly, I shove it in my mouth before I say or think something stupid. To my surprise it does taste like ocean candy.

I give a little smile. She's getting better with her magic. I'm proud of her.

My chest swells as I watch in awe while she uses her magic effortlessly to clean then heal Beck's little legs. She then sits on the ground and pulls Beck into her lap, cooing at him and rubbing his hair. Bourne moves to tuck into her other side.

"You see what happens when you have fun without inviting me?" she teases.

"We wanted to play with you. We were told you were busy," Bourne says.

"Who told you that? I'm going to soak them and make them pay. No one gets my favorite boys hurt and gets away with it," she says.

The little traitors both look at me and point their little fingers at me. Billy gives me a mischievous smile and stands up, placing Beck on his feet.

"Let's get him, boys," she sings.

In the next breath she has a water gun in her hands

chasing after me. The boys' laughter fills the air and it's like music to my ears. Their hearts sound happy.

We spend about two hours throwing water balloons, sliding down a water slide and feeding the boys and myself ice pops. Billy and the boys look happier than I've ever seen any of them. This is what they all need.

I'm going to make this their normal.

Billy

Trained Assassins

Two months later ...

"**S**ek sek," I hiss as I throw a combination punch then spin away.

These assassins are fast as shit. I've had to beef up my conditioning just to keep up with them. The first few weeks they kicked my ass.

I'm getting better though. I summon my naginata and spin it in my hand before settling into a low side lunge, holding my weapon out to my side. Three of the assassins have me surrounded, but I still have a little smirk on my lips.

"Patience, Billy. You don't have to rush. Allow your weapon to guide you. Give Intikam room to breathe and become a part of the fight. You are not alone. Take this advantage," Kenji coaches.

I listen to what he's telling me and allow Intikam to rise its head. Kenji says he's been cloaking Intikam's presence

within me because Ardan might get pissed off. I don't like lying to Ardan, but if he can't feel it, am I lying?

Yeah, I know. It's a lie of omission, but I can feel something is coming. Kenji won't reveal what it is, although I get the feeling he knows.

Ardan is still acting as if everything is fine as long as his stone doesn't come up missing. I, on the other hand, want to be ready to protect what's ours. Our people, our boys, our home, my man. I love Ardan with everything I am. I promise you someone is coming up missing if they fuck with him.

I'm stronger, faster, and more lethal than I've ever been in my life, and it's only been eight weeks since I've been training with Kenji and the *asashin*. I love the way that sounds in Japanese. It makes it sound so much more badass—which these women are.

"It's time to test the true form of your naginata," İntikam says.

"What do you mean?"

"The weapon will become whatever you will it to be. Sword or swords, bow and row, pistols, what will you choose to get us out of this?"

"Let's find out," I reply and choose my weapon.

I stand up straighter and toss the naginata in the air to catch the handle at a lower angle. I then press the release to separate the blades. Willing my power through it, a chain forms between the two blade handles. I grab the chain with my free hand and begin to spin the loose end.

The assassins move into action. One runs at me, dodging the spinning blade. She drops to her knees and leans back as she slides at me with her own blades in hand. I don't even flinch.

I elongate the blade that I'm using as my anchor. The sharp edge extends right through her side like a lengthened shard of ice. I stump down on her and turn the blade before I pull it out.

"Good, no mercy. Well done," Kenji croons.

I don't have time to gloat in his praises. I swing the chain as I lengthen the links once again and slice through the other two without giving them a chance to attack.

Kenji claps his hands as if I didn't just obliterate three of his assassins without batting a lash. Not that they were permanently taken out of commission. Kenji will fix them up and they will be back to training in no time.

"Very good, Billy. You have shown great progress," Kenji says with a bright smile. "How do you feel?"

"I feel great. İntikam is starting to feel like a part of me. Like more of a thought than another being."

"Ah, this is good."

"Can I ask you something?"

"Yes, of course."

"I think I understand what you're not telling me. İntikam was not a gift from you. It is a gift from the gods but why?"

"Beautiful and smart. Let's see if you can figure it out," he replies. "A master creator was once in the middle of weaving perfection. His work was interrupted and only two of his creations were completed. He then had to make away to finish the other two master pieces, but all of his old tools were forbidden from his use."

"I should have known you weren't going to give me a straight answer. Your riddles suck, by the way."

He releases a roar of laughter. "What would be the sense if they were simple? What kind of trickster would that make me?"

He freezes and his eyes begin to glow white. I gasp and step forward to reach out to him but he holds a hand up to stop me. I drop my hand and wait for him to tell me what's going on.

When his eyes stop glowing, he has a frown on his face. I get the feeling this isn't good. He looks pissed.

"What is it? Is it the stone?"

"It's the scumbags trying to work their way around my barriers. They have been trying harder and more frequently these last couple of days," he bites out.

"You mean whoever is trying to reach the boys." He gives a curt nod. "What can I do? How can I help?"

"You are doing what you can for now. Their hearts are filled with happiness these days."

"Is that really enough?"

"You will play your part when the time is right. For now, you and Ardan have words that have not been spoken but linger in the air."

I look down at my feet. I have worked with Kenji to come up with the perfect date. It took some time for me to learn enough about Ardan, to come up with something I know he will enjoy.

I've learned so much about his past and eras he enjoyed most. I finally felt like I had it nailed two weeks ago, but something keeps coming up when it's time for me to surprise him with the date. I've gotten my hopes up so many times only to have them deflated.

"Tonight will be the night. I've ensured there will be no distractions," Kenji says as if reading my mind.

"Thank you."

"As I told you before, you are family." He gives my arm a gentle squeeze. "I am going to my meditation chambers.

"All you have asked for will be ready for your date this evening. Ardan will be busy until you are ready. I have made certain of it.

"Enjoy your evening. And Billy?

"Yes?"

"Be sure to tell him your true feelings," he says and leaves.

I try to get excited about the date, but I can't stop thinking about someone trying to come after the boys. I

think of their happy little faces and my veins start to pulse with my powers.

"Easy, young master. We don't want to go down that road. We will flatten all in its path and there will be no return," İntikam warns.

AMADEUS

I CAN FEEL my mate as she pours a steaming cup of tea before me. I want to open my eyes and address her and this elephant in the room, but I already feel the cracks forming in the illusions.

I double down my efforts and remain focused on my task. I believe my grandfather has me overreaching. I had no idea I would have to hold up so many illusions at once for so long. I had been fine until my grandfather began to enter and exit the illusions at will.

I thought the original plan was for him to stay here in this realm with me and Kai as I created our images back in reality. I understand that Ardan might become suspicious of him.

I don't know my grandfather as well as Ardan and I was bound to make a mistake. Ardan arrived suspicious of Kenji and with good reason.

"You are doing well. Relax. We are nearly done," Kenji's voice floats to me, telling me he has returned.

I still don't open my eyes. My hold on things is slipping. Right now, the slightest change and I will lose it all.

"You can do this. I have faith in you. Let's check in with each illusion so you can regain control. I've already rein-

forced the barrier around the boys, so that magic will not interfere with your tasks."

I give him a nod of acknowledgment. It is all I can offer at the moment. Then I focus on my hands to weave the right strings to tighten each illusion as he goes.

"First, the temple. The stone must be sensed within the vault. He cannot sense that it has been moved. If he walks into the vault, it must appear to be there."

I weave the illusion carefully, reinforcing the cracks that have begun to form. I am careful not to set off any triggers as I work. In my mind's eye, I can see Ardan and the others keeping watch.

Ardan turns his head toward the door of the temple, and I freeze. I hold my breath until someone calls his name and he looks away.

"Slowly, he can feel higher magic. You have to move slow," Kenji coaches.

Slowing down, I finish weaving and release a breath as I'm done. I nod to signal for my grandfather to continue. I grow frustrated when I hear him sipping tea.

Of course he is relaxed. This is second nature to him, while I'm trying not to break a sweat. However, if I lose my temper, I will lose it all.

"Good, you are calm and ready to move on to the next. The stone. It's true presence must remain concealed as should the presence of the other with it."

Again, I take my time to weave the thread of the illusion. In my mind, I can see the gold strings I need to pull and thread together. Time is space and space is time. I weave and thread them with my mind.

This one is harder because the power coming from the source stones is so strong. I have to increase my strength to close the final loop as the stones fight against me.

"Very well done. Let's move to the next. Billy and İntikam

have gotten stronger way faster than I thought. Lock them down, before he senses the change. Be careful with this one.

"They must fully merge naturally. They must awaken as one for Billy to attain a true transformation. They are not there yet, and your magic cannot interfere. Take your time."

I think his words over, allowing the gold threads to dangle before me before I reach for them and begin to weave. This will need to be thin but strong. Impenetrable but nearly invisible.

Taking a calming breath, I begin. I use an intricate design and take my time to thread each loop and strand, making sure not to touch anything that's not my own magic.

"Excellent. Done like a true master. Now, the last one. You and Kai must appear as normal.

"He cannot sense you are here and the two out there are illusions. Your grasp on Kai has been slipping. Don't allow whatever you are feeling to get in the way of this. You can deal with your situation with your mate once this is all over."

I grind my teeth bitterly. My emotions begin to rage. I didn't have time to deal with any of my personal feelings.

"Get a grip. This is not the time. The gods don't make mistakes. You will have time to lick your wounds after our job is done," Kenji snaps.

I growl. Not at him but to gather my emotions and reel them in. He is right, I will be able to address the problem later.

I begin to weave the threads needed to sure up the illusion of Kai. Grandfather wanted someone I know and trust here with me. Someone who's also a warrior who can watch my back. That could only be Kai, so she has to be here—no matter how awkward the situation.

"Very nice. The illusions are stronger than before. You learn fast. Your powers are growing stronger.

"You should be able to relax now. Have some tea. You must keep up your strength."

I open my eyes to find my grandfather sitting across from me with his own teacup in hand. He sips at it as he looks over the cup at me.

"How much longer?" I take a chance and speak.

"Tanrı will let us know when. We are almost there. The journey is almost complete."

"Let's hope we still have a friend when this is over."

"We will," Kenji says with that wolfish grin he gets.

I'm not so sure he's right, not after what has been done to his mate.

Ardan

I Am Here

"Good night," Beck yawns.

Bourne is still brooding over losing at chess as he lies bundled in his bed. I've already had a talk with him about being a sore loser. He reminds me so much of Bradan when we were little.

"Good night, buddy. I'll see you in the morning."

"Tell Queen Billy I said good night and I'll see her tomorrow," Beck says.

"Why don't you tell me yourself?" I turn and do a double take.

Billy is standing in the doorway, dressed in a tight black minidress. She has on these sexy black heels that wrap around her ankles, running up her calves like jeweled coils. The straps across her feet are jeweled too.

"*Billy*," Bourne coos and perks up. He opens his arms and sits up.

The little stinker. He wouldn't even talk to me a moment

ago. Billy goes over and sits on his bed, and he wraps himself around her neck. She hugs him tightly and he melts into her.

I can't even get upset. I think Bourne is the one who needs Billy most. That little temper of his might be a concern in the future.

She kisses the top of his head and ruffles his hair. Bourne kisses her on the cheek. "You look pretty and you smell nice like Mommy used to."

"Thank you, Bourne. Are we still on for our date tomorrow. I'm ready to bake some cookies," she croons as she palms his little face.

"I will be ready. I'm going to be a good helper so I can get extra cookies," he says with a smile.

"That means you need to go to bed and get a good night's sleep. Good night, sweetheart."

"Good night, Mo … Queen Billy," he says, catching himself before calling her Mommy.

I close my eyes and stifle a groan. This is what I knew would happen. I can't put this talk off any longer.

"Night, Beck."

"Night, Queen Billy. See you in the morning," he replies sleepily.

"Are you spending the night here or coming with me?" I open my eyes as Billy places a hand on my chest and whispers the words.

I search her face, wanting to take her sweet lips but knowing I need to wait. They are painted with a shiny gloss that makes her full lips pop. Placing a hand on her hip, I lead her from the room.

"What's this all about?" I ask as we walk out the door.

"You will find out. Just follow me."

I lace my fingers with hers as she leads me through the main building. I feel like things have been strained between us since we arrived here.

I want to get back to the connection we were forming before we had to come here. Back then it felt like we were building a life. I was making my way through Billy's walls, little by little.

"You don't let me into your thoughts anymore. Are we okay?" Billy asks softly as we make our way up to the tower.

"Hey, baby, we are. I'm just not sure you want in on everything I have going on in here."

"You sure it's not all the *T* and *A* around here?"

I release a laugh. "You need me to remind you that you're the only one?"

"Maybe after this," she says as we step into the open tower on top of the main building of the complex. Lanterns are hanging all around the area, lighting up the panoramic views. In the center of the space is a table set for two.

"You know I'm a sure thing. You don't have to feed me first," I tease.

"You're totally ruining this," she laughs.

I throw my hands up in the air. "I'm all yours. Where do you want me?"

"Come sit. I have dinner for us."

I follow her to the table and pull out her chair then I take the seat across from her. She causes the domes over the plates to vanish.

The food smells damn good. It reminds me of a steak house I used to frequent a long time ago. As the place transforms to look like the old speakeasy, I know Kenji helped her with this.

"I see you have made a friend here," I say with a smile.

"I might have."

"To what do I owe all of this?"

"I think it's time we talk. You're hiding your feelings from me for a reason. I think part of that reason is because I haven't been straightforward with how I feel about you.

"Am I still scared to death of commitment? Yes, I think I will always fear giving others the power to hurt me. When I first found out I had sisters I was afraid to let them in, but the computer screen we all hid behind made that easier for me.

"They were my little secret. I got to decide if and when I wanted to meet them. I'll be honest. I was nervous and excited to see them in the flesh, but when the time came, I was ready to force myself to do it," she says.

"That's just the thing. I am fine with you taking your time to let me in. I saw your memories, your past.

"I understood it. However, you've arrived in my life at a time when my people need me, the little titans need me to figure things out for them, and the gods are up to something I know is going to challenge me.

"My greatest concern is how I will handle Beck and Bourne. This is one time when I can't split myself in two to fix things. There is no reflection of myself that can fix this." I pause and swallow, knowing that's a lie.

There is. It's her. I just won't allow myself to ask her.

I frown at my thoughts. "You are always honest with me, so I'm going to be honest with you. I've had a lot of time to think about this and have been in my feelings about the answers I've found.

"I'm afraid you're going to reject me, not the boys. So much time has passed since my mother and father abandoned me and my brothers. They didn't die. They weren't killed. They abandoned us.

"We weren't allowed to go where they are, and they never came back for us. We were four children raising each other. I know your fears firsthand, Billy. I have lived them too.

"I know what it's like to be small in a cruel world. To go unloved and forgotten. I … I don't want that for them, but I don't want to feel rejected either," I finish.

"Ardan, I am here. I'm not going to reject you. I can't reject you. Not because of some bond, but because I'm madly in love with you. I've been falling from the beginning.

"I didn't know marriage was an option, but if you asked me. I would say yes in a heartbeat. You make me feel safe, you listen to what I want and need and you're always protecting me even when I can protect myself.

"As for the boys. Aren't they ours? Why would you think I don't want them? They need a mother. They only trust me fully.

"I've seen how they are wary of others. Kai tries but they don't take to her the same. I would protect those babies with my life. I'm here, Ardan. I'm all in.

"I'm not going to abandon you or our people. I want it all with you. Beck and Bourne, little ones of our own, the wedding, the 'Property of Ardan' cut and tramp stamp. Sign me up for the package deal, I've thoroughly enjoyed the trial version. I was made to be yours. I love you," she says with a wide smile.

I stand and swipe the food from the table, causing it to vanish. In the next motion I have Billy in my arms as I kiss her passionately. She laces her fingers in my hair as I devour her mouth.

"Say it again," I breathe against her lips.

"I love you."

"No, tell me you want to have my babies. Tell me you want me to fuck you and knock you up."

"I want to make cute little magical babies with you. I want you to fuck me until my toes curl and I'm so filled with your cum it's coating my insides for weeks."

"That's my little nasty girl. Whatever you had planned for the rest of the night, we'll do it next time," I say and teleport us to our room.

"Ardan," she whimpers as I squeeze her ass and take the flesh on her neck into my mouth.

"Thank you, baby. Thank you."

BILLY

ONCE ARDAN RUSHED to end our date, I wasn't expecting him to make love to me. I was expecting him to fuck me hard and fast. I didn't think he would take things slow and be so methodical.

He has taken the sensual route, but I can't say I'm complaining. Ardan is giving a lovemaking clinic for sure. Like right now, as he feeds me his dick, he's touching me sensually while alternating between neutral-temperature toys and ice-cold ones.

As he pumps his hips into my face, he's gliding his cool fingertips against my belly. None of the toys he's using are as large or filling as he is—only building the anticipation for the real thing.

I hum around his large dick as a new flavor hits my tongue. He's been using his magic to cause his length to taste like different-flavored ice pops. I've had grape, pineapple, and mango so far.

The craziest part has been the brain freeze, as if his dick were a real popsicle I'm trying to suck down too fast. Even then, I didn't stop taking him in greedily. I happily lie here on my back, allowing him to take command of my body.

Ardan removes the metal toy from my pussy and I'm expecting him to reach for the glass one in the bowl of ice,

but he reaches to bend my legs in toward my chest and dives in with his tongue instead.

I moan around his length and am rewarded with a new flavor. I squeal happily as I realize it's strawberry. I try to get as much of my tongue on him as I can.

"Fuck, you're making me so hard. Are you ready for me to be inside you?" he croons.

I nod my head against his thrusting as best I can. He pulls out and takes a step back before spinning me to face him while still on my back.

I'm expecting him to feel cold when he enters me, but he fills me with a hard warm thrust that curls my toes as he pins my legs against my chest and holds onto my butt cheeks.

"Oh God, you always feel so good," I whimper.

"Not as good as you do," he says as he grinds his hips in that slow, soul-stirring way.

I'm still in awe of how gentle he's being. I'm so used to his rough, passionate sex, this is almost confusing me. I claw at his back as he picks up the pace slightly.

Shifting a little, he brings my foot to his mouth and sucks my toes between his lips. His tongue is cool as he swirls it around my big toe, bringing my senses back to that place where I'm aware of everything happening to my body because of the contrast in temperatures.

He grabs my hips and groans long and deep as he pushes in and out, bowing my back off the surface he has me on. Sliding his hands up my sides, he reaches my hands and laces our fingers together.

"I would do anything for you," he breathes into my mouth then kisses me passionately.

"I love you," I say as I feel his seed fill me.

Those words are like a trigger. He lifts me into his arms and begins to bounce me on his length as he holds me in a vise grip. I cling to him as I lock my ankles over his ass.

I don't know how long he spends making love to me in the most sensual and passionate way, but I'm spent by the time he places me in the bed and climbs in behind me to spoon me.

I'm almost fully asleep when İntikam speaks softly in my head.

"Congratulations."

"For?" I ask sleepily.

"He has given us an anchor. New kings will be born, and I will be redeemed."

I'm too sleepy to ask what that means. I have cookies to bake in the morning. I'll figure it out later.

Ardan

Time to Go Home

A month later ...

I'm on first shift today. Kendrick and the others are having church but there's a huge time difference between us. I came to get the others settle before I pop in for the meeting.

I let Reilly know I have business with Kenji, but I will be there when I'm done. Kenji said he would meet me here so we could finish the conversation we were having about my potential departure. He also said he has something he wants to share with me.

Although Kendrick told me not to rush back, I'm feeling like it's time to return. My gut says this is no longer where I'm needed.

For three days, I've been reading and analyzing that page with the prophecy. Billy and I have discussed it, and still, I'm not sure I believe my father is on our side.

Why? What's his motive after all this time? What good will this do for any of us?

I find I'm becoming more and more bitter with each day. I try not to let it show and to keep an expressionless face when others are around, but this is all festering on the inside.

"Are you okay, My King?" Dracon asks, causing me to notice I've been grinding my teeth.

I look up and something shifts in the air, grabbing my attention. I turn to look at the door to the temple where the vault rests and the shift happens again. I curse and storm over to the temple. Pushing my way inside, I inhale.

Magic permeates the air. I wave my hand before me and the illusion falls away. The door to the vault seems closed but the magical seal is broken. I move forward and yank the door open. The stone is not sitting where it was when I arrived and Kenji let me in.

The scent of the area says there's been magic going on here for quite some time. I begin to growl. It's not Kenji's magic, but there aren't many with the type of magic that can handle a trick like this.

"Brother?" Dracon says worriedly.

"I've been played," I seethe.

"I don't know if this is a good time to tell you this, but Kenji was walking toward this way, but then this guy appeared in his place," Hudson says as he shoves a shaking little guy toward me.

I release a snarl. "Everyone out," I bark.

Grabbing a hold of the frightened being, the team leaves out. I stand with my palms facing up. I need to know what happened here, did my friend betray me?

"Ben kralım," I rumble.

The space ices over and water begins to surround me, then begins to spin counterclockwise as it encircles me. I watch and wait.

The vault door now sits closed before me. Suddenly, a figure appears. They are large and covered with a hooded cloak. The figure moves swiftly. To my surprise, waving a hand to open the vault, they then enter.

As the figure rushes to leave, the asashin surround the exit. The figure moves with such fluidness. Their fighting style reminds me of my own and my brothers'. There are little nuances that come from our people in the way this being moves.

The asashin are holding their own, but this being keeps a slight upper hand although it seems like they are taking care not to kill anyone.

Just when I think the assassins are about to close in, a light comes out of nowhere and the figure and the stone vanish. Time seems to spend forward as I continue to watch on. The stone reappears and the vault door closes.

I pause the vision and run it back to replay it in slow motion. There … right there. I can see the threads of magic to know this was a trickster's work. It's not Kenji's signature, but it's someone who has his skills.

It sinks in that the stone has been gone the entire time I've been here. I release a roar that rises from my toes and shakes the ground beneath my feet.

BILLY

"THANK YOU," I say as I take the bottle of water offered to me after my training session. I just got finished fighting off twenty of Kenji's best.

The next group will be starting soon, but I have time to catch my breath. The sun is beaming down in the courtyard we train in. It's been nice enough to train outdoors lately.

As I get lost in thought, I amble over to have a seat. I start to think about that prophecy Ardan got from Kendrick the last time they had church.

I've read it multiple times, but I'm still not sure what it means. İntikam's interest has been piqued each time I review it. Which I find very interesting.

I take a gulp of water as I sit on a bench under a cherry blossom tree. At least I finally know what's coming. A war. A war of gods at that, but I don't know what that means for all of us.

I can't believe it's been three months since we've been here. It's strange but I miss home. I haven't spoken to my sisters much. I'm assuming they are all as busy as I have been.

Mack checks in once a week. I think he's starting to worry that Ardan has kidnapped me. I'll have to go see him as soon as I get back. Ardan has been toying with heading back soon since there haven't been any disturbances, and the stone is safe.

My suspension was extended as if I give a fuck. I have truly been wondering why I'm still a cop. Monsters get away with murder even when I nail them dead to rights.

I'm so tired of walking onto crime scenes to find babies as victims—that goes for young teens as well as small children. With the power I have now, I can do so much more good in the world.

"Mom, Mom," Bourne and Beck call as they come running out to the training area where I am.

I wipe a hand under my nose to clean the blood off. Looking down, I find there are a few nicks on my arm, but they will heal up. I did a whole lot worse to the other side.

If I hadn't taken so long to call for my weapon, I probably

wouldn't be this banged up. Once I see there's nothing too alarming going on with me, I open my arms with a smile for the boys to run into them. They are growing so fast. These are not the same little boys I first met on that dais.

"Hey, what's all the excitement about?"

"We finished training early today. Dad said if we were good and got our worksheets done and finished our training, we could have ice cream and watch a movie with Ren and Ford," Bourne says excitedly.

Ardan has begun to allow them to call him Dad. I don't know who is happier about that. They haven't call him King Ardan since.

Some days I think they call him Dad just because they love the way it sounds. Same with calling me Mom. Their little faces light up with the words.

"Wow, that sounds like fun. Too bad I still have another session. I'm going to miss out on the movie."

"We will save you a seat for when you're done," Beck says giving me a cute little smile.

"Aw, thank you. We'll see what happens."

"Training is important. We understand," Bourne says.

I give him a smile and ruffle his hair. He's not wearing his ponytail today, causing his long blond locks to spill in his eyes. So stinking adorable.

"I heard you two are going for your next belt with Master Kenji this evening. You two might have to become my tutors."

They both laugh and hug me. İntikam sighs in my head. I can feel the love it has for the two of them. I once thought İntikam was a male spirit, but as of late I haven't been sure.

There's this maternal instinct that comes from the spirit. Male, female, İntikam is a protector and nurturer. I think we both want to see these two happy and healthy.

"Speaking of your dad, have you seen him?" I ask, hoping the four of us can have lunch together after my next session.

"He said something about going to church, but he didn't go into Master Kenji's temple," Beck says with a frown.

I snicker. "It's not that type of church."

"Oh, so he didn't tell a lie?" he says, looking at me cautiously.

"No, he didn't. He went to meet with the other kings."

"He doesn't lie to us anyway. You have to pay attention. Master Kenji took him some place. They walked off talking while you were messing with your shoe," Bourne says and rolls his eyes.

"Oh, I missed that."

"It's okay. We'll catch up with him later."

I'm a little disappointed but we'll catch up with him when he's not busy. It's been a while since Kenji has been a part of my trainings. I haven't thought much about it but for some reason it sticks out to me now.

"Can we go to church next time? We want to see King Bradan," Bourne says, pulling my attention.

"No, maybe when you get older and become Iron Brothers you can, but for now you will see your uncle Bradan when we go home."

Bourne's eyes light up. "I can't wait to become a prospect."

"Are we going home soon?" Beck asks, hope filling his eyes.

"I think we are."

Suddenly, a bone-chilling roar fills the air. I lift my head and jump to my feet. İntikam lifts its head. I hold out my hand to my side as I call for my weapon.

"Get behind me," I command.

"But we can fight," the boys say and take a stance.

"I said, get behind me now," I demand with more force.

They quickly run behind me and hold hands. Power hums through me as I feel the glow of İntikam surging through me.

"Mom, you're glowing blue," Beck says in awe.

"What was that?" Bourne whispers.

"I don't know. Just stay behind me. I will keep you safe," I say.

My eyes widen as Ardan enters the courtyard with all six of our guards. He looks pissed, but the moment he sees me, his face contorts with so much fury and rage, I take a step back.

Billy

Vengeance Denied

Ardan wasted no time bringing us all back home after he reported in with Kendrick and the others. He didn't even bother searching for the real Kenji to say goodbye.

I know he's upset. Not just with Kenji or about the missing stone. He knows. He knows I've been keeping a secret from him.

We haven't had time to talk, but I can feel his anger even now. He spent enough time with me to get the boys settled in their new room he created for them and then he was off to handle club business without a word to me.

So much has happened since we arrived. I'm still numb. When we stepped through the portal, Kendrick informed me that Candido was killed.

A part of me feels robbed. I will never get to look him in the eyes and tell him why I hate him before I get to watch

them cart him off to a jail cell where he could suffer. Death was an easy out.

Someone stole the revenge that was mine. Yes, he's dead, but this feels wrong. This feels like a disservice. Kendrick says Ray is torn up over this.

She would be. That bastard was some type of father to her. While I have no sympathy for the man, I can't help sympathizing with her plight.

My stomach churns and my mouth waters. I've been getting nauseous since we teleported back. The trip back seemed a little harsher than the one there.

"Hey," I turn to find Lee with her head poked into the front door.

"Hey." I wave her in. I was just about to call Mack and let him know I'm back.

The boys tired themselves out exploring their room and having their run of the clubhouse. They are going to be a handful around here. We'll be setting boundaries in the morning.

Lee comes in and takes a seat in the living area with me. She looks around, taking the room in and then looks back at me. I look her over. She looks good. There's a glow about her.

"It's funny to see their different tastes. This place is nice. How many floors has he made the place so far?"

I laugh. "As of today, we have four stories. Magic is something else."

I shake my head and look around, still in awe that all of this is behind that same door a single room used to be behind. My life has changed so much since I first walked into this clubhouse.

"How are you feeling? I mean, I know you had the least attachment to Candido, but he was our father for all intents and purposes. Do you want to talk about it?"

"We can talk about anything but that man."

"How about we talk about our cousin, or we can start with our uncle," she says as she looks me in my eyes.

"Huh?"

"Those babies aren't the only thing extra you came back carrying," she says knowingly.

"You do know this is the reason I have such a hard time liking you. How do you always know so much of everyone else's business? You're like that noisy-ass auntie no one wants around," I say and roll my eyes.

She laughs at me and shrugs her shoulders. I purse my lips and fold my arms over my chest. Quickly, I remind myself not to shut her out.

"Everything around us is a cycle of life, trying to fit the right pieces together from a time when they all fit together perfectly. We're all moving toward a moment. A single moment of harmony when it all made sense and felt right," she says while studying my face.

"Right. You know, you sound worse than Kenji," I snort.

"So you have spent time with our cousin," she says with this shit-eating grin.

"What? And before you start with that riddling shit, my stomach hurts, I'm getting a headache, and I'm tired. So be straight with me. What the hell are you talking about?"

She laughs and waves me off. I glare at her to let her know I'm not playing and I'm not in the mood. She bites her lip as if in thought.

"I guess it's time." She shrugs. "Our uncle from our original birth is living inside you. You know him as İntikam. His original name was Sevimli. He was our father's twin brother.

"When our father Yakışıklı was killed, Sevimli became vengeful. He became stuck in a single form. The form of a sea creature. He lured people to their deaths all in the name of vengeance. That's where the name İntikam came from.

"The gods knew they should put him to death, but Su-Vaha couldn't bring herself to do it. He was her creation and her lover. No other god could do it without starting the wars all over again.

"Tanrı had already made the ultimate sacrifice for peace. He gave up his sons. Su-Vaha had to figure out something to stop her lovers tirade. It lasted for years before Su-Vaha gifted her grandson with special powers. Do you know what powers she gifted him?"

I sit as my mind races. The pieces all fall into place like a puzzle. The war, the magic, İntikam. I clench at my chest as I feel İntikam's pain.

"Yakışıklı," İntikam roars in my head.

"Easy now, İntikam," Lee coos as she looks into my eyes.

I turn away and catch my reflection in a mirror across the room. My eyes are glowing blue. I close them and try to reel in the emotions coursing through me.

"You're in control, Billy. İntikam is here to help you, but you have all the power."

"If I have all the power, why is there a water dragon living inside my head?"

"Because you and Taylor were never marked by Tanrı like you were meant to be. Your blessing was snatched from you when our father was slaughtered and the war was started.

"Tanrı only had time to bless Ray and half bless me before he had to go help Mom. The four of us were meant to hold so much power. The world was meant to be a happier place because of us and our love.

"Kenji, the soul keeper. Su-Vaha give him the power to master souls. He is Sevimli and Su-Vaha's grandson. He is our cousin.

"He didn't just help me because I'm Ardan's mate. I have his grandfather's spirit inside me and I'm his cousin. That's why he kept saying we are family."

"Yes, Kenji and Tanrı have been trying to right things for Su-Vaha for a long time."

"What happened to our mom?"

"Like a phoenix she will rise again. Nothing lost, nothing wasted. So many sacrifices are being made for us to come to the intended outcome of who we are."

I sit and allow my thoughts to gather. I have so many questions and emotions swirling through my head. İntikam is sobbing so deeply in my head it almost bows me over.

I can feel all his memories coming back to him. The pain and sorrow are so fresh. I want to shut it all down.

Suddenly, İntikam begins to roar and the vengeance within him begins to push forward. I jump to my feet and ball my fists against it.

"Stop," I scream in my head and push him back.

"See, you're already doing better than the others. It's in your blood to master him," Lee says as she watches me closely.

"Why give me a spirit of vengeance? Why place this burden on me?"

"At the heart of İntikam's pain is love. A deep love. You have the capacity to love deeply. You just have never given yourself a chance to.

"Kenji and Tanrı believe you have the soothing balm to redeem İntikam and make his spirit whole and useful once again.

"They believe you have the power to heal what was broken. It's what you needed, what Ardan needs, what Beck and Bourne need, and what İntikam needs. You also need his presence to transform to this battle that's to come.

"You were marked when you were Zander, my little sister. However, Tanrı once again didn't get to finish the blessing. Kenji sacrificed his familiar in the process.

"İntikam once lived inside of him. That's why you see him as a water dragon and not the monster he had become."

"He placed his grandfather's soul in his magical pet?"

Lee smiles and snickers. "You can say that. Familiars are more than pets. They are a part of their owners. This is why you probably feel a connection to Kenji."

"Okay, I think I'm with you, but how is İntikam supposed to help me ... transform, right?

"Yes. You will understand what that is when your heart is ready. İntikam will bridge that gap when the time comes. He will allow you to peak. The rest is up to you."

"So what do I do now?" I say and frown.

"Feed those boys, for goodness sake. Your stomach sounds like you're carrying gremlins," she says and bursts into laughter.

I look at her like she's crazy. It's the second time she's implied I'm carrying a child. I place my hands on my hips and look down my nose at her.

"What do you know now that I don't?" I mumble.

"You don't know?" she says and looks shocked.

"Don't know what?"

"I'm sorry. You should ask Ardan. I think it's time I go. I've overstayed. Reilly will be busting down your door looking for me soon."

"I bet," I mutter as my phone rings.

I wave Lee off as she scurries off before I can grill her any further. When I look at my phone, a smile comes to my face as I see it's Eddy. I feel like it's been forever since I've talked to him.

"Hello," I sing into the phone.

"She's alive," he croons on the other end.

"Oh, shut up and stop being so dramatic. I finally took a vacation like you guys are always telling me to do and you all freak out. Thank God I'm home. Papi can relax," I huff.

"You're back? I was just calling to see when you were heading back. I leave for Japan at the end of the week and thought we could hook up there, but if you're home, you can come out and hang with us for a few beers. Carson is here."

"Bro, I'm exhausted. Besides, Ardan has a lot of catching up to do. Maybe another night."

"Since when can't you come out if some dude can't make it?"

"Since I have a man who's crazy about me and I'm crazy about him. No, seriously, I want to hang, but I'm *sooo* tired. I'm going to drop in on Papi in the next few days. I'll see you then?"

"Yeah, I'll be around. Listen, kid, you should call Carson. He's pretty messed up. I'm not saying you're wrong to be happy and living your life, but the guy just wants to talk. You were his everything before this new guy showed up."

"He's going to have to get over that. This guy isn't going anywhere, and I never made any promises that I've broken. This isn't fair to me.

"I'm finally happy and starting a family with the man I love. I don't ask for much, but I'm asking this once for everyone to chill."

"Wow, starting a family? I didn't know it was that serious."

"Eddy, come on. I've been away for three months with the guy. I would say, considering we're talking about me, that's pretty damn serious."

"I'm happy for you and can't wait to meet him. Papi already loves him. I'm proud of you, Billy. You never settled. You deserve nothing but the best. I'll see you later. Love you."

"Love you too, Eddy. Thanks."

I hang up with a smile on my lips. I want to take the boys to meet Mack. I don't know if Ardan will be okay with that, but I plan to ask.

I can already see the look on his face as I introduce my two sons. Placing a hand over my belly, I smile wider. What if Lee is right? I could be carrying Ardan's baby.

No. That know-it-all said sons. Plural. Their daddy is a twin, so I wouldn't be surprised.

"Well, little demigods. I don't know about you, but I've had enough excitement for one day."

Ardan

"You want to talk about it?" Reilly asks as he comes to sit by me at the bar in the main hall.

"No, not entirely sure I do."

"Well, as my big brother, you can listen. Having a mate isn't as easy as I thought it would be. I mean, I love her. Gods, I love her. I didn't think I could love anyone or anything as much as I love her."

"So why do I hear a but?" I murmur.

"Because I'm still learning. I smother her because it would kill me to repeat the past. This time, she's my mate.

"That would finish me, but I'm starting to see she was designed to be my match. I can go all alpha and shit, but Lee is the real fucking deal. If all our mates are as powerful as she is, this war or whatever is coming is already won," he says thoughtfully.

"That's the least of my problems. Worrying about how powerful she is. I already know the answer to that. Billy is scary powerful. I think she would need to wear more iron than me to lock all that power down."

"Then what's the problem? Why have you been down here sulking instead of being upstairs with your mate and your two boys? Congratulations, by the way. I think it was the best decision."

I'm still too pissed off to talk about it, so I show Reilly what I found in that courtyard after finding out my stone was gone. My head is still spinning. All this time, while we were looking for that water spirit, he's been living inside my mate.

The worst part is, I think I brought him to her, but Kenji had to have a hand in binding him to her spirit.

Reilly releases a low whistle. I can feel he's speechless. So was I. I didn't know who to be angry with.

"I'm not mad at Billy. I'm mad at myself. I knew what could happen taking her there. I've known Kenji for too long to have fallen for any of it.

"I don't want to admit it, but I think he's behind all of it. Somehow, he masked his involvement, but this has him written all over it. I just don't understand why. Why risk centuries of friendship on one of his games?

"That weakling couldn't have been pretending to be Kenji all that time. If he were, how did Billy end up with one of the most powerful water spirits ever inside of her?

"There are answers to everything. I believe the entire picture will show itself soon. We will all be home within the next few days, and we can sort it all out.

"If Kendrick is right about Father, it will make sense in due time," he replies and pats me on the back. "You should go talk to your mate. Let her know you're not angry with her.

"I can feel your children growing, this is not the time for her to question your feelings or to be upset."

I smile. I've been waiting for Billy to sense our children. I already have names in mind for them.

"You are right. Thank you."

I stand and head for our apartment to let my mate know my ire is not with her. I was just angry to see İntikam in possession of her.

***

I FIND Billy in our bed, fast asleep. I stand with my arms folded across my chest as I watch her. I love this woman so much.

I will kill Kenji if that monster inside her brings her any harm. I was too young to remember how İntikam came about. Kenji should have been too.

I only remember when Kenji brought the spirit to me and asked that I lock it away. I remember his somberness and reluctance to hand him over. However, at the time, I thought it was the right thing to do.

"You better have a good reason for this," I growl under my breath as I undress while walking the stairs to get to our bed.

I will have to change the design of our room again with small children living with us. So much in my world is changing. I climb under the sheet and splay my hand on Billy's belly.

"We will be okay, my pretty mate. I love you."

Billy

Acting Weird

I sit next to Ardan on the bleachers at Hydra, wondering how this has become my life. I've told Mack and Eddy about my biological sisters, and I've shared that I don't think I'm going back to the force.

I was shocked when Ardan agreed to allow me to bring the boys to meet them. Although it had to be under three conditions. One, he had to be with us. Second, we had to explain to Beck and Bourne that Mack and Eddy are human and a part of the human world, so they couldn't reveal what they are.

Third, at least two members of my guard had to come along. I had no problem with any of that. The boys are smart and seem to understand our secret. Although, I have concerns with Beck. He's so innocent and overshares at times as he wants to make friends.

"Grandpa Mack, can we go swimming?" Beck asks, eyeing the doors to the swimming pool area.

"Not today, maybe next time," Ardan answers for Mack.

I look around and my heart swells. Mack took to the boys as soon as I told him they were my sons. No questions asked.

I've never seen him this happy. Eddy has taken to the two as well. That's not surprising at all. Eddy just has a warm nature about him.

"You boys know how to swim, or will I need to give you lessons?" Mack asks with a wide smile.

"We can swim," Beck replies. "Like fish in the ocean."

"In that case, you can come by anytime. Come box, come swim, just come by to hang with this old man. Hydra is your second home. My doors are always open to my grandsons."

"You hear this, Billy? I don't remember ever having free rein in this place. Now look," Eddy teases.

"You weren't as cute as my boys are," I toss back.

"So what was your excuse?"

I glare at Bourne as he bursts into giggles. He's been sitting with Eddy, playing chess at a table Papi brought out. I roll my eyes and ignore them both.

I want to see Bourne laugh once Eddy beats him. Then again, the last thing we need is for him to turn into a titan after losing. Damn, the kid is a sore loser. We'll be working on that.

We spend another hour talking and laughing as Mack dotes over me and the boys. Hudson and Dracon have been taking advantage of the gym as they try to look normal. There are only a few people in today.

Suddenly, the air shifts in the gym as the scent of Cuban food fills the air. Ardan stiffens next to me. I turn to find Carson has walked in with bags of food and beer.

I reach to place a hand on Ardan's knee and give it a squeeze. He stops growling in my head and turns to look at me. I shake my head at him.

I'd rather leave than cause a scene. It doesn't escape my notice that Beck and Bourne have stopped to glare in Carson's direction. They are now watching him cautiously as if ready to attack if provoked.

"Carson," Mack croons. "Now all my family is here. Come meet your nephews."

"I have to go to the bathroom," Beck says.

Bourne turns his attention back to the chessboard and acts as if nothing else exists. This isn't good. I may have my issues with Carson at the moment, but I hope we'll resolve that and get back to normal.

"Come on, little buddy. I'll show you to the bathroom and we can get cleaned up for dinner," Mack says to Beck.

I watch as Beck takes his hand and follows him just like I did the night he found me. I can't help remembering how safe I felt in that moment for the first time in … I don't think I felt safe before that.

"Are you okay?" Ardan mind-links me.

"Yeah, just thinking."

"Do you want me to get you something to eat? It doesn't have to be his food. I can make it look like Hudson or Dracon went to get you something."

I laugh in my thoughts. *"You don't have to do that. I don't think he would poison me."*

"Do you want to take that risk with our children? They are still very small, demigods or not, if he—"

"Oh my God. You've known? So I am pregnant?"

"I knew from the time I planted them in your womb. You are carrying our sons. Have been for about a month."

"And you weren't going to tell me?"

"I wanted you to sense it for yourself first. I will always know when I have gotten you pregnant the moment it happens. I didn't want to rob you of that moment when you figured it out."

"Next time, I'd like to know too, buddy."

Before I can fully get the words out through our link, he has my lips crushed with his. He drinks from my mouth like he desperately needs my air to breathe.

"What was that for?" I ask breathlessly.

"Next time?" he says and lifts a brow.

"Oh, these two and Bourne and Beck, that's all you want?"

"We can have as many as you want and can take," he replies, looking at me lovingly.

I slide closer and snuggle into his side. My stomach growls, reminding me of his initial question. That food does smell good.

"I'm going to make a plate, you want one?" I ask.

"Billy, I told you I would make you one," he says and frowns at me.

I lift my shoulders to my ears. "Old habits?" I squawk.

He kisses my forehead and stands to head for the table Mack and Carson are setting up while Beck watches on. I sigh in relief as Carson gives Ardan a nod and looks like he offers him a beer.

Happy we're not going to have to cut the visit short, I stretch out my legs and lean back on the bleacher behind me. Placing a hand on my belly, I smile. We're having babies.

***

A FEW MORE HOURS HAVE GONE BY. Eddy and Bourne are still at it with the chessboard. Eddy has been taken aback by my tiny chess player. Beck has become Mack's shadow, much to his pleasure.

I had to go to the bathroom. I'm making my way back out

of the locker room when I find Ardan with his head back and his arms across his chest. Placing a hand over his heart, I sag into him and place my head over it. He lifts his head and wraps his arms around me, palming my ass.

"Are you tired?"

"No, I just need to be near you," I reply.

"I've needed to be near you too. There's so much we should talk about. Not just what we talked about this morning but our plans.

"I'm not waiting around for that prophecy to come to pass without living my life. I've waited so long for you. I won't be robbed," he murmurs.

"I'm going to resign. Candido is dead. I'm not going to see him behind bars and I'm slowly beginning to accept that.

"With him gone, I have no motivation for the job. It's taxing and that can bleed out into civilian life. I don't want that for our family."

"I feel you, baby girl. I feel you. I'm here for whatever you need."

"I know. Thank you."

He kisses my forehead and hugs me tightly. I'm thrown off balance when he pushes me out of the way and catches a stumbling Carson under the arms before he can face plant on the concrete floor.

"Hey, you all right?" I ask as I turn to see what's happening.

"I don't feel right," Carson mutters.

"Dude, were you sneaking into the hard liquor? I saw you drink like four beers. You're no lightweight like this," I tease.

"Does he still smell strange to you?" I mind-link Ardan.

"No, not as strong as before. It's very faint now."

"I don't feel strange either."

"No, I only had the beer," Carson groans.

He looks like he's going to be sick. Concern begins to set

in. I look around. There's no one left in the gym we don't know.

I don't think anyone here would slip him something. Ardan holds him up with ease as Carson's knees give. I rush to Carson's side to help even though it's clear Ardan doesn't need me.

"Is there somewhere we can lay him to rest this off?" Ardan asks.

"Yeah, our old rooms are upstairs. Follow me," I say.

Ardan takes the brunt of his weight as I lead him upstairs to where the apartment is. Carson is panting and sweating the entire way. Once we get him into his old room, Ardan sets him down on the bed.

"Thanks. I don't know what's going on. One minute I was fine the next everything started to spin."

"Where is Beck? Hudson and Dracon don't have eyes on him."

"I think Papi took him to show him around. They took off before I went to the bathroom. Why? What are you thinking?"

Ardan shakes his head at me. *"They have him. I think we should leave soon. We've been here too long. I shouldn't allow them to be exposed like this for so long."*

"You think this has something to do with magic?"

"We can never be too cautious."

"Billy, I want to apologize. I see you're happy," Carson says pulling us from our conversation. "I've been a jerk, but I want to see you happy, even if it's not with me."

"I know. We don't have to talk about this now."

"No, it has to be now. You've been slipping away, and I didn't know how to stop it. You have always been the prettiest girl in the world to me.

"I was the one who found you that night. Did you know that?"

"What do you mean?"

"The night Mack found you digging in the trash cans. I

saw you first. Even as you rummaged through the trash, covered in dirt, I could still see how pretty you were.

"I raced back inside and got Mack. He was always so sad and broken before that night when it was just the two of us. Then you came and everything changed.

"You were our light. You made this a home for us both. I get it now, why you mean so much to him. You were his second chance to raise his daughter."

"Huh? What daughter?"

"You know the picture in his office of the girl in the boxing gloves?"

"Yeah."

"That's her. She was killed by a drunk driver. Mack and his wife got divorced after. A few years later he found me and took me in, but he didn't start to get better until you came along."

"How do you know all this? He never answers questions about that picture."

"Not while he's sober. He told me about a year ago. She was the same age as you were when you arrived."

"Wow."

"You see? You have always been everything to us. I thought we would grow up and you would see we belonged together.

"I didn't change my last name back to Ramirez to honor my family. I did so I could change your name from Salvado to mine. I was working to buy us a house and ask you to be my wife.

"When you came to me to ask for that favor with Ricci, I thought you were finally opening up to me. You were leaning on me like you do with Eddy. You were allowing me to be there for you … finally.

"I thought you finally understood I would sacrifice any

and everything for you. Then this guy showed up and ... and ... Fuck. I can't remember."

Ardan growls in my head. I can feel his temper rising. I look to him and shake my head.

"Easy. He's no threat to you."

Ardan grunts in response, but he stops the growling. I look at Carson and note the confusion etched across his face. He continues after a few beats.

"All I know is I've been so angry, and you disappeared, and I couldn't find the flight you used to take off and you stopped going to your place. Everything is so jumbled."

"Car, maybe you should lie down. We can talk about this tomorrow or when you're feeling better."

He shakes his head. "I just want you to know I'm sorry. I would die for you, but I would never get in the way of your true happiness. I haven't been myself and I'm sorry things got as far as they did.

"All I have ever wanted was to be your person. I've always been jealous of the bond you have with Eddy. I tried but you were never like that with me."

His words hit their mark. I feel bad for always holding him at arm's length. I thought it was best once I realized he didn't see me as a sister. Not that I would have been big on showing affection if he hadn't shown interest.

"You will always be important to me, Car," I say as I tug him in and give him a tight hug.

"You will make a great mom. My nephews are cute. Don't forget you have a family here too. Don't make me have to become a biker. I don't really think your dude likes me and I might never earn a patch," Carson jokes sounding like the brother I know.

"How can I forget the boy who saved my life? Thank you, Carson. Thank you for going to get Mack and getting me a home."

"Anytime, sis. I'd do it again in a heartbeat."

I release him and stand as I can feel Ardan's agitation through our bond. He's trying and failing to block the emotion from me. I move to his side and lace my fingers with his.

"Come on, let's head home."

Eden

Setting the Play

I have never forced myself into a body this small. However, I don't have time to adjust to his size. I need to find some useful information I can take back.

When the bishop gave me this assignment, that Carson guy felt like the right vessel. His obsession with her and the way he reeked of her scent caused me to choose him. I was sure he would get me close to her.

My luck, she cut him off the same day I possessed him. He will be lucky to survive all the time I've spent occupying his body. He'll be dead by morning, being a human and all.

Ah, bingo. I won't need to remain in this one long, but I will use him to set up a play, just in case.

I knock the little boy out so I can take control of his mind and body. He will wake when I exit. For now, I need full control.

"Grandpa Mack?"

"Yes, Beck." The old man looks up from the drawer he's digging through.

"Will you come to see us at the clubhouse?" I ask.

Thankfully, I won't have to be in this body long because I don't think I would get used to the tiny voice. It would drive me crazy after a few hours. However, he was the easiest vessel to take over without notice.

"We'll have to see what your mother and father think of that. If it's fine with them, I would love to."

"Good. I have something for you. It will help you get into the clubhouse. They will know we invited you and they'll get you right to Mom and Dad."

I reach into the little boy's pocket and pull the coin from inside. The old man looks at it and hesitates. I think fast in order for my plan to work.

"They would want you to have it. We all have them. If ever something were to happen to Mom, you would be able to get in during a lockdown if you have this."

This gets him to take the coin from my hand. I smile, pleased with myself. I will return to His Grace with solutions and not empty hands. I can't help wondering how my brother has fared.

Asher doesn't have the same patience. Knowing him, he has abandoned the mission for another realm—not doubt the vampire realm, his favorite—and he will return when he senses I have.

"Thank you, Beck."

"No problem. I hope we see you soon, Grandpa. I had so much fun with you today."

"Come give me a hug, little buddy. You have made my day."

With a cunning smile on my lips, I go to hug the old man.

The bishop will be pleased.

***

I ENTER the bishop's office with confidence and pride. However, I do note something is off. I don't feel many of my brothers here. That's strange. This place is always filled with life. Even when many of us are out hunting or on assignment, there's always so many of us around.

"Your Grace," I say as I place the coin down on his desk.

I stole this one as I passed by the other baby titan. I was nearly caught as that woman and the abomination sensed my presence. I only got away because they rushed for the boy not knowing I had already released him.

I jumped right into one of the humans and walked out the front door in their person. I'm sure my plan will go off as effortlessly.

"You come in here at a time like this with a coin? Do I look like I'm in the mood for a fucking offering?" The bishop spews.

I take a step back, startled. He's never spoken to me like this. As one of the only original queens of my kind left, he has treated me as special among our lot.

I still believe he would have killed me if I had not been just as special as my brother. While Asher has the power to clone others, I have the power to invade their beings and access their thoughts. He couldn't have one and not the other. We are a package deal.

"Y ... you told me to come to you straight away when I had something," I stammer out in shock.

"Not three, four months later. Not after nearly everyone is gone."

"What? What do you mean, Your Grace?"

"What do you mean, Your Grace?" He mocks in a whiny

voice and moves his head tauntingly. "I needed something useful two days ago. Your brothers are all dead. Well, the majority of them. Our numbers have been depleted."

"Asher?" I ask with a shaky voice.

He looks at me and glares. Something crosses over his face quickly. I hold my breath, fearing his next words.

"He gave a sacrifice for the greater good. I wouldn't have used him if I would have known she would kill all the rest of them."

My heart crumbles. My brother, my twin was all I had felt. I have served this cause as a nun for longer than I can remember. Asher never wavered in his support, he may have detoured to enjoy his life, but he always returned.

"In that case, I'm glad I have this news to give you. This is not just a random coin. It will grant us access to the head-quarters of the Iron Brothers.

"I've been inside the boy, so I can trace my essence to where they are. Although I have set up a better plan if you're willing to listen," I say.

He gives me a dark grin. "I am listening."

CARSON

WHAT THE FUCK is wrong with me? I feel like I'm dying. My body feels so heavy, and I'm soaked with sweat.

I groan as I try to toss and turn to get some relief, but this ache is in my bones and feels so heavy I can't move. It's not like I've been sick. This just came out of nowhere.

Although for months, I haven't felt right mentally. Even

now, I can't fully remember a lot. My thoughts are all jumbled up.

"Carson. Carson Ramirez."

I can't open my eyes, but I don't think the voice is in the room with me. It sounds more like it's in my head. I groan in response, thinking the angel of death is here for me.

"Are you listening, Carson?"

"What do you want?" I reply in my mind.

"I want to help you."

"Help me how?"

"I can heal you."

"Why would you do that? Who are you?"

"I'm a friend. I want to help you come into your true potential."

"Bro, I can't even think right now. There's nothing I can do for you, and I don't think I'm going to live long enough to come into anything."

"Yes, you need reassurance and relief. I understand."

Suddenly, the crushing pain lifts from my body. I lift a hand to wipe some of the sweat from my face. Feeling like I can move now, I sit up in bed and open my eyes.

"Now, that's better," the voice says before some dude appears standing in my room before me.

I jump and reach for my piece, then realize this isn't my apartment. I don't have my gun on me, I'm off duty. The one I usually carry when I'm off is in the glove of my car.

"Do you mind if I sit?" he says, pointing to my old desk chair in my old bedroom.

I take him in as he moves to sit without my response. This guy is dressed like some priest or bishop or something. His blue eyes are cold, and he has this vibe coming from him that throws me on the side of caution.

I want to allow him to speak, so I know his motives before I engage him. I remain silent and watch him as he watches me. A part of me believes I'm losing my mind.

"Now I think we can talk and have a productive conversation," he says.

"About what?"

"Billy Salvado and the biker she's with."

I ball my fists at my sides but give no other reaction to the mention of Billy. I knew that biker was going to get her into some shit. I calm down to pay attention to figure out how to get her out of this.

"She never picks you. Over and over again, she chooses someone else. Anyone else but you. Don't you think it's time you become the choice?"

"Once Billy has made up her mind, there is no changing it. I don't know what all this is about, but I don't think I'm your guy."

He stands and snaps his fingers. The pain and sweats return instantly. I grind my teeth and grip the sheets.

He snaps his fingers again and the pain stops. I double over and gasp for air. When I catch my breath, I scramble back. This shit ain't normal.

"What the fuck are you?"

"I am your salvation."

"I highly doubt that."

He gives a maniacal laugh. This guy looks unnatural. What the fuck has Billy gotten herself into?

"You still don't understand you're dealing with something greater than your fleeting human life. You will do this willingly, or I can force you to do what I need."

I go to tell him fuck him, but I quickly remember a few moments ago and the pain I was in. I need to know what it is he wants with Billy so I can understand how to help her.

"What exactly is it you need from me?"

"I want her to choose you."

I sigh. I'm a fucking detective. A damn good one. This

motherfucker is lying. He knows she won't choose me and that's what he's banking on.

"Okay, how do we make that happen?"

He gives me a sinister grin. Nothing good for me will come of this. I can feel it in my bones.

I will always protect you, Billy. Always.

THE BISHOP

I NEEDED a quiet place to act out my mission, so I went to my prayer quarters with a renewed step. My lord was right. Eden presented herself useful.

Her idea is brilliant. We will walk in with the upper hand and if all else fails, I still have an ace in my back pocket.

Her plan is solid, but I have taken things a step further. Eden gave me more information than she knows. Once I told her Asher didn't make it, I knew she would.

By the time she finds out the truth, I will have completed my mission. I left none of my valued assets behind. Not even my hunters know who made it out and who didn't. I purposely split them up for my plan to work.

As I'm done with Carson Ramirez, I return to my body waiting in my prayer quarters. I lift my head and stand from kneeling before the stone. Power still courses through me even after the energy I've expelled. He will play his part nicely.

"That went well," I murmur to myself with a satisfied grin.

I have planted the necessary seed to get my desired

results. I now have a pawn in play. My numbers may be down, but I have the critical players still at my fingertips.

I have lost one battle, not the war. This is still mine for the taking. I've always been in this for the long game.

Remembering my purpose, I pull out my cell phone. I lift it to my ear and wait as the other line rings. It doesn't pick up until the third ring.

"Hello," the voice on the other end comes through gruffly.

Good, he sounds detached. I believe I have the perfect timing. Invoking insanity is my strong suit.

I snort to myself. The water wielder's mate has the spirit of İntikam. They're making this all too easy.

Very well done, Eden.

"Bardo. It is time. I have your task for you."

Ardan

Intruders

"Go upstairs with Dracon. We'll be up as soon as the ceremony is over," I say to Beck and Bourne as they pout because they're going to miss the ceremony.

"But we promise to be quiet," Bourne tries one more time.

"Why do you want to be down here with all those old folks? The ice cream and cake are all upstairs. My mom is in the kitchen. I can get her to sneak us some snacks," Dracon says, trying to help me out.

"*Yes*, come on, Bourne," Beck sings and takes off.

I shake my head and stand to my full height. We better get this show on the road before those two eat their weight in sugar. I'm not dealing with that shit for the rest of the day and night.

Billy comes up to me and slips her arms beneath my cut and T-shirt. She runs her warm palms up my back as she smiles up at me. Dipping my head, I take her lips.

When I break the kiss, I lift my hand to pull her shirt aside and look at the spot Taylor singed earlier with her flames. Billy covers my hand and gives it a squeeze.

"It's fine. It's already healed, thanks to you. Come on. They're waiting."

I turn and look around at everyone gathering. This has already been a long day, and it isn't halfway over. I feel like we haven't stopped since getting back from Japan. Bradan showing up on death's door has caused me to think about how grateful I am for my mate and her powers to protect herself and our family.

Bradan is looking more and more like himself. He's been joking and is as lively as ever. We're looking more like a family around here. I've never known where I belong more.

"Shall we get started?" Nuvos asks.

Nuvos, the eccentric golem, oversees all weddings, blessings, and bonding ceremonies like this one. He will perform the naming ceremony for my sons. That will be one proud day for me. I can't wait.

"Yes. They're setting up for a celebration upstairs. We shouldn't keep them waiting," Kendrick replies.

"Ah, yes. I was informed there would be a stone cake for me. Let's be quick," Nuvos says happily.

My brothers and I move to our respective locations on the crest engraved on the floor. I tug Billy to stand before me and look into her eyes. I can see the love she has for me in her gaze.

I get choked up as the look overwhelms me coming from this woman. A few months ago, she wouldn't let me help her carry her groceries up to her apartment. I could barely hold a door open for her.

But now, she's standing here looking at me with so much trust and love. Nuvos steps into the center of the crest, getting into his position, ready to begin. I smile down

at Billy, ecstatic to finally bring her fully into our community.

"Wait, oh god. Does this mean that one water fairy who talks too much will be able to bust in talking all the time?" Billy asks through our link, causing me to laugh.

"No, you don't have to let anyone in you don't want to. They know the rules. It's not a social line. It's for community business and emergencies. Unless there's a bond with someone who wants to talk, you can shut them out like you do me."

"Shut up before you're the only one I don't let in."

I give a laugh and smile at her. Our life will always be entertaining. *"I'm so glad I found you. I love you, Billy."*

"I love you too."

Nuvos begins and we fall silent. The temple is filled with excitement. The queens are finally officially taking their thrones. This is huge for the community. We can definitely use the boost in morale around here.

No sooner than I have the thought things begin to go wrong. Our mates begin to lift into the air. Their heads are thrown back and their mouths open. This shouldn't be happening like this.

My thoughts go to our babies. I don't know what to do as panic I've never felt before fills me. My brain is trying to process what's happening.

"Nuvos, what's happening?" Kendrick is the first to demand. "*Nuvos.*"

I look to Nuvos to see he's still chanting. Confused, I turn my attention back to Billy. She and her sisters now have their palms turned out at their sides. Water jumps from Billy's palm into Lee Ann's palm and from Lee Ann's palm flows sand into Ray's and Lightning jumps from Ray's palm to Taylor's. I watch as flames jump from Taylor's palm to Billy's. Then the cycle continues.

A beam of blue light surrounds Nuvos as the sisters

remain suspended above us. I'm so enthralled as I watch what's happening, I'm taken by surprise when Dracon mind-links me and the rest of the guard.

"Bardo is here. I tried to fight him off, but he has the titans. He's not alone. We're under attack." His voice sounds weak.

"Ocean, find Dracon and get him to the infirmary. Ren, assist her. Hudson and Ford, find the boys. The rest of the team, you are needed in the temple."

As I finish the mind link intruders rush the temple. I only have an instant to react. Kendrick has thrown a tornado of wind around the sisters as they are still floating in the air. Bradan follows with a wall of fire. Quickly, I throw up a wall of ice.

Before I can release and go on the attack, I'm hit with something so heavy it carries me back and pins me to the wall. I hit my head against the wall, and I'm dazed at first.

When I regain my focus my first instinct is to fight against the web of chains. However, I look to Kendrick and Bradan and see it's futile. The more they fight, it's like their powers are attacking them.

I look to Reilly, and he has gone still within his confines. I do the same. The way to help my family is to remain calm.

BILLY

THE STRANGEST FEELING comes over me and I'm thrown back in time. Nothing feels familiar to me. It's like I'm seeing through someone else's eyes. Then I realize I am.

"Su-Vaha wishes for you to enter the ceremony through the path of the gods. Come this way."

This is Sevimli. I can feel it. His excitement for his brother is flowing through me. We follow the man who seems off to me, but I'm not in control to stop Sevimli.

We come out of the path, and I can see what looks like a ceremony happening below. Tanrı. He is leading the ceremony. I know right away who he is.

Suddenly as we watch Tanrı lift one of the babies from the basket, two men jump out and grab Sevimli to restrain him. He fights back, but they overpower him.

"It's time to pick a side, Sevimli. Tanrı and the losing side or go against your brother and Su-Vaha will be spared."

"How dare you? You will not get away with this. Release me. Release me now," Sevimli roars.

"Let me put this another way. Your son or your brother? Choose now," the man who led him this way says as he holds up a small child.

A strangled whimper comes from Sevimli's throat. He reaches out his arms and the child is placed within his embrace. In the next breath, one of the men releases a ball of energy down below.

"We are gathered here to bless these four—" Booms loudly from afar before the words are cut off.

I know right away the voice is Tanrı's. The next sound I hear is the strangled sob of Sevimli.

"Yakışıklı, Yakışıklı. My brother. No, Yakışıklı."

A chill runs through me. They snatch the child from him, but a woman appears and flashes a beam of bright light.

I'm snapped back to the present and I can feel İntikam writhing in pain inside my head. He watched his brother die. He was given an ultimatum between those he loved and lost his brother.

Rage rises through me so fast and strong, I can't stop it. I

fight to catch my bearings. I'm hovering above the room with my sisters. I can feel their power as if it were my own. There is a pulsing of energy surrounding us like nothing I've felt before.

I throw my arms and head back and release a sound I don't even recognize. İntikam joins in, lifting his head and stretching out his power within me.

"I understand, İntikam. I will get your vengeance. You can rest now. Thank you for your sacrifice. It will not go wasted. Be at peace, my friend."

"Honor our past, young master. Don't allow my brother's death to be in vain. Do better than I did. Be worthy of the gift of the gods. Thank you, young friend. Thank you."

I open my mouth and blue smoke flows from my lips. I can feel my skin humming. It's like İntikam infuses into my soul.

I reel in my rage and emotions and focus. As I do, I absorb the wall of ice surrounding us after the other two barriers disappear. I land on my feet in a side lunge, my arm out to my side with my naginata in my hand.

The weapon is glowing blue and hums within my palm as blue smoke raises from it and me. My eyes harden the moment I see Ardan pinned to the wall.

My power pulsates in my veins. Ice-cold magic beats within me. I can feel I'm skating a thin line trying to harness this power, but I'm in control.

"Don't let the vengeance control you. We have a purpose beyond that day," Lee says in my head. *"This was our destiny. The Council of the Phoenix and the fire sirens will rise again. Born of ash, risen through song."*

"Then let's fucking sing," I growl.

I snap my gaze to the asshole standing before me when I hear Beck's whimper. Looking up through my lashes, I glare at Bardo as he holds Beck in one hand and Bourne in the

other. Wrong fucking move. I'm going to drop him and get the guys free in one breath.

"They are strong, but this is our house. Bring them down," Lee Ann says in my head.

"The fire bitch is mine," Taylor snarls.

"I will get our mates free," I seethe.

However, as I launch forward, everything around me changes. I freeze as a woman holding my father comes into view. Carson stands beside her with his wrists bound.

I know right away we are in an illusion. I look to Bardo as he glares back at me. The boys are now in a cage floating high above us.

This motherfucker should have kept them in his grasp to keep me off his ass. I don't know who this bitch is, but she's going down just the same.

"Who's up first?" I snort and smile.

Bardo charges forward like he's skating on ice. I'm ready for him. He pulls an ice sword out of thin air right as he gets up on me.

I dip back out of the way. The cold of the sword breezes by my chest and face. I come up and turn to face him.

He swings his sword at me again, trying to take advantage of his long reach. I block it with my naginata and shove him back, taking him by surprise as he stumbles back.

"So I shouldn't underestimate you," he says as if he's amused.

"Do whatever you want. I'm going to fuck you up either way. You hurt my boys, I'm going to make you pay for that."

His big ass laughs at me. "Your boys? I don't remember my brother giving you that right."

"So what? You murder your brother and think it's your right?"

"You know nothing about me," he bellows like a madman.

He charges at me again angrily. This time as he glides

toward me, I release the button on the center of my weapon and pull the two blades apart. I move past him in a flash and slice his arm and side.

He roars as blood drips from his side. "You bitch."

"That's Queen Bitch to your ass, asshole."

I knit my brows as the wounds I just caused heal up and look like ice is replacing the flesh I broke through. Quickly, I put my blades back together and spin the weapon above my head.

Out of the corner of my eye, I see a shard of ice heading for my face. I bring my naginata down to block it. The blades on my sword change, lighting up blue.

My instincts kick in and I blast him with the light. It shoots out a blade of ice that hits him in the shoulder and shatters. I adjust and send more power through on my second blast.

This one hits him and lodges in his shoulder. I grin to myself. I guess I still have more to learn about this thing.

Suddenly, this motherfucker grows by like four feet. I watch in awe but shake it off quickly. He drags his sword across the ground, making this piercing sound that hurts my ears.

I note he's slower in this form. This time, when he comes at me, I flip out of the way and shoot another shard of ice at him. However, when he knocks it away, it comes spinning back in my direction, cutting me across the cheek.

"Come on, Billy. You've got this," Carson calls, reminding me he and Papi are here as well as that woman.

I'm thrown backward as I'm momentarily distracted. When I look up, Bardo is bringing his sword down on me.

"Shit."

Beck

Split in Two

*"T*hat's Uncle Bardo. The dreams were real. He is an ice titan,"* I say to Bourne through our mind link.

"I know."

"Does that mean he really killed Mom and Dad?"

"Look at what he's trying to do now."

"But why?"

"I don't know. He's taking everything from us. Mom, Dad, our home."

Anger fills me as I watch my uncle fight my mom. I don't want to lose another mommy. Billy is good to us.

It hurts so much when you lose a mommy. I don't want to feel that hurt again. I squeeze my eyes shut when Uncle Bardo sends a shard of ice flying at Mommy.

"Don't worry. I'm not going to let him take her from you," Bourne says.

"What are you going to do?"

"I'm going to fight him myself. For Mom, for Dad, for you."

Before I can stop him, he starts to transform. I can't let him do this. Bourne is needed as a sea guard. If he does this, he's going to become an ice titan like Uncle Bardo.

The cage we're in begins to lower as the weight of Bourne's titan form makes it too heavy to hold us up. I go to transform too, and the cage drops faster.

"Wait, Bourne. We're not supposed to reveal we can transform at will. Kenji warned us," I try even as we both transform.

"You stay here. I can fight him myself."

"He's an ice titan. You shouldn't. Not alone."

"He won't just kill Mom. He'll kill our brothers. I have to kill him first," Bourne growls.

I look to our mom and that's when I feel them. I knit my brows and tears come to my eyes. I can't allow this.

I won't lose my family and Bourne won't be the one to lose his heart. I begin to shiver as a chill fills me. I snap my eyes open as I feel my powers moving through me.

"Get away from my mom," I roar as I step from the destroyed cage.

"Beck, *no,*" Bourne cries out.

ARDAN

I SLOW my breathing as I center myself. Billy and the boys are in an illusion with that bastard, but it's nothing like one of Kenji's illusions. I'll be able to force my way in, I just need to split in two.

This is different from astral projecting. I need to be by Billy's side in the flesh. I need to protect her and our family.

I have my mind's eye on the fight as I work to send a part of me outside of this blessed iron cage. I'm not sure it's even possible, but I need to try.

Billy is holding her own, but I know what ice titans are capable of. Bardo is playing with her right now. I need to get to her before he turns things up.

Suddenly, everything moves in slow motion. Beck and Bourne have transformed and are surrounding Bardo. Beck is blocking Billy with his frame.

No.

He has transformed into an ice titan. We have lost him. My heart fills with so much pain and sorrow.

He's just a child. He has become my child. How can I banish him now?

So much rage fills me, I split in two with ease. One half of me remains in the blessed iron while the other heads for the illusion.

"Ben kralım," I roar as I bust through the illusion.

I drop to one knee to slow my momentum and call on my sword to dig into the ground and stop my forward motion. As the sword halts my forward movement, I swing up and land on my feet.

The titans move to my sides as if to battle with me. I want to tell them to stand down, but this is their battle as much as it is mine. They have lost so much because of their uncle.

Their innocence, their parents, their home. The chance to just be two little boys. I will not take this from them too.

Beck is swift as he glides across me and Bourne to slice across Bardo's middle with his ice sword. Bourne works in tandem with his brother, gliding by to slash Bardo from the other side. I go to run him through, but he drops to one knee.

A grin comes to my lips as I find Billy landing in a crouch, blood dripping from her blade. It is then I notice Carson. He is writhing in place.

I figure out quickly that my knights won't deploy because I'm half of myself. I can't send them to protect Billy and my unborn children. I need to end this fast.

Carson breaks free from his restraints, and in the next instant, he doubles in height as the woman beside him vanishes into thin air.

"Shit," I murmur.

That woman is one of my kind. A gifted one. I know with all my heart she just possessed Carson. He's now at least eight feet tall which would be the woman's natural height as a queen.

"Don't attack him," I command.

To keep him from attacking, I surround him with a block of ice until I can figure this out. To my surprise, the woman reappears outside of the ice in her own body once again.

She pulls a sword and aims it at the block of ice I placed Caron in. She has her other hand wrapped around Mack's throat. My heart races. If she strikes that ice, Carson will shatter into a million pieces. One wrong move and she will tear out Mack's throat or pierce it with her claws.

"No one move or I will kill them both. Ice titan, get up and finish your job," the woman says.

I shake my head at the twins as they look to me as if they are going to make a move. Billy will be destroyed and İntikam will be unleashed in all his fury if something were to happen to either man. My mate will lose her mind. I will lose two people I love to insanity in one battle.

"We need to melt the ice," Billy's voice comes through the mind link.

"I can throw an ice spear," Beck replies.

"No. You will do the same thing she's threatening to do," Bourne says.

Bardo stumbles to his feet. He attacks Bourne first. I'm

proud of Bourne as he holds his own. Billy goes to assist him, but the woman tightens her grasp on Mack's throat.

"Move and he dies," the woman barks at Billy.

"I think I get what's going on here. They are trying to cause me to choose. It's how İntikam was created. Sevimli was forced to choose between his brother and his son."

I growl. It seems she's right. Billy will not lose any of us or her mind. This is a cruel tactic. Our hands are tied.

"What do we do?" Beck asks, sounding like the little boy he is.

"We save our family," Billy replies.

Billy

Ben kraliçeyim

My back has been placed against a wall and I hate it. My babies are under attack and my family is in the middle of something they probably don't understand. Kenji's voice fills my head.

"You are not who they think you are. You are who you know you are. That's the difference between a winner and someone who's willing to lose."

All my life, I've been told who I could be. Who people thought I should be. Every time, I've proven them wrong.

I'm not about to let these people take my life from me. I'm not going to allow my family to be taken away. I have children, I have love, I have a safe home.

"Ben kraliçeyim."

İntikam voice fills my head for what feels like the last time. *"That you are. Well done, young master. Finish them."*

ARDAN

I CAN'T BELIEVE my eyes. Billy transforms right before me. It's such a beautiful sight.

Her avatar awakens and stands behind her in all her glory. A crown on her head covered in ice and surrounded by flowing water just like mine. The avatar reaches to straighten her crown and winks in my direction.

A glance out of the corner of my eye tells me the woman is standing with her mouth open, too transfixed to move. I take that moment to fluid the block of ice Carson is in— melting it.

His true human form begins to fall to the floor. Beck glides toward him to catch him and bring him to the ground safely.

A popping sound fills the air—like the sound of two guns going off—causing me to turn my focus back to Billy. I find her spinning two smoking pistols, one in each hand. She then slams and twists them together at the butts, causing her naginata to reappear as it gleams in her palm.

Billy pops her hip out and nods in satisfaction. She then holds her arms open and squats. Beck and Bourne rush into her arms back in their natural forms. She stands with them in her arms and smiles at me.

"We will fix him. We will bring back his balance, or we will love him as he is," she says through our link as she repeatedly kisses the top of Beck's head.

"That we will."

I look around and find Mack shaking and sobbing beside

Carson. The woman lies on the floor with a bullet hole and blue smoke coming from her forehead. I wouldn't give her the respect of calling her a queen. A puddle of water rests where I last saw Bardo.

The illusion vanishes and we're back in the middle of the temple where the real battle is happening. My brothers and my other half are still trapped. I need to get them free.

Suddenly, the room begins to shake. The ceiling is crumbling, falling to the floor. At first, I think this is another illusion being forced. Then, a spine-tingling cross between a growl and a grunt fills the air.

"Holy shit," I breathe as I turn my head toward the sound.

ABOUT THE AUTHOR

Blue Saffire, award-winning, bestselling author of over seventy contemporary romance novels and novellas, writes with the intention to touch the heart and the mind. Blue hooks, weaves, and loops multiple series, keeping you engaged in her worlds. Blue writes for her own publishing company, Perceptive Illusions as Blue Saffire, as well as Royal Blue.

Blue and her husband live in a house filled with laughter and creativity in Long Island, NY. Both working hard to build the Blue brand and cultivate their love for the arts. Creative is their family affair.

Blue holds an MBA in Marketing and Project Management, as well as an MED in Instructional Technology and Curriculum Design. She is also an NLP Master Practitioner.

ACKNOWLEDGMENTS

I gave my all in this one. I mean, really. I love this entire universe and it's giving me life, but *babyyy*! I gave a piece of me for real. We are almost there. I want to say this was the last cliffhanger, but you may interpret it differently.

I really think that subconsciously, I'm writing this series for my mom. A mother's love hits different and the more I write, the more I see her in this. I think that's why I'm so emotional at the end of each. Love, love, love writing these, no matter how challenging they have been.

Thank you again, readers, for coming on this new journey with me. Thank you for your patience and continued support. I'm not going to release a book that doesn't feel right to me. So I have missed the timelines a few times. I thank you for rocking with me as I get it done right, not just get it done. We are almost there. Thank you for the encouraging emails, videos, posts, shares, and DMs. Bless you all for being instruments in keeping me going.

The way I love God. The way He pours into me to keep me going when I don't think I can. How can I not? Thank you, God, for continuing to allow me to demonstrate your glory through the works of my hands. Thank you for giving me life and the wisdom to do what I love. Thank you for showing me the way when the course needs to change. As always unapologetically blessed and highly favored.

Next! *Reilly. He's about to have me all in my feelings.*

THANK YOU

Wait, there is more to come! You can stay updated with my latest releases, learn more about me, the author, and be a part of contests by subscribing to my newsletter at www.BlueSaffire.com
If you enjoyed *King of Tides*, I'd love to hear your thoughts and please feel free to leave a review on my website. And when you do, please let me know by emailing me TheBlueSaffire@gmail.com or leave a comment on Facebook https://www.facebook.com/BlueSaffireDiaries or Twitter @TheBlueSaffire

OTHER BOOKS BY BLUE SAFFIRE

PLACED IN BEST READING ORDER

Also available....

Legally Bound

Legally Bound 2: Against the Law

Legally Bound 3: His Law

Perfect for Me

Hush 1: Family Secrets

Ballers: His Game

Brothers Black 1: Wyatt the Heartbreaker

Legally Bound 4: Allegations of Love

Hush 2: Slow Burn

Legally Bound 5.0: Sam

Yours 1: Losing My Innocence

Yours 2: Experience Gained

Yours 3: Life Mastered

Ballers 2: His Final Play

Legally Bound 5.1: Tasha Illegal Dealings

Brothers Black 2: Noah

COMING SOON...

King of Gods Book 4: Immortal Iron Brothers Series
King of Past Book 5: Immortal Iron Brothers Series
Kevin or Nothing: In Deep Book 2: The Blackhart Brothers
series

OTHER BLUE SAFFIRE SERIES

Other Blue Saffire Series

Hold On To Me Series
My Funny Valentine
Be My Valentine

Hitter Squad Series
Remember Me

Work Husband Series
Unexpected Lovers
My Best Friend's Wish
The Ones Left Behind
The Last Ones Standing

The Lost Souls MC Series
Forever
Never
Always

The Moran Brothers Series
Love Notes
Stay With Me

The A**hole Club Series
Pit Book 1: The A**hole Club
Ox Book 5: The A**hole Club
Kelex Book 6: The A**hole Club

Immortal Iron Brothers Series
King of Knights Book 1
King of Inferno Book 2
King of Tides Book 3

Check out Blue Saffire exclusives on the
BlueSaffire.com website
The Fixer
His Miracle Baby
Razor
Dane
Trip
Professor Jones
Room 112

**Other books from Evei Lattimore Collection Books by
Blue Saffire**
Black Bella 1

Destiny 1: Life Decisions
Destiny 2: Decisions of the Next Generation
Destiny 3 coming soon…

Star

**Other books from Royal Blue Gay Romance Collection
written by Blue Saffire**
Kyle's Reveal
Beau's Redemption

I0670182

MURDER AT GOLDEN COVE FOREST

CATHY PICKENS

A Blue Ridge Mountain Mystery Book 3

Originally published as *Hog Wild*